midnight & indigo
celebrating black women writers

Speculative Issue no.3

EDITED BY:
Ianna A. Small

midnight & indigo
PUBLISHING

midnight & indigo

VOLUME 3
978-1-7379332-6-7

midnightandindigo.com

———————

MANUSCRIPTS AND SUBMISSIONS
Whether you've already been published or are just starting out, we want to hear from you! We accept submissions of short stories and narrative essays written by Black women writers. View complete submission guidelines and submit your stories online at *midnightandindigo.com*. No paper submissions please.

Cover design by Asya Blue Design. www.asyablue.com
Cover image: Victor Torres/Stocksy

Printed and bound in the United States of America.
First Printing October 2023

To us.
That's it...that's the dedication.
'cause we deserve it.

midnight
&indigo
celebrating black women writers

SPECULATIVE ISSUE no.3

8

midnight
&indigo

celebrating black women writers

Story Summaries

From a mysterious swamp to a haunted highway, new wishes granted to past lives revisited, we are excited to introduce our third speculative fiction issue. Eighteen emerging and established Black women writers across the U.S., the Caribbean, Africa, and Europe share tales in which secrets are exposed, mysteries unravel, and the human spirit shines in unexpected, often supernatural ways.

In **"Crepuscular Hour"** by Lorraine Rice, it has always been Evie and Lili, two selves vying for dominion over one body. That is, except for the twilight hour of each day, when girl and double are made separate and whole. As an eleventh birthday approaches, heightened tensions tip the scales.

When her silver jar of wishes starts running low, Jasmine wishes to become a unicorn in **"If Wishes Were Horses"** by Azure Arther. Unfortunately, it isn't quite what Jasmine thought it would be.

In **"The Revelation of Laila Dupont"** by Desiree Winns, babies all over the world are being born with wings—those of an angel or devil. Theories circulate about what the wings mean for humanity, and whether the actions of the mother impact which their children receive. Two sisters wait to see which their babies will be graced with.

In **"A Dirge without music"** by Fatima Abdullahi, a desperate father races against time to save the life of his only child, riddled with guilt over the knowledge that the situation was caused by his own hand.

An unwelcome customer stops into a local restaurant at closing time in **"Sunup Town"** by Hou Rhyder. In a homogenous municipality that welcomes others at night but expects them gone by day, sometimes saving grace is a little kindness and reconciliation. And other times, it's a spare tray of mac and cheese and a fresh banana pudding.

In **"Buyer's Remorse"** by Toni Jones, a telepath and an empath get into a relationship. They must contend with how their powers have impacted their past relationships.

In **"In the Middle of Air"** by Ashley J. Hobbs, First Lady Marvette Lee Royster is struggling to fit in with the congregation of Mount Moriah Pentecostal Church and nurture her gifted daughter. When an influential church mother wages war against the child and her gift, First Lady Royster has to determine what matters most.

In **"Healer of Herself"** by Elnora Gunter, Cora has a secret she shares with her husband Tim. When Tim abandons her, she sets off for the swamp. What she finds offers something redeeming—and terrifying.

Unable to cope with the absence of her pilot father, a young girl finds refuge in her imagination in **"Mama Said"** by Karla Tiffany. Between her oppressive, Bible-thumping mother, the beautiful but antagonistic Delilah, and boy troubles, coming of age hasn't exactly been a walk in the park. All she knows is that she wants to fly away, just like the slaves in *The People Could Fly*. When the mysterious Amadaius appears, she just may get her wish—for better or worse.

A witch finds herself becoming the new bride to a vampire prince in **"Two Halves Of A Whole"** by Camilla Andrew.

In **"Spanish Moss"** by Nortina Simmons, three Black teenagers take an afternoon road trip to a haunted highway. When they get there, they find there may be more truth to their ghost stories than imagination.

Precious is the only Black girl in her prestigious boarding school in **"Bleeding Marble"** by Megan Baffoe. When her best friend falls pregnant, rumor transforms the infant boy into a savage "Beast."

Blind in one eye with a scar around her neck from nearly choking to death while being born, Kayri has never been able to see much of the world around her or understand it in the same way that others have, in **"And She Cried Out, Unseen"** by A. A. Blair. When a new world opens up to her, the handicap may just be the one thing that saves her mother's life.

In **"Mud"** by Jasmine Griffin, Monica must host her would be mother-in-law while grieving the death of her fiancée. When she becomes enamored with a sculpture she makes of Gwen's likeness from bricks of red Alabama clay, things come to a head.

In the backwoods of 1960 Alachua County Florida, Gina meets with a rumored root worker in the hopes that she might keep Gina's past from being uncovered, in **"The Witnessing"** by Kayla Cayasso.

In **"Welcome"** by RJ Joseph, a widow with an empty nest ruminates on her loneliness and inadvertently changes her status.

A girl becomes a woman and has to make certain sacrifices in **"Flower Girl"** by Oubria Tronshaw.

In **"The Favor"** by Jennifer E. Jones, everyone wants that ride-or-die friend, the one you'd call if you need to hide a body. But what happens when you get that call?

Once again, we are so proud to travel this literary road with you. If you're interested in reading additional stories by Black women writers, visit midnightandindigo.com, check out previous print issues, and follow us on social @midnightandindigo. Thank you for your support. Enjoy!

Crepuscular Hour

Behind the forsythia, fluorescent yellow arched against the brick-side of the house, a child crouches in wait, gripping her knees. Twilight is blooming—the in-between hour, Evie's favorite time of day. She hears the mother singing along to the radio, the clatter and clink of dishes in the sink. Light from the overhead window suffuses her hiding place with a gossamer glow.

Evie can just make out the impressions on her skin where her fingernails dig in. The sting momentarily soothes, but she is acutely aware of night's gathering momentum. "Lili, hurry," she calls.

A breeze whispers through the leaves in answer, summoning sleeves of tiny bumps. Then, a sudden absence of sound is followed by another whisper, too close in her ears.

"Scared you."

Startled, Evie falls into a tangle of branches. She is relieved to see the mirror image smiling down at her, but reluctant to let her twin off the hook so easily. "Why'd you wait so long?" Which sounds more whine than gruff.

"You know I always come." Lili shrugs and pulls her up. "Don't be such a baby, Evie—And quit that!" She slaps Evie's hand, then runs a finger along the ridge of raised skin on her arm. "I'm here now."

Lili grins and Evie eases; the two make the most of the dying light. They sit cross-legged behind the bush and play hand games—*Say, say, my playmate. Come out and play with me...* They pluck the yellow flowers and decorate their thick black braids while Evie chatters. Lili is hungry for news of the day. Who was mean at school? Did Evie walk home alone again? Did the father come back with gifts like he promised? And always she wants to know about the mother.

"What does she say about me?"

"Well," Evie searches, "we passed a man selling flowers from a cart, and she said, 'Lilies have always been my favorite.'"

Lili nods to herself, the edges of her mouth twitching toward a smile.

Evie sighs, relieved she came up with a suitable answer, something to please her twin and sate a voracious appetite. She imagines her cleverness has opened a space wide enough for her own hunger to slip in and asks, "What's it like—the other place?"

But Lili is fading, lines and features receding, as night consumes the gloaming. The mother calls, and for half a second the withdrawal is halted.

"Stay," Evie pleads. "Sometimes she stares at me, looking for you."

"Won't find me." Lili's form flares for an instant, "You're just you—for now."

To be two—not halves of a whole, but two selves vying for dominion over one body. It has been this way for as long as Evie can remember. Always together, but in contention, except for the hour when they can be themselves, see themselves as no one else does. There was a time when Lili held the most hours in the day. They were very young, and it was before Evie understood the intricate workings of memory. But Lili, born knowing, remembers everything.

When or why the coin was flipped and one twin went under, is a mystery. Evie sometimes tires of the struggle and yearns to hand the days over to Lili. Especially those days when the other children won't leave her alone, and the teachers pretend not to notice; when the mother cries after yelling into the phone for hours at the father.

She knows Lili thinks she's missing it all, but Evie envies her twin's invisibility, and dreams of elsewhere—if Quiet was a place.

When the mother tucks her in that night, a birthday party is proposed. "Eleven is nothing to sneeze at. Invite some kids from school." The mother touches two fingers to Evie's forehead, as if to smooth her own worry lines from the child's brow. "All the time by your lonesome."

"I'm not alone. I have Lili."

Barely more than a breath, but the words wreak havoc.

The mother's legs buckle and she bumps the nightstand, toppling the lamp, which goes out, and in reaching to keep it from crashing, she knocks over a glass that smashes into shards, now bloodied as she collects them in the dark.

The last time Evie uttered Lili's name in another's presence, the mother had shaken her shouting, "Enough! You don't have a sister," before collapsing into sobs and sorries, covering the four-year-old's face with salty kisses. The taste of pond water still lingers.

This time the mother says nothing as she leaves the room, cradling broken glass. Evie lies perfectly still in the darkness, and pictures Lili watching from a corner.

Over the following weeks there is a shift of seasons between them, like the warm front moving in, promising the slick and blister of summer. It isn't only the inconsistency of Lili's visits, now loosely tied to the crepuscular hour, but also the plague of lost things, which begins with holes in all of Evie's pockets. Among the lost: five oxblood marbles, three exquisite bottle caps, and a genuine two-headed penny. Doesn't matter if she checks in the morning before dressing. By nightfall, there is a hole and another missing treasure.

Worse yet, Evie has had to go rummaging for her favorite books. When she finds them—behind the radiator, under the porch, in a rusted bucket at the back of the shed—their pages are rippled, some torn in half. She won't allow herself to blame Lili, but does not mention the missing in her daily reports, lest her twin give herself away with a grin. Evie stows the books under her mattress to smooth the paper and keep them safe.

One day in the forsythia, Lili breaks off a branch and peels away the young bark in long, thin strips. "I'm sick of being stuck in this in-between time." Only just arrived, she is already threatening to dissipate, like a roving cloud.

Evie wants to reach out, grab and hold her twin in place, but a tingling sensation ignites in her fingertips, travels up her arms and warns against it. She bites her lip and claws deeper into her own skin, making tiny crescent cuts near her elbows. "You can't quit coming," she rushes.

"Can do what I want. Almost my birthday."

"Our birthday," Evie says.

Lili snaps the stripped branch in half and looks up to the window where the mother's voice is ringing. Evie follows her gaze.

"She's planning a party for us."

"For *you*," Lili corrects. "But no one is coming."

"You'll be there." Evie says to the space Lili has left behind.

The eve of her eleventh birthday, Evie does not linger in the hiding place.

She leaves the yard altogether and follows a trail of dropped sunny blossoms through the neighborhood, to the pond she has not visited since she was too young to remember. Lili has often tried to stir the memory of sneaking out to see the ducks, recounting, with relish, every detail from the dusky blue sky to the cool muddy squelch. But the digging always makes Evie itch to change the subject, to shake the lingering taste of pond.

Lili is by the water, waiting. That is what surprises Evie. Not the fact that her twin is wearing the party dress intended for *her*, but that Lili is waiting for Evie.

"Like it?" she twirls in a violet whir.

"You look nice."

"I know."

"Why are we here?"

"You'll see." Lili grabs Evie's hands, "Come on," and yanks her toward the water.

"We're not allowed."

"Who says?" Lili pulls harder. "Nobody told me."

Evie tries to free herself, but Lili's grip is fierce, cuffing her wrists, dragging her to the pond's edge, tugging her right out of her Keds which the muddy shore claims.

"Lili, please."

With all her weight, Evie throws her body backward, slipping and sliding in the sludge until her head is under water.

By the time she screams, her mouth is filled with sediment, plant bits, water mites, seed shrimp. No one hears, not even her twin, smiling from above as she holds her under. At least, Evie thinks it's Lili—hard to make out the dwindling features through murk and heavy indigo. Only the white grin of a waning moon.

Flashlight beams, bouncing off the trees and cattails, reach her before the voices calling. The sharp edges of fear and anguish are dulled, muffled below, so that it sounds as if her mother is simply calling her home for the night. When the small crowd of bodies surrounds her, faces split into light and shadow, the child starts to cry, tearless, air-sucking wails.

"Found her," someone yells. "She's here."

Her mother pushes through and gathers her up, holds her close, weeping.

The child is limp, cold, and wet, clenching clumps of water weed in her fists. Party dress, ruined. But her mother rocks and coos until breath and beat are at last in sync, in sync.

If Wishes Were Horses

Wanted: A wish. Any wish. Just one. We don't have a lot of money, but we'll pay the going rate. Contact: AB1-JK5-L245.

For Sale: Empty Wish Canister. Silver Level. Refills for 30% off. $10,000 or best offer.

For Sale: 10 Nature Wishes. Good protection for outdoorsy folks. Great for bad weather, snake bites, mosquitoes, and rough rapids. Bought for an adventure trip that I have to back out on. Everyone got the same package, so no one wants to buy my 10. $1000. Firm.

***

On Saturday, Jasmine wished to be a unicorn.

Her silver jar of wishes was running low, and she wanted every one of the last wishes to be good ones. She had already wished for the maximum of money, which was based off a percentage increase of her prospective lifetime earnings, a thing she didn't really understand. She had also wished for a new house for her parents, for a long and healthy life for her pets. She had acquired the skill of playing the piano, was fluent in five languages (also the maximum because she definitely would have chosen more, if she could), and she had lost the capped amount of weight.

Her hair was large, an afro that reached for the sun, and her brown skin truly did glow whenever the daylight touched it. *I woke up like this* was no longer a daydream, but a fact.

The only problem with a bottle of wishes, and really, it wasn't a true problem, was that you couldn't wish for love or more wishes. But you could wish to be a mythical creature for a day, sometimes a week, and if you were favored and lucky, maybe longer, though anything longer than a week required approval from the wish company and they were free to deny you, however that usually didn't happen. It wasn't a bestial wish, but an embodiment, and the disclaimers did cover accidents, though none ever happened. The wish business was just that—a business.

This was why Jasmine decided nothing, absolutely nothing, beat being a unicorn for a night, and on Saturday evening, when she stepped out of her house, perfection radiating from every pore, her clothing effortlessly couture and chic, and her makeup flawless, she thought, *Nothing is better than being a unicorn.*

That night, she met Harley, a golden-skinned, cat-eyed, Egyptian goddess, and Harley took her back to her place, a penthouse suite that smelled of smoke and incense and spoke of money and decadence. But in the morning, the wish had worn off, and Harley chalked up her interest in Jasmine to the alcohol.

She was kind, but Jasmine could see the luster of being a unicorn had faded, and with it, Harley's interest.

Jasmine rushed home and used another wish.

"I wish to be a unicorn for as long as possible."

When the confirmation email came, her wish had been granted for thirty-seven days. It was a random number, but Jasmine didn't care. She dressed, applied her makeup, and left to find Harley.

Thirty-seven days was long enough for someone to fall in love, for a woman to realize that she had met her soulmate.

Thirty-seven days was just long enough for the layers to peel back and the acceptance to ride in.

Thirty-seven days was plenty for Jasmine to receive her just desserts.

Only, it wasn't.

Thirty-seven days was just enough for Jasmine to get her heart broken, and not enough to not be embarrassed at the fact.

Wished for a pet and now it's too much? Here at Danny's Devil Dogs, we take 'em all! From dinosaurs to Cerberus, poison dart frogs to talking rabbits, there is no pet that Danny's won't take off your hands! Wished for animals require a signed contract releasing wish to DDD.

Wanted: Minor wish for school bully. I just want her to trip in front of everyone. I've only got $15 bucks, but help a kid out, okay?

For Sale: A bed you can sleep forever in. Literally. I almost died. Buy at your own wish...or risk.

***

"Did you hear that there was a compound wish recently? Not a really big one, but like an 11-wisher."

Titan grunted in response and glanced up at his co-worker. *Susan? Sarah? Sally?* S. He would stick with S.

S was leaning over his cubicle wall, a beeline straight down her shirt available for his sight. He would look, but S wasn't hitting on him. She was just her, naturally attractive and appealing to others. She was a type, just not his.

"The Confidentiality department won't say what the wish was for, but I'm hearing it was a mythic beast." S popped her gum and grinned at Titan, her perfect, pink lipstick framing her bright white teeth. "Chancy, that. You don't get to specify with a compound wish. It's a high risk."

Titan grunted again and continued typing. If he could just finish this last report, he could clock out and go home.

And then. Titan smiled to himself as he typed a period and hit enter.

"Vacation," he said, quietly, his deep voice still loud.

"Oh, that's right. One paid vacation wish. I used mine for my birthday." S smiled at him, big and wide, her blond bouffant going perfectly with her sweet smile. "Know what you're gonna wish for?"

Titan shrugged and focused on shutting down his computer.

"Well, no matter. You'll figure it out. Enjoy your time off, big guy."

Titan nodded, packed his few things: briefcase, reusable snack and lunch bag, water bottle, coffee cup, jacket. He stood, looked around at his neat desk and pushed the chair up to it. He paused and looked up at S' bright blue eyes before carefully saying, "Two weeks."

"Ooo. I thought you were only on a seven dayer. I'll see you in June then!"

Titan nodded as he walked away. He could almost feel the brightness of S' smile at his back.

***

Wanted: SM, 27, seeking unwish-enhanced partner of any gender. Must not have used wishes to enhance self AT ALL.

Available: minor wish nanny. I will give your little ones the best dreams! NO CHANGELING WISHES. I will NOT change your child. Full benefits required and min. of 2 nights off per week (studying for next nanny levels). CPR and wish-danger certified.

For Sale: Empty Wish Canister. Silver Level. Refills for 30% off. $7,000 OBO.

***

On Sunday, Jasmine awoke with a migraine. Harley's snores didn't help, so she slid out of bed, slipped on the silk kimono Harley bought her when they were in Japan last week, and padded barefoot to the bathroom.

There, she opened Harley's ornate mirrored medicine cabinet and shook out a few pain relievers. She swallowed them dry and rested her palms on the sink, not wanting to look, even though she knew she would have to, eventually.

This time, it had only been eighteen days.

The last time, she had made it thirty-three. Then her hair had turned white, iridescent, and in truth, the sparkling sheen had illuminated her brown skin, adding to the otherworldly glow. Her afro wasn't really bright or silvery white, though at first glance it appeared to be. Instead, it was a rainbow of colors, each strand shifting with every movement, dependent on the light.

Jasmine had played with the hair, styling it in large afro puffs, in braided styles, sleek ponytails, and flat-ironed it straight. It was beautiful regardless, and even when the unicorn wish faded, the hair stayed, luminous, flawless, perfect.

The hair wasn't the only change though.

Before the hair, the wish effects had only taken six days. There was no rhyme or reason to how the wish affected her.

That time, it had been her eyes and she was blind for close to a month. When she could finally see, her irises were rings of purple, starting with English violet closest to her pupil and changing, gradually lightening to an almost clear mauve before reaching the sclera. It was pretty, and definitely eye-catching, but still, she argued with the company that she wasn't able to enjoy her wish due to the side effect, and they had agreed, based on her signature of a non-disclosure agreement, to give her three more wishes or one gold level wish.

Of course, she'd chosen gold level, which was why, at this point, she didn't understand the side effects, especially this quickly.

This was the gold wish, which came with an inset wish reversal, and she was a guaranteed unicorn for a full year. That was plenty of time to get Harley to propose. Plenty of time to make her love Jasmine. A year was enough for a thousand possibilities, but not if she was horrifically disfigured, not if she had a horn growing out of her head.

Please don't be a horn. Please don't be a horn. Please don't be a horn.

Jasmine opened her eyes and squinted through the pain. There was no horn sticking up through her iridescent strands, but her afro was wild. She reached up and parted her hair with her hands, starting in the middle, and ran her fingers through the shimmering curls, lightly touching her scalp.

Nothing.

She winced as the migraine spiked and shifted her fingers forward a bit more.

Nothing.

A bit more, still nothing.

She sighed with relief and went back to bed, nuzzling Harley's back. The other woman turned over, her long hair tangling around her face as she opened her eyes. Jasmine smiled at her, and Harley blinked.

"Hey, baby. What time is it?"

"Not time to get up. I just had to use the bathroom."

"Mmm. Come here." Harley opened her arms and Jasmine sank into her, pressing against her chest. Harley pulled the sash of Jasmine's robe and smiled mischievously. They kissed, and Jasmine pushed the headache to the side.

Harley was everything she wanted, everything she needed. Worth the pain. Worth the wishes.

***

Got my new wish! #new car #wishyoucouldbeme #goldlevel –feeling amazing

365 likes, 47 Comments, 23 Reactions, 4 shares

Most Active Comment:

Sierra: That's not a gold level wish car.

Andrea: Do you really believe she has gold level? Try basic.

Hilary: C'mon guys. It's possible. I mean, it's not she's platinum.

Sierra: Ha-ha. Platinum doesn't exist.

Sierra: No, seriously. Does platinum exist?

Sierra: Hilary?

Hilary has been banned from access.

Sierra: Whoa. Platinum must exist then @Andrea.

Sierra has been banned from access.
Comment removed.

***

Titan's vacation started with an incredibly careful, well-thought-out, extremely specific, foolproof plan (he had a friend in the department), insured (it had to be since the job provided it) wish. His wish went like this:

"I wish for a very relaxing, but not unhealthily relaxed, sunshine-filled at a balmy level of 86 degrees max with a full sun cycle, including normal nightfall of at least 10 hours, where stars are in the sky and do not fall, vacation at a normally-populated with no food poisoning, poor construction, coincidental accidents or criminal activity high-end resort with a sandy, not rocky beach that does not include aliens, monsters, disasters or any other unnecessary, dangerous, or ridiculously unrealistic occurrences, particularly in reference to plague, unnatural silence, a "rapture" event, or being too intoxicated to recall, for the duration of my 14 days of leave, which does include safe arrival, departure, and arrival at my home residence without lost luggage or any other malfeasance."

In the olden days, when wishes were first being sold, if a person took too long a breath between words, the wish would be considered final. The next wish innovations were contained in snap capsules, but upon breaking them open, the wishes sometimes escaped and flew away, to be caught by random people or to land on people who accidentally wished for things that they couldn't take back. That was also when people still used, "I wish" as a random saying, though in the decades since, the usage had definitely been removed from colloquial terms.

These days, wishes were kept in two click squeeze bags. The first squeeze activated the wish listen, while the second click finalized the wish. Thus, in a quiet room, with no distractions, Titan lightly squeezed with his large fingers, took one deep breath and several small ones in between the words, and voiced the carefully created, practiced, and finely enunciated wish.

Then, he closed his eyes, squeezed the tiny bag tightly, and felt the wish burst out of the perforated baggie and coalesce around him.

When he opened his eyes, he was in the lobby of a swanky tropical resort, the scent of salty ocean air, sunscreen, and cleaning supplies surrounded him. He looked down at his clothing, and realized that, even though he hadn't included attire in his wish, the word "vacation" must have covered it because he was wearing khaki shorts and sandals with a tropical shirt to match. The lobby, decked out in gold and cream, tropical oranges and yellows mixed with vibrant green plants, and ocean blue furniture and uniforms, was moderately full of people checking in and out, coming and going, or just lounging.

Everything looked normal, but Titan knew the possibility of someone else's wish marring his perfectly crafted one was a possibility, and a disclaimer that came with any wish, including his. However, the job gave away one vacation wish per year to every employee, and in ten years, Titan had never taken his.

This year, to everyone's surprise, he did.

Even though he hated people. Even though he was self-conscious about his size. Even though he always felt like people were staring at him, that they knew he worked in wishes, that they were going to mob him like they mobbed that lady from HR last year. Though, really, that was her fault. You had to agree not to disclose you worked in wishes when you were hired on, not just for the company, but for yourself as well. She learned the hard way. Still, Titan was conscious of others finding out that he worked in wishes, as well. That woman was a cautionary tale.

Even though Titan was large, he was more wide than obese, more muscled than fat. He was also tall, with lightly tanned skin and vague features that made his race hard to decipher. He kept his hair slicked back in a ponytail, though when it was wet, it was just curly enough that he was suspect, but just fine enough that he could pass for Jewish. As he considered this, Titan supposed that he was likely overthinking his appearance and should find his room key. He walked to the desk in a few strides of his long legs, already considering that he might have missed some portion, some loophole to disaster in his wish, and hesitantly waited his turn.

"Hello!" The perky young woman, well-tanned with sun-bleached, brown hair, looked up at Titan with what could only be described as joy. "How can I help you?"

"Uh, a room, for..." Titan hesitated and mumbled, "Titan Undertid."

"I'm sorry? It's a bit loud here. What did you say your name was?"

"Titan." He looked around.

"Titan?" The woman's name tag said Sarah, and Titan considered that Sarah was a nice name. "Is that the last name, sir?"

"No." Titan muttered a bit louder.

"The last name, sir?"

"Check under U. Titan U."

"Titan...U...is U the last name, sir?" Sarah's voice had a bit of a bite to it, a slight impatience that he was sure came from having to repeat herself.

"Undertid." Titan said firmly.

"Titan...Undertid." Sarah looked up at him and her green eyes were a bit less joyful, a bit more concerned, possibly confused. "Tighten under tit?"

"Yes." Titan sighed and looked away. "But please, call me Mr. U."

"Oh. Okay."

Sarah was quiet for a moment, and Titan was sure his face was red. When she spoke again, he could tell she had made up her mind about something.

"Alrighty then, Mr. U. You were in one of our best suites, but I've upgraded you to the penthouse. I see that you are one of our premier members, and you are going to have an amazing time. Your luggage arrived before you and is being transferred to your new room. Here are your key cards, a map of the island, a list of activities, and the Wi-Fi password."

Titan reached out for the brochure, key cards, and map, his large fingers comically fumbling them. He frowned as the items flew into the air by no control of his own. Sarah, in the middle of suggesting a bellhop and giving him his room number, stepped back in surprise when each neatly fell to balance at the tip of his nose. A few people near snorted but kept moving. Titan collected the papers and key cards, smiled politely at Sarah, and headed to the elevators.

On the way there, he tripped and banged into a wall. Once inside the elevator, all the floors lit up, even though he hadn't chosen them, and the next couple who ran on, suggested by the bellhop because they too were going to the upper floors, glared at him as if he had chosen to make sure the three of them stopped on seventy floors.

Titan fumed. Something was going on.

And that's when Titan felt it. His wish was fighting him.

If you knew what to look for, wishes sometimes rode on you while you were under their influence. For some people, it was a fullness inside, a pinch in your heart, a muted eardrum or stopped up nostril. For others, it was a full body coverage that felt like you had a film over your skin, or something tiny, like a grain in your shoe.

For Titan, it was a target on his back, right beneath his shoulder blades.

Not every wish did this, only the ones that wanted to run free, or wreak havoc, or were just too tightly constrained. The easier wishes were more open, but that openness was dangerous. Give Titan a tightly controlled wish any day, but this wish wasn't controlled. It was bucking, and wild.

He ran over the wish in his mind, trying to figure out what he'd forgotten.

"Undue embarrassment." Titan said aloud, surprising the couple. "I forgot to say no undue embarrassment, but that should've been covered by no ridiculously unrealistic occurrences."

The couple eyed him and got off on the very next floor.

***

Tired of your wishes going wrong? Need help with how to phrase them? Let us help you! Here at My Command Writers, your wish is OUR COMMAND. Minor side-effect contract required.

Wanted: Wish-enhanced people for a wish party. Let's mix our wishes and see what occurs! Cannot be organization or activity-specific wishes. Must be silver level or higher. The more beast wishes, the better. Let's get furry. Kink-friendly.

For sale: Birthday wish dragon. Used to be my roommate. He refused to revoke the wish or use a new wish to stop the process. Now, I can't wish him back. Make your offer.

***

The horn took six months to fully rise from Jasmine's widow peak.

It was silver and complemented her glittering hair. There was an oil-slick shimmer to the spirals, which were thick near her scalp, but tapered into a wicked point at the top. It was also hard, harder than diamond (they'd checked), harder than anything that existed (they'd tried to have it surgically removed), and harder still on Jasmine's self-esteem. She could have wished the horn away, if she were willing to give up being a unicorn, but she would just wish to be a unicorn again because—Harley. And besides, Harley, still enamored by the unicorn wish, found the horn charming even though Jasmine was horrified, embarrassed, humiliated, and a host of other emotions.

People enjoyed the horn until they realized it was real, then they assumed she had wished for it. Some found that brave. Others found it disgusting. Or strangers realized that it was a side effect and either pitied her or made fun of her. Mainly because of jealousy. Anything above bronze level required money, and Jasmine was a silver-level wisher. She had used the inheritance from her grandmother's death to buy a large jar of silver wishes, and she had enjoyed them, up until now, but even stranger's looks were not enough for her to be truly embarrassed.

Mainly, as with everything else, it was Harley that Jasmine worried about.

Her horn shredded the roof in Harley's gorgeous, pearlescent Lamborghini. Harley laughed and said, "Well, I guess it's time to get a new one."

She cut Harley's stomach during intimacy one night. To which Harley, after wincing and gasping from the alcohol they put on it, said, "Ooo. War wounds and scars. You're stuck with me now."

When she leaned over too fast to rinse her mouth, and cracked the expensive, gilded mirror in Harley's gargantuan bathroom, the other woman just shrugged and rubbed Jasmine's back. "Darling, fuck that mirror. As a matter of fact, let's just break some other shit."

But Jasmine couldn't be as fickle as Harley. She was ashamed of the horn, and no amount of arguing with the wish company fixed it. Jasmine hated that her girlfriend had to deal with the looks, the whispers, and the jeering laughter. She despised Harley's friends' quick jibes, or the way that the love of her life had to constantly come to her defense. Most of all, she obsessed over how she looked when she saw herself in any reflective surface.

"I'm going to take you on a vacation," Harley said, kissing Jasmine on the mouth. She tilted her head when she did so, her dark chocolate eyes flitting up to the horn. She smiled against Jasmine's mouth, then reached up and stroked the horn, her long fingers following the spirals of silver iridescence. "My little unicorn. You were already a unicorn when we met. I just...I screwed it up so bad that first night and then, when I saw you again...what happened that first month. I'm still sorry."

When Jasmine didn't respond, Harley kissed her again. "I don't know what I would do without you."

Jasmine pulled back and smiled slightly. "You'd find another me in a heartbeat."

Harley rolled her eyes. "No, I wouldn't."

"I love you." Jasmine saw that Harley was gearing up for a fight.

"I love you, too," Harley said, serious. "You know you're not replaceable right?"

"So, where are we going on vacation?" Jasmine quickly changed the subject.

Harley's eyes strayed, often, but she tended to focus on Jasmine rather than act on her interests. Still, her wandering gaze did nothing for Jasmine's insecurity, especially with the addition of the horn.

"I was thinking somewhere tropical. Maybe a resort. Let me call my assistant and see." Harley smiled, full lips and dark gaze. "Then, to bed with us both. I have a unicorn to catch."

***

For Sale: Empty Wish Canister. Silver Level. Refills for 30% off. $5,000 OBO.

Need a lift? Ask and you shall receive! Here at Beggars Would Ride, we have a variety of conveyances for you. Just wish for: "a BWR" speak your intended location, and your ride will appear! Log onto the BWR website and commit payment info prior to first wish.

Crave higher-level wishes, but can't afford them? Never going to make it to one of those over-priced wish clubs? Come to Ambiance, the first wish-enhanced, virtual-reality studio. Here, in one-to-three-hour blocks, your deepest wish can be experienced.

***

Titan spent the first ten days of his vacation dealing with one embarrassing blow after another. His shorts fell off while he was swimming, a waiter tripped and covered him in spaghetti, he got horrific gas from a meal.

On one hand, he was miserable. But on the other, he was also falling in love.

Sarah, the concierge, seemed to always be there when he was struggling with something completely mortifying. Yet, every single time, she was empathetic. Kind, even. He liked her, probably too much, but he didn't question it. Something about this vacation had to be perfect, and Sarah was it. He had worried about her working for the resort at first, but she had laughed.

"Whatever I do in my downtime is my downtime. It doesn't become a problem until we make it a problem, and I don't think we're going to have any problems, Tit."

To which, Titan agreed.

"Wanna go dancing?" Sarah asked. Her green eyes twinkled with mischief, and she spun around the penthouse suite in her bikini, flashing tanned skin, black and white fabric, and sun-bleached hair. It alternated. Flash. Skin. Spin. Fabric. Blur. Hair. Repeat. "I know the greatest spot in town. It's a hole in the wall, but it's perfect."

"I thought we weren't supposed to leave the resort." Titan rumbled from the couch. The penthouse was large and set with sea colors of differing shades of blue with a plush couch and chairs, wide screen TV, partial kitchen, and two bedrooms. It was the only place Titan hadn't had an embarrassing occurrence. Still, there was always a possibility. "The brochure says it is safer to stay on the property."

Sarah laughed at him, her voice melodic. "Of course, you can leave the resort. That's just what we tell people to make sure they spend the most here."

"I think I'd rather stay in the resort."

"Don't be a fuddy." Sarah grinned and came over to him, sliding into his lap. She wasn't a short woman, but she was petite in size and weighed barely anything. She wiggled her hips and slung an arm around his beefy neck. "I want to show you around."

"No." Titan said. He carefully lifted her and set her on the couch next to him. "I am suffering under a recalcitrant wish. I will not release this chaos on another party."

"Ooo, but you can. We can go to a wish party. With a suite like this, your vacay wish has to be at least silver, right?"

Titan studied Sarah before nodding slightly. She grinned.

"Technically...a vacation is an event-specific wish, but it is just wide enough..." She thought carefully. "Let me make a call. You want to go?"

"What is a wish party?" Titan asked. He looked over at her, his bushy eyebrows coming together.

"You've never been to one?" Sarah smiled brighter than before. "Oh, this is going to be so much fun! Basically, a bunch of people under the influence of active wishes, it has to be silver or higher, get together and the wish powers mix. It's super cool. The effects don't last, but you never know how they're going to mix."

"And that's...safe?" Titan frowned. "Legal?"

"Technically legal, and technically safe, but definitely fun."

"Oh."

"So, you'll go?" Sarah asked. She tilted her head to look up at him.

"I don't know, Sarah."

"We don't even have to go anywhere. I know where someone is having one in another penthouse."

"I..." Titan could see Sarah on the verge of disappointment, her pouty mouth slowly downturned and he sighed. "Yeah. I'll go."

"This is going to be so cool!" Sarah squealed. "I've never been to a wish party either!"

***

Side effects got you down? Fine print torturing you? You need a wish lawyer! Contact Wish Gone Wrong to get your just desserts at 555-555-WGWL.

For Sale: One talking car. It never shuts up and has an opinion on everything. It's not my wish, so I can't revert it.

Be Magical. Be You. Bewished Makeup Line for the nights that plain old make-up just won't do. Located in all major department stores and online at Bewisheddotcom.

***

Harley threw a wish party in their penthouse suite. Anyone under silver wish influence or higher and one guest were invited, and so many people came, spilling into the opulence of their penthouse suite, eating, drinking, dancing, socializing, and of course, sharing wish power.

The unenhanced became enhanced. The bad wishes became good. Good wishes became bad. One man sprouted bat wings and flew around the room, cackling. Another woman's skin was dusted with glitter, making her appear ethereal. Hair grew, makeup changed, eye colors switched. Most of it was minor. Some of it was just a feeling of joy. A few people were upset until they imbibed in a drink or something stronger. Everyone was having a great time.

Except Jasmine.

Jasmine hated it.

From the second other wish-enhanced people arrived, Jasmine's unicorn wish had been misbehaving. Her horn glowed, then her hair straightened, then coiled, then grew to her ankles in massive, boisterous curls. At one point, a tail burst out of her pants, long and silky, and almost immediately stepped on.

But the worst was when her skin turned into horse hide.

"I want them to leave." She cried to Harley. "Make it stop."

"Loosen up and have some fun, baby!" Harley stroked her cheek. "I did this for you."

"I don't want it." Jasmine snapped, and Harley, her feelings hurt, went to dance with a sun-bleached blond who came with a massive man whose wish wasn't apparent. He appeared to be enjoying himself immensely and had been all loud laughter since he arrived. It was his arrival that had caused the tightness in Jasmine's back, just beneath her shoulder blades. It felt like a target, and she was jumpy and spooked easily.

And the feeling didn't stop when the party ended.

Harley went to bed, turning her back on Jasmine when the other woman tried to make up. Jasmine lay on the mattress staring at her lover's spine and the golden skin she admired. Harley had never been wish-enhanced. She'd never needed it. She didn't know what it was like to be Jasmine, who had always fought to lose that last twenty pounds, dealt with horrible acne, had never been able to get her hair to do what she wanted. Harley didn't know what it was like to be poor or to struggle. Harley didn't understand the need for wishes. They were a paltry thing to her, a party favor, an entertainment.

But the wishes were everything for Jasmine. She had poured everything she had into that jar of silver wishes, with their carefully laid out rules but seductive abundance. And it had been worth it, until she realized she was alone, and honestly, with Harley, Jasmine often still felt alone.

She reached out for her girlfriend and froze, staring at her hand. The nails had fused together, though her fingers beneath them were still separate. The pain in her back intensified. Jasmine opened her mouth to scream, but her tongue felt too big in her mouth and all that came out was a gargled whine. Her jaw cracked as it grew larger, longer. Jasmine stumbled out of bed, flailing, and arching her back. Everything hurt, from her eyes to her feet. She fell and lay on her side, trying to curl herself into a ball, but she couldn't. She couldn't.

When the pain finally stopped, the first thing Jasmine noticed was her own scent. She smelled like happiness, warm vanilla, and toasted marshmallows one moment, chocolate the next, sunshine and sugar a few seconds later. It kept shifting, but every shift was someone's version of perfect happiness. She tried to look down at herself, but her eyes hurt, and she blinked a few times once she was able to open them.

Her skin was covered with a fine layer of white fur. Her

hands and feet had formed into hooves, and her body had transformed. She stood, shaking, on four legs, rather than two and slowly walked to the full-length mirror that stood in the corner of the room. She wasn't surprised to see a full unicorn looking back at her. She sighed. The wish reversal was going to take everything away from her, but that was the risk she had taken. Now, it would be up to Harley to decide if she really wanted Jasmine or not.

"Harley." She tried to say, and only a whinny came out. Jasmine gasped. Words had to be used for a reversal wish. Words that she had to say.

"Harley." She tried again, forcing the unfamiliar, thick tongue in her mouth to touch her teeth to form the L, but no matter how she moved her lips and mouth, the word wouldn't form. This time, when the whinny came out, she screamed.

***

Headline: Wish company worker that was mobbed by the public finally wakes from coma.

Wanted: A unicorn for my daughter's birthday party. We can't afford a wish to buy one, and really, how would we take care of it? No one has one to rent. Help?

For Sale: Empty Wish Canister. Silver Level. Refills for 30% off. $3,000 OBO.

***

Titan spent the last four days of his vacation in bliss. Something about the wish party had removed the wish wrangling, and he felt amazing. Sarah had been just what he needed and wanted for the vacation and more, but she had ended things with him as soon as he checked out.

"Oh, I don't think keeping in touch would be a good idea, Tit." Sarah smiled at him. "Long distance never works out, but it's so sweet of you to offer."

"I like you though."

"Oh, you probably love me, but that's just the work wish working on you."

"Work wish?"

"Oh, yes. The resort has a minor wish on all their employees to be seen as helpful, but I've noticed that the longer you work here, the more likely people are to not just like you but love you."

She gave him a bright smile, and Titan felt it then. It was just a slight nudge that he hadn't even noticed in his nervousness when he first arrived, and definitely not when he'd thought she was interested.

"Why...then?" He flailed for the right words.

"Oh, I like you, too!" Sarah laughed. "Don't question that. I knew when I first saw you walk up. Ooo. He is a tall, strong, drink of man."

"Then keep in touch." Titan grabbed her hand.

"I don't know, honey." Sarah bit her lip before finally nodding. "Okay."

"Okay then." Titan said. He smiled, a toothy grin that few people ever saw on his solemn face. "I'll call you when I get home."

"Is your wish returning you?"

"Pretty sure it is."

"Oh good. That's always so fun to watch. One second, you're here and the—"

Titan popped back into his apartment and laughed when his cell phone rang. It was Sarah.

"One second, you're here and then, pop! You're gone."

"I miss you." Titan said.

"Already?"

"Yes." He waited for her to respond.

Finally, she spoke. "I miss you, too."

Monday, when Titan returned to work, S was all smiles.

"Did you enjoy your vacation?" She leaned against the

cubicle wall and struck a pose, her flawless figure outlined. Titan smiled.

"I did. I met someone."

"Ooo. What's her name? Tell me about her?" S came into his cubicle, something she'd never done before and perched a hip on his desk.

"Her name is Sarah." He waited to see if this name resonated with her. He still didn't know S' name and at this point, he thought it would hurt her feelings if he asked.

"Oh! I love it." S smiled at him. "Look at you with two girls now. Well, you tell Sarah that your work wife wants to meet her."

S giggled and Titan stared at her.

"And what name should I give Sarah for my work wife?"

"Titan, you're so silly." S laughed. "Let me catch you up on what happened while you were gone."

S started talking, equal parts gossip and work, and Titan mentally shrugged. Maybe he'd just call her W for work wife. Or GW for gossipy worker. Maybe that should be GCW. Gossipy coworker, but S didn't mean any harm.

"And then, Danny's Devil Dogs confiscated her. Girlfriend is having a fit, threatening to sue, big money being thrown around, and Danny's is being Danny's. They have so many unicorns that we can't figure out which one is actually her."

"What?" Titan asked.

"The lady. Um...Jasmine something. We still haven't figured out which unicorn in the stable is actually her. Legal says, because it was a gold-level wish, she can't be forced to remain a unicorn, but we can't find her in the stable, and Danny's is being...well...Danny's, like I said. And you know how they're protected from having to forcefully give up anything."

"Want me to go?" Titan usually volunteered for field work.

"No, honey. You just got back." S smiled at him. He noticed she had highlighted her hair red again. He liked it that way. "So, I was just catching you up. I'm headed out in just a second."

"Okay." Titan nodded. His phone chimed, a text from Sarah,

and he smiled, much to S's pleasure.

"Well, now. You go on and grab that text and I'll catch you up on this unicorn drama when I get back.

***

Free: Teething Wishes. We were gifted way more than we needed at our baby shower and want to do something nice for someone else. They really do work. I have 20. Please don't ask for more than you need.

Quote of the day: Wishes aren't for fairytales; they're for real life. – A wish fairy.

For Sale: Gold-Level, members only wish catalog. Serious inquiries only.

***

"Why's the unicorn look sad? I want a non-sad unicorn, Mommy." The little girl, Tabitha, stared up at Jasmine, her big eyes full of tears. It was her birthday, and her mother had requested a unicorn from DDD. The kid wore a sparkly dress with fairy wings on her back, and her mother had given her a whole container of basic paper level kid wishes. Minor things that wouldn't stay for longer than 24 hours. She had already wished ribbons and flowers into Jasmine's mane and personally shined her horn and hooves herself. She was a cute kid. As brown as Jasmine once was, with pigtails and bright eyes.

It wasn't the kid's fault that no one knew Jasmine was human. She had been with DDD for almost six months, and in that time, the wish company had been to the stables twice. No matter the level of reversal wish, Jasmine, in all her cleverness when she wished her gold wish, had made it nearly impossible for anyone but herself to reverse the wish, which meant that no human woman had popped out when the wish company people had come.

"Can't I make you happy? Unicorns aren't supposed to be

sad." Tabitha said, rubbing Jasmine's chest.

The unicorn woman sighed and tried to muster some happiness for the child, to exude the joy that she knew would roll off of her in waves, rather than the miasma of depression that she felt, but Jasmine was a human, and a human stuck as an animal could no more pretend to be happy than, well, a human stuck as an animal.

She nuzzled Tabitha's hair, instead, and the little girl hugged her. "I wish you could talk."

"You and me both, kid." Jasmine said, and gasped. Tabitha giggled and opened her hand to show the dissipation of a wish capsule.

"Yay! Now you can tell me what's wrong so I can have a good birthday." Tabitha danced around her.

Jasmine laughed. "You're about to have the best birthday."

And Tabitha did, but the highlight for the little girl was when Jasmine turned into a unicorn woman with iridescent hair and purple eyes. Tabitha's mother gave her some clothes. Jasmine squeezed Tabitha tight before she left. "You'll never know what you did for me, little bit."

Jasmine walked home, refusing to wish a ride, refusing to do anything more than enjoy the stride of her own to legs, the swing of her arms, the wind in her hair. When she arrived on her property, she expected her animals to be dead, for her house to be in disrepair, but the lawn was manicured, her dogs were in the yard. Music played from inside the house.

She stepped through the gate and, using the keypad, entered her home. There, she found Harley, who screamed with joy and cried when she embraced her.

"No more wishes." Harley said.

"I won't be a unicorn anymore." Jasmine said, stepping back. "And I'm okay with that. You're gonna have to be, too."

"I've always been okay with that." Harley said. "It was you who wanted to be more. I think you're amazing."

Jasmine nodded and looked around. "No more wishes."

"No more wishes." Harley agreed. She stared at Jasmine with her dark eyes. "Wanna get married?"

"I need a shower and some therapy first," Jasmine said and they both laughed until they cried and laughed some more.

***

For Sale: Lizard skin pants and shirt that turns you into a lizard. Getting out of the fit is the only way to revert, but I can show you how to do it. $900 OBO.

Need a day away from a world of wishes? Come to Reality Central and experience how things used to be. We promise you'll appreciate things a bit more when you leave.

For Sale: Empty Wish Canister. Silver Level. Refills for 30% off. $1,000. Seriously. Why doesn't anyone want this thing?

The Revelation of Laila Dupont

I knew this much; I was having a boy, and he was going to have wings. In the bile-yellow light of the airport bathroom, I saw a woman in the mirror and did not recognize her, because she was pregnant, and in my mind, I was still only one person. Pregnancy, like death, was something that was supposed to happen to other people. Pregnancy, like death, was supposed to be so distant that even thinking about it was as dumb as worrying about when the sun will explode. But there I was, swollen with child, staring at myself in that mirror. I knew I would die one day. I knew I was pregnant. And I knew that as soon as my parents saw me waddling down the terminal, those fates would collide catastrophically. I felt the kid flutter. I could only hope they were feathers, in the same pathetic way we can only hope we'll die warm and old in our beds.

Waiting would only prolong the inevitable. I grabbed my suitcase and shuffled out of the bathroom, making my way to the exit as slowly as I could manage. Around me, scattered kids clinging to their grumbling parents, families chattering away in languages unfamiliar, fellow college students returning home from abroad to make their families proud. I had my university sweater on, and it itched as if to remind me of the irony. On the televisions looped continuous news reports about the strange miracle, babies born with wings all over the world. They still didn't know the cause. Something had happened, radiation or revelation, or maybe just some odd new step in evolution—the scientists were scrambling to figure it out. Closeups of tiny shoulders brandishing tufts of soft, goosey down, or gnarled and crooked gargoyle hooks folded into the babies' backs filled the screens.

My hand slid to my stomach. I saw people eyeing my belly as I passed, and the questions on their grimacing lips. My breath left my mouth, loud and rushed. Something poked at me from the inside. It felt sharp. Feathers could be sharp at the tips. At the exit up ahead, a crowd of people waiting with handmade signs.

My only mission was to study well and come home with a white coat. I had failed. I wanted to turn around. I wanted to go back into the bathroom, hazy and yellow, and drift back to the innocence of only knowing about pregnancy, death, and failure. But my feet were too fast and my mouth was already loaded with the onslaught of apologies I would shoot.

I'm sorry. It was an accident. It's too late. I will go back to school as soon as this is over, as soon as I get it out. I'll do better. I'll—

"Laila?"

There stood my sister, Nayeli, her belly just as round as mine, her smile as bright as the sun.

Behind her were our parents. Baba, his mouth open and slack, his bald head twitching as that angry vein squirmed under his skin. Mama, her hand holding a "WELCOME HOME" balloon, bobbing like an unanswered question above their heads. Their eyes on my stomach.

Nayeli laughed out loud, her hands pressed against the small of her back. I didn't know what she was laughing at. I looked at her belly as she admired mine with a smirk, and wondered if the cousins could sense each other, like submarines in a hopeless sea.

***

Mama and Baba did not yell, and that was the worst part.

The ride home was quiet. Nayeli still held that stupid grin on her face. Baba's eyes were closed, and Mama's fingertips massaged her temples as the driver took us through the rough area of the city surrounding the airport. I looked out of the window, watching the broken houses and back alleys turn into mansions and manicured golf courses. Once we were home, it was like a funeral procession as we all stepped out to enter, the door wide open and ready to swallow us whole.

Inside, Mama and Baba let me speak, and I did so shakily in our cold living room. I could see our dinner being set out by our maid, Luisa, who watched me with pity. All of my favorites: chicken with orange sauce, potatoes au gratin, dirty rice, were steaming hot for my return. But I knew they would grow cold.

I explained, with my hands on my trembling stomach, as Mama and Baba sat on the couch, absorbing every word. Nayeli sat beside me, her hands knitted in front of her belly. Her smile was gone, but I knew she was enjoying this.

I said it was an accident, after a short fling with another pre-med student. I said I had a plan to put him up for adoption and return to school right after I recovered. I said I was sorry, and that it would never happen again.

They were silent for a long time. Then Baba cleared his throat and stood. He crossed the room, bones cracking with the effort of his joints, and poured a glass of syrupy bourbon from his cabinet.

"Was it worth it, Laila?"

"S-Sorry?"

"Your little party with the pre-med student. What's his name, by the way?"

"Samuel."

"Samuel." Baba tasted the name and chased it with a sip of his drink.

I glanced over at Mama worriedly. Her lips were pressed in a firm, purple line, her eyes avoiding me completely.

"Samuel what?"

I looked at the floor. Baba nodded.

"And is Samuel planning to help you pay for your prenatal expenses? Check-ups? Adoption processes? Therapy?"

"No, I told him I would take care of it."

"You told him you would take care of it. Well, your white coat must be in your luggage, then. You must be a doctor who can afford all of those expenses, now. That's what we sent you to school for, isn't it?"

"Yes, Baba. But I'll be going back to school as soon as this is over."

"As soon as this is over."

Baba took his time returning to his seat beside Mama. He swirled the small spot of bourbon left in the glass, taunting it. His eyes shifted from me to Nayeli, and back.

"Was it worth it, Laila? Our moving to this country for your education? All the time and money we spent getting you tutors? All the effort we put into making sure that you could become something, wasted for one night of fun?"

"No, Baba."

"What will the church think, their pastor's daughters come crawling home with demons in their bellies?"

Nayeli sucked in a breath.

Mama spoke up. "We don't know what they are, yet."

"These children are a *sign*. We're being punished! Laila's having a child with a man whose last name she doesn't even know. Nayeli, well, Nayeli and her bastard of a husband—"

"Don't talk about Amir," Nayeli warned.

Baba ignored her. "We already know what's going to come out of *that* disaster."

Nayeli gritted her teeth and took to her feet, teetering as she struggled to balance herself. "Believe me, after he's born, you won't have to worry about it." She waddled out of the room, groaning as she passed the decorated table.

Mama sighed delicately, the same way she always did after an explosion shattered our fragile peace.

"I'm sorry," I told her, and tears burned my eyes. "I just lost focus for a second because I was stressed. But if this has taught me anything...I'm going to work even harder after this is over. I won't disappoint you again."

Mama didn't answer. Baba faced me, the hardness in his features softening a bit.

"We weren't expecting this from you, Laila."

A warmth bloomed within me. I wiped my eyes.

"We will allow you and your sister to stay here until you give birth. After that, you go back to school and redeem yourself. As for your sister..."

He shook his head, as if the very thought of her was pointless.

I nodded, my throat squeezed tight. I thanked them, excused myself, and rose to leave.

Luisa's gentle hand touched my shoulder as she helped me up the stairs. Behind me, I heard Baba sink back into the couch.

"Stupid girl. No one is going to adopt a child with devil wings."

***

Nayeli perched on her bed as the moonlight spilled through the blinds. For a moment, she looked just like when we were kids, picking out stars and naming them when she couldn't sleep. But her belly gave her away, the same way mine had. We were no longer children, innocent of knowing, now the very horrors we had been warned against.

"I thought you were in mourning," I asked, as I settled on my bed, across from hers.

"I am. His family didn't want me there."

I cringed as the baby punched my kidney. As I braced my side, I glanced between our sides of the room. Mine, a museum of science and math awards, golden trophies adorning the shelves like hunters' prizes, photos, newspapers, and certificates framed for all to see. Nayeli's, cluttered with record albums, thrifted books, stuffed animals she had adopted from sketchy markets in the city, love letters crammed into her drawers. I could see the secret box beneath her bed, full of hash and rolling paper. She caught my eye on it and kicked it back under the bed with her heel.

"Don't be stupid," she said. "I was just reminiscing."

"How many months are you?"

"Seven. You?"

"The same."

48

"Huh?" she chuckled. "I wonder if we—"

"No, no," I groaned, not even wanting to think about it.

Nayeli cackled, the moonlight hitting her teeth, making them glint white above her perfect dark skin.

"I never thought you'd end up pregnant. Hell, I didn't even think you had sex."

"Well, I never thought you'd ever come back here."

Nayeli twisted the gold band on her finger. "I guess we're both surprising ourselves, then."

"Mama and Baba, too."

Nayeli sighed and pulled her heavy legs onto the bed. I eased down onto the floor.

"Do you really think they'll have devil wings?" I asked.

"I don't think it matters."

"It will matter to Mama and Baba."

"You care too much what they think."

I scoffed. "You never have. That's why you're—"

I bit my tongue. Nayeli challenged me with her eyes.

"I didn't have this baby with them. I'm having him with Amir." Her hand rubbed her stomach gently. Her voice cracked, "He was so excited to meet him."

Another hard kick to my side. I hissed, and leaned my head back onto the mattress.

"He can feel your stress," Nayeli diagnosed. "You should try singing to him."

I was in no mood to sing. I climbed into bed, ready to sleep, until I remembered that I was still wearing the clothes from the plane. I forced myself up and headed toward the bathroom. Nayeli, still in her jeans, tucked herself under her blankets and began to sing.

In the bathroom, I studied myself in the mirror. I saw the dark line slicing across my middle, like a firm ripeness on a summer fruit. I prayed for feathers.

Please, please, God, let him have feathers. Pure white, perfect angel wings. It just may be the only thing to soften the damage I've done.

I held my stomach in my hands, squeezed my eyes shut, and mumbled aloud to anything that might hear me.

A gentle kick came, to assure me, or maybe a warning to keep it down.

***

Our lives became endless checkups and ultrasounds. The ultrasounds showed us typical, boring things, like the babies' health and brain development, but our boys gave no hints about the wings they would have. The doctor explained with an uncertain look; the wings were contained in a sort of caul, a protective covering that only fell off when they came into the world.

We were given small photos. It still seemed unreal. In that fuzzy, gray picture was the face of the baby inside me. His profile was like Nayeli's, a short, curved nose that resembled the snout of a piglet. His forehead looked like mine, firm and flat. I peeked at Nayeli, who was tenderly wiping the spots that her tears had left on the photo. I did not have a name for mine. But I wouldn't need one. Whoever adopted him would come up with something much better than anything I could think of.

Mama and Baba were uninterested after they learned the wings were invisible. Baba would not allow us to come to his church in our current state, so when he came home, he took off his collar, went upstairs to his study, and ignored us for the rest of the day. Our parents became ghosts in our house, only appearing to send a look of silent disapproval when we laughed too loudly or ate too eagerly. I spent my days planning my return to university, calling the registrar, arranging my delayed graduation, sending apologies to professors. Nayeli left with the driver every day to pick out tiny clothes and shoes, finding toys for his first Christmas and hats for his first winter. She even tailored a jacket with holes in the back that would allow his wings to poke out, in case he ever had the urge to fly away.

I learned what I could about the wings from the news. There had yet to be one child born without them, and the theories came spilling forth from a vault of confusion.

Politicians said it was a sign of one political party's internal corruption being exposed. The Pope said that he was still consulting with God. Some fanatics believed the children born would become the armies of angels and demons that would fight over the fate of mankind. A few parents, upon seeing the bat wings, attempted to cut them off. But the wings were composed of bone and muscle, and any effort to remove them resulted in a painful, bloody mess. A few more of the babies with bat wings were thrown off of bridges or suffocated.

Ornithologists found that the "angel" wings perfectly resembled the anatomy of a goose. Biologists discovered that the "demon" wings were actually those of a fruit bat. Doctors said that there was no difference in the behavior of bat wing and goose-wing babies, that their responses and cognition were perfectly normal. They all laughed when tickled, cried when pinched, and latched eagerly to their mothers' breasts. They were, quite literally, just babies with wings.

A few commentators dared to wonder publicly if the mothers had anything to do with it. Comics quipped that hoe phases had produced the demons. Pregnant women flocked to confession, their ankles and wrists swollen with sin. Grandmothers prayed over the bellies of their daughters and interrogated them for the most risqué stories that might put the child at risk.

I had nothing to admit. Mama and Baba had not asked, anyway. But one night I overheard them in the living room, when I came downstairs for water.

It was strange, to hear and see them so close, as they had not made themselves visible since the ultrasounds. In muted tones, they were talking about Rachel, who lived down the road. I stopped on the last stair, listening as Baba mumbled.

"Rachel's pregnant with her third child. By a third man!"

Mama sucked her teeth. "That child will come out with claws and horns."

"God help us. These girls, running around and giving it away to any man who's willing. This is a reckoning for all they have done."

"This is a lesson," Mama continued. "Like the flood or the plagues. It will expose, and wash away the wrongdoing. It will be all right in the end."

"But what do we do now?"

I stood silently on the stairwell, swaying, too tight to breathe.

Baba spoke again. "I thought we taught them better."

"We did," Mama insisted. "It's not our fault."

***

For the next few weeks, I spent hours on my phone, researching. I looked for answers about the wings. I tried to find confirmation, signs, any way to tell what kind of wings the kid would have. All I found was speculation. Some people wondered if the bat wing babies would grow up to be psychopaths, the goose-wing babies to become saints. Now it seemed we could easily point out the good and bad of the world, depending on the wings they carried.

"That's as stupid as thinking anyone with blue eyes is evil," Nayeli sucked her teeth as her knitting needles clacked away at a pair of socks.

I was on my laptop, researching adoption agencies. Most of them were shut down, refusing to take any newborns until the wings were figured out. My chest tightened.

"I think people are just scared. They're always trying to put meanings on things." She scoffed, as if everyone in the world were idiots except her.

I tried to focus on my laptop. It was just like Baba said. No one wanted a baby with devil wings. The baby jabbed me again, and I felt a wave of nausea.

I ran to the bathroom, and shoved my face into the toilet, retching up everything I had eaten that morning. Nayeli followed, and rubbed my shoulders until it was all out.

"Are you good?"

"No."

"Do you want some tea?"

"No."

I sat back on my heels, my head in my hands. Nayeli hovered above, unable to join me on the floor. We stood there, bloated, staring at each other. Nayeli, like with everything else, was absolutely fine in the flurry of chaos. But she was looking at me pitifully as if I didn't know something obvious.

"We'll get through this together."

Together was for something we could hide from our parents, like a tattoo. Together was for picking out stars and naming them. Together was for stupid, silly, childish things. I could not afford to be stupid, silly, or childish. I could not afford to be Nayeli.

"How are you so calm?"

She blinked. "What do you mean?"

"You're nearly nine months pregnant. Your husband is dead. Mama and Baba won't want anything to do with you or your son, especially if he's a fruit bat. You're alone, and it's your own fault! Why are you acting like everything is fine?"

Her mouth trembled with an answer she could not reveal, or did not have. Her fingers twisted her ring.

"You always act like you know better than everyone else." I snapped.

Nayeli was silent. I stood up and left her. I finally understood what had always irritated Mama and Baba about her. She didn't accept reality. She thought she could fall in love and run away and ignore her responsibilities to our parents. I had worked my whole life to become everything they wanted. I had ruined that for myself. Now, I was demoted to the same place as my sister.

I saw the way Baba looked at me. I felt the way Mama ignored me. I had to distance myself from Nayeli. I had to prove to them that I wasn't like her.

After that day, I dove even deeper into my search. I found doctors who wanted to study the babies over the next eighteen years. I collected their contacts. I researched their facilities, all of which promised excellent care. I gathered my information, the numbers, the services, a selection for my parents to choose from. I went to Mama and Baba and showed them what I found.

"As soon as he's born, I can hand him off." I told them. "They'll take care of the baby for eighteen years. They'll feed him, clothe him, raise him, and he'll be okay. I can go back to university and graduate in three years, and then go to medical school right after."

There was quiet between them for a moment. Then, Mama spoke.

"What will happen to him after eighteen years?"

"He'll be an adult. He'll do whatever he wants."

Baba leaned back and crossed his arms. "So you'll release a demon into the world, and carry on as if you had nothing to do with it?"

"They don't know if they're evil or not. That's the whole point of the study."

"I see," Baba said.

Baba only said "I see," when he could see right through me.

I see, Laila, you're desperate to redeem yourself after your irredeemable mistake. I see, Laila, that you don't know what you're doing.

"Did you hear? Rachel down the road just gave birth to a girl with devil wings," he said.

Mama shook her head.

My mouth opened, then closed. An emptiness bubbled in my stomach. I felt, right then and there, that I was begging them for forgiveness. And I knew I would receive none.

***

"How could anybody think a baby is evil?" Luisa said as she mopped the kitchen, moments after I dropped the vitamin shake she had made for me on the floor.

I was trying to read comments on an online forum of pregnant women who were predicting what they might have. One mother insisted that her morning sickness was proof of bat wings. Another was sure that her uneventful pregnancy was certain to produce an angel. I had been kicked, painfully, but other than that there was not much to report. What did that mean? I had just finished typing when I tripped, and sent my smoothie sprawling. I apologized to Luisa and tried to clean it up, but she refused.

I wiped up the edges with a paper towel.

Luisa continued to talk about babies being a gift from God, having received three of her own, and I could not pretend to listen. I scrubbed. Nobody would want this baby. I scrubbed. My life had been cut short by some cruel irony, a devil child brought into the world by a devilish act that didn't even last more than a minute. I scrubbed. I would suffer the same exiled fate as Nayeli. Tolerated, but no longer preferred.

The dam inside me cracked, then burst.

I bawled, ugly, loud, wretched.

Luisa came to me, and cradled me, asking what was wrong.

"I can't mess up again." I choked.

Luisa held me.

From Baba's study came a yell for silence.

***

It happened at night.

Nayeli and I were suddenly awakened by sharpness stabbing our groins. We sat up at the same time, our bodies connected by pain. We looked at each other, and knew.

We screamed, and Luisa came running. She took us downstairs, one at a time, and it wasn't until we were both wailing at the front door that Baba emerged from his bedroom.

"What's going on?"

"They're going into labor," Luisa huffed, dashing about the foyer. "I'm getting them to the hospital. Where are the keys?"

Baba stood frozen at the top of the stairs, his hands clenching the rail.

"Mr. Dupont! Where are the keys?"

"There are doctors at the hospital that go to the church," he muttered. "Take them to the master bathroom."

Luisa escorted us to the master bathroom. It was the one bathroom in the house that Nayeli and I were never allowed in as kids. Two clawfoot bathtubs, gold etchings, faucets glinting silver, soap dishes flashing opals. We used to peek under the door and take in as much as we could. Now, we were right in it, gasping on the floor.

Luisa ran warm water in both tubs and checked the temperature with her elbow. She pulled off Nayeli's pajama pants, then mine, and hauled us each into our own tub. She prayed for a moment, then announced that she was going to get towels. She promised she would be right back.

The tubs were right beside each other, installed so two lovers could gaze into each other's eyes as they soaked in rose petals, or two sisters could pretend they were sailing boats into a churning sea.

I turned my head and saw Nayeli crying as her contractions ripped through her, and I felt them as if they were my very own.

My sister, who used to follow me around and beg to play with me and the other big kids. My sister who, when I pushed her away, learned to do whatever she wanted, not caring about my parents' reputation or mine. My sister, who ran off, married Amir, and loved him so much that she never called or came back home until now.

Now, I knew what she meant when she said it didn't matter. I didn't care if I never went back to university, or if I never became a doctor. I just wanted the pain to end.

Lightning burned through my belly, and the water bloomed red between my thighs. All at once, the life that I so desperately wanted flashed before me.

I saw my graduation. I saw the wingless child that I would have one day with a sturdy, handsome doctor who would forgive me. I saw the golden halo that I would have again after I made my practice, after I won Nobel Prizes and established charities that would feed angel children all around the world. Baba's church welcomed me with open arms, and their smiles told me that I had earned their holy awe. I reached out to them, to Baba, to Mama, to whatever ancestor would receive me, and I yelled for help and asked for forgiveness and cursed all at once, and then someone took my hand.

I opened my eyes and saw her. Nayeli, using what little remained of her strength to smile at me and squeeze my hand.

I remember Luisa yelling push.

A towel, covering Nayeli's forehead as her head slumped backward, and her breathing became shallow.

Hands on my shoulders, on my thighs.

Something leaving me, rushing into the water.

Twin splashes, someone running between the tubs. Then, two cries, joining as if they knew the other's pain.

A warmth placed into my arms. I focused my eyes.

Nayeli's nose, my forehead. Screaming, pink gums.

Dark, bat wings.

Luisa smiled at me, but there was uncertainty in her eyes.

In Nayeli's arms, a child cried as if he knew everything this dark world had waiting for him. On his back were feathers. Bloody feathers, but between those red splotches were pure white. Nayeli's eyes were closed. She was alive, but the birth had taken her right to the edge.

"Nayeli?"

She did not answer. I looked at her baby, his little eyebrows furrowed as he yelled, his perfect little wings fluttering.

Luisa spoke breathlessly, something I could not hear.

"What?"

"Your parents are coming."

Alarm slammed in my chest. Footsteps creaked above, crossing to the staircase.

I held my baby up to Luisa. "Give mine to Nayeli and hers to me."

Luisa blinked. "Laila—"

"Please!" I begged. The stairs groaned.

"I—I can't."

"Nayeli won't care. I need this more than she does."

Footsteps in the hallway.

"Luisa, please!"

Luisa hesitated, her mind battling itself. Finally, she gathered the baby from my arms, and carefully rushed to take Nayeli's. Nayeli, in a daze, didn't even notice. Luisa placed the demon in Nayeli's arms, and gave the angel to me. He screamed even louder.

Mama and Baba came in a second later. Their unimpressed faces brightened as soon as they saw the bundle of feathers in my arms. I smiled tiredly. Mama came forward, cooing.

"An angel," she breathed.

I sighed, relieved.

Speechless, Baba walked toward the tubs. He glanced at Nayeli, who was just now beginning to come back to the world. He saw the hideous bat wings on her new baby, and sneered.

Baba turned his back on her and admired the crying baby in my arms.

Luisa, shaking, blood on her hands, stood back.

"We have to call an agency," I raised my voice over the baby's shrieks. "To take him."

Mama's hands were raised to her mouth, and she glanced up at Baba with tears in her eyes. "Oh, Michael, it's an angel."

Baba nodded. Something, silently, transferred between them. An unease lifted in my throat.

"We have to call the agency." I reminded them again.

"Laila, don't be ridiculous," Mama said. "How could you just give away a child with the wings of an angel?"

My lips trembled. "But what about university?"

Baba muttered, "We will figure out a way for you to go back. But we cannot refuse a gift from God either."

The angel screamed, loud and shrill. I forced a smile.

"He's perfect," Baba said.

"An angel," Mama insisted. "A gift."

The baby kept crying, as if he were trying to explain. His grandparents adored him, pointing out his nose or his perfect curly hair. Luisa turned away.

In my arms, Nayeli's child wailed. And I knew, as the child knew, that one day the sun would explode, that one day we would both die, that one day he would grow up and I would grow old, and that between now and then there was no hope.

I looked at Nayeli, now fully awake. She saw the crumpled bat wings and touched them tenderly. The baby wheezed and whimpered, and she cradled him closely with a smile as tears pooled in her eyes.

"Hello, Amir," she sang softly, and kissed his wet forehead.

A Dirge without music

The train rumbled along on creaking wheels, its cramped compartments filled with tired and jaded passengers returning to the quiet corners of the countryside and their weary lives. In the watery light filtering through the window panes, the titanium-coated steel of the train car seemed almost black. Only when closely observed could Saif make out the tell-tale hint of cobalt, the color of the ocean in a storm.

Saif sighed and pressed his face to the dirty glass, sleep licking at the edges of his consciousness with the caress of a tentative flame, undaunted by the worry etched into the creases of his brow, or the rocking sway of the train as it streaked past, set on its course. He had been told several times, by his own father and grandfather, of the tiredness that came with trying to counter the blasted curse, but he hadn't quite expected it to feel like this. The constant weariness that suffused his limbs and mind and made him feel like he was trudging through molasses.

He rubbed his swollen eyes, watching the empty stretches of land that had accompanied his journey suddenly give way to derelict housing units. And as the train slowed on its approach to its final destination, Saif caught glimpses of things that filled him with a quiet sort of ache: crumbling backyards with clothes lines strung up from wall to wall like uneven stitches; the back entrances of factories and carpentry shops where exhausted men gathered on their breaks to smoke and watch the cars and buses roll along; trash littering roadsides and graffiti lining walls; all things that spoke of lives well established, written by people who refused to let their memories be extinguished. A life quite different from his own.

Saif stood up before the train stopped completely at the

station—nothing more than a small ramshackle building made of faded wood that looked like it had endured for generations—and hurried to the nearest door to avoid the imminent crush of the crowd. The sky was the azure of a cloudless summer, the white hot light of the sun baking and bleaching all within its sight, immediately making him break out into a sweat.

He sought the temporary shade of the station's awning, holding a hand to his face to better search for his quarry, and found her almost immediately, for she could not be anyone other than who he was looking for. Even excluding the way the other passengers' eyes seemed to slide right off her, with knee-length silver hair offset by eyes and skin that glowed like starlight, her appearance made it clear she was not quite fully of this world. And because no one met women like her on the side of a road at two in the afternoon just standing about and cooling their heels. You met witches and spirits, the fae and the forbidden, and in all the stories they tell about this sort of thing, they warn the listener to never get close, to not speak to them, and to never ever give them power over you. More than they already had at least. And yet, here Saif was, about to do all three.

She raised her hand and beckoned to him, crooking smooth fingers until he started toward her, then abruptly turned and walked away. She didn't even check to see if he was following. She probably knew he had no choice.

He followed her carefully down a solitary path until they reached a small hut set in front of a thick forest that almost swallowed it whole. His companion motioned him to a straw mat, and he sat down slowly, trying to fight through the fear in his heart.

The woman sat opposite him, cold and pale and beautiful, a shard of winter impervious to the entreaties of the fire in the hearth behind her. He had not known what to expect when his fumbling requests and bribes to the scant believers in the otherworldly led him to her, though he could hardly remember the time when seers and soothsayers had not been his usual purview.

She watched him idly, looking slightly amused at his hesitance, her hand twisting and twirling a silver chain around her neck that held a long slim rod. He'd seen it before on other soothsayers he'd frequented but still didn't know how it worked—whether it drew from its owner's unfaltering form, or had a power all on its own. It was bone white with three black marks on both top and bottom, and Saif watched it, hypnotized, noting its natural curve and the uncanny way it seemed to cleave to her fingers as though it belonged in her hand and nowhere else.

"Your trepidation is misplaced," she murmured as she squatted before him, her hair flapping behind her like a banner. There was no breeze to have caused its movement, and yet there it was, trailing behind her as if it had a life of its own.

"I am not afraid"" Saif said, the hitch in his voice exposing the falsehood.

The woman smiled indulgently, and reached out to push his locs back from his face.

"Yes, you are. But I will not hurt you. I am only here to give you the answers you seek. As you are here to seek them."

"Yes," Saif said, feeling his shoulders relax in resignation. "As I am here to seek them."

All his life Saif had worn his name like a badge of honor, and never thought to wonder why holding his head above others came to him so naturally. He had been born into privilege, and to him, wealth and the admiration of his peers had been not so much a constant companion, but an obsessive stalker. When she'd lived, his wife had once accused him of acting as though kingdoms rose and fell based on the decisions he made. Even when he was young he had been followed and looked to, whether by kids at his school or strangers on the street. When things went wrong—a fight breaking out, a house on fire, anything where a firm and steady hand was needed—faces turned his way and people he'd never really talked to asked him, "What do we do?" And Saif would raise his head and square his shoulders, and try to answer them. It was easy for him. Natural. And then he had turned twenty-five and his son had been born, and his father had sat him down and told him about their family's blessing, and their curse.

It was what was at the forefront of his mind as he held out his palms to the seer, watching her closely as she grasped both hands in hers and unfolded his fingers like a blooming water lily.

She traced his lifelines with the white rod, the chain still around her neck, and Saif watched as his blood broke skin to follow the path she made. There was no pain. She poked and prodded at his flesh for several minutes—Head. Heart. Life. Fate—then raised sad eyes to his and said, "I'm sorry, what has already begun, cannot be stopped. It is done."

Saif felt his throat close up with the force of his despair. He wanted to challenge her, to tell her to look again, but she was the thirteenth seer he had visited in the last year who had given him the same verdict. Nothing could be done.

"He is my son," he whispered. "My son."

"I know, but the Anatiyan are old magic. Steeped in the strength of familial blood and lineage, and from the time of the Founders of magic themselves. Some even say they are the Founders. Their will cannot be countered, only endured. I am sorry."

The tears he'd sensed a moment before sprang up and spilled over. He thanked her quietly and got up to leave, his steps unsteady beneath the arresting blue of her sorrowful gaze, and suddenly, a memory surfaced in his mind, raw and visceral, of when he had last seen that exact color.

It was the summer after Oman graduated Primary School—when they had gone on a trip to the beach, just the two of them. Saif closed his eyes and remembered the ocean as it had been that day, blue as a Robin's egg, the warm sand beneath their feet and the fine mist that had settled over the world and wrapped them in a gauzy grey blanket. He had been so carefree then, so sure that there would be a counter or a cure, that nothing would destroy his happiness, and there would be no cold spot to soil the paradise of warmth he had found with his son. How very wrong he had been.

He spent the journey home in a daze, the sights that had so captivated him earlier lost to his troubled mind.

When he finally reached his home, standing majestically in the middle of lush grounds, Oman rushed outside to greet him with an enthusiasm that better suited a child of six rather than his seventeen-year-old form. But Saif had no complaints. Nowadays, he clung to every moment he got with him, his only child, because he knew exactly how long they had left together.

Oman pulled back from their embrace, face falling at the wetness around his father's eyes.

"Is everything all right, Adda?"

Saif looked at him, tracing his every feature with quiet desperation, trying to memorize lest he forget.

"Yes, everything is fine." The lie almost burned his tongue on its way out.

Oman did not look like he believed him, but he squeezed Saif's shoulder and tugged him toward the towering mansion. "Come, Adda. Come see who came for a visit!"

Saif allowed himself to be tugged along, even as his heart was breaking anew, and Oman led him to the parlor where the sour face of one of his friends sat glowering.

"It's Dean!" Oman announced grandly. "His parents finally let him visit again, isn't it great? I thought we'd never see each other again after we moved."

Oman was the only one displaying any enthusiasm at the reunion, while both Saif and Dean eyed each other with distrust.

Saif did not understand what his son saw in the other boy. Dean was an outcast, even among his peers, with no other friends apart from his son. But then that was always Oman's way, daring to step where others would not tread. It was what Saif himself had cursed him with, so he swallowed his complaints and extended his hand for Dean to shake.

He watched Oman bundle his friend up the stairs, swinging

his luggage over his shoulder and chatting a mile a minute, and whispered a silent prayer to whoever was responsible for upholding the prayers of fathers for their sons: *Let me keep him*, he whispered. *Please. Just let me keep him.*

Child of the Anatiyan, the light-eyed mage called Duna had said, holding his wrist loosely from where she knelt by a fire somehow made out of wet wood, and clad in clothes that smelt of the cave she dwelt in, dark and damp, like all things borne of old magic are. *Son of the darkness, blood of the Founders, come and seek the fate of the one that comes after you.*

And like his father before him, his grandfather before them both, and like all the men in his family going back over a thousand years, he had sat with his newborn son cradled in his lap, and held out his hands.

The story his father had told him of the Anatiyan and their ties to his family, had seemed nothing short of fantastical at first, and even with the proof of their power seemingly affecting the course of his life and his many successes, at the time, part of Saif had only really agreed to seek Duna to humor him. He had not wanted to believe. Because to believe was to question whether anything that he'd ever done had been a product of his own free will or if it had been preordained. Had he merely gone along for the ride all his life, swept up like a leaf in a storm and carried along on the journey to the end of time? No, Saif had not wanted to believe.

But curiosity had led him to sit in front of the mage and watch as she arranged small tablets of tubali in front of him. There had been ten in total, each with different markings etched deep into their center. Perhaps it was their weathered forms that had started to chip away at his doubts, or perhaps it had been the heaviness that had settled in his chest the minute his fingers brushed at them. If nothing else, the calm certainty in Duna's eyes as she gazed at him—utterly aware and in control of her own power— had almost done away with it altogether.

The first tablet was Courage, followed by Beauty, Wealth

and Humility. In the middle were Wisdom, Empathy and Prestige, and the last, Kindness, Loyalty and Love.

Even as he thumbed them warily, he acknowledged the one his father must have chosen for him. Prestige. The reason why no matter where he went, his presence made itself known, and his influence lingered.

Looking down into his son's slumbering form, filled to bursting with love and pride, he could think of no better character to grant him that would shape the course of his life for the better, but courage. Because courage was strength, valor and perseverance. It was fearlessness and heart, and Oman's life would be richer for it.

Yes, he would give his baby boy courage for the ages.

Remember, Duna had said, *you cannot alter your choice.* And Saif had nodded, content, until he turned the tablet over, and saw the two numbers etched on the other side: "one" and "eight," and had been told then, that by choosing a character trait to define his son's life, he would also be choosing when that life would end. He had just condemned his precious boy to death at the tender age of eighteen.

Saif had dropped the tubali in his shock, demanding to know why he hadn't been told earlier. Duna had merely shrugged. *Magic is both blessing and curse, child. And you would not have come otherwise.*

Seventeen years of trying to find a cure or a counter, and he had been left with nothing but the bitter taste of fear and regret, and the lingering question of what would have happened if hadn't listened to his father after all.

On the day he left for his fifteenth trip to see his fifteenth seer, desperate for a verdict that did not make him want to tear out his own heart, Oman met him on the steps of the house, wearing an oversized robe and looking old and frayed around the edges like an aging photograph. "Another trip?" he asked softly.

"I won't be long."

"Will you tell me where it is that you go? You never used to travel so much before this year. I miss you Adda, what is going on?"

Saif paused with one leg in the car, the worried note in his son's voice arresting him in motion. What could he say? *You are near death and I am trying to prevent it?* Or, *I wish my father had kept his knowledge to himself?* How do you tell your only child that you are responsible for the fact that he will not live to see past his eighteenth birthday? And that his heart will never fill out enough to bear the weight of the courage it carries?

He turned around and reached out to cup his son's face. "I am sorry," he said, meaning it with every fiber of his being. "I am so sorry."

Oman watched him drive away with hurt in his eyes, reflected in his father's.

"You are running from something that cannot be escaped. You seek something you have already found. There is no hope for you in all the corners of the world, my child. You must accept your fate, and that of the one whom you love so. The *Anatiyan* have spoken."

"He is my son!" Saif roared at the wrinkled sorcerer, throwing away the cup of bitter tea he had been handed, but he only received pity in return.

"The *Anatiyan* have spoken," his fifteenth sorcerer said again, "and you have run out of time."

As Oman's eighteenth birthday loomed like a black cloud threatening rain, Saif thought of escape, of grabbing his boy and moving to a city so distant that no one would ever find them—that if the earth were in indeed flat, they would teeter on the very brink like a coin balanced on the edge of a table. But it would accomplish nothing. Even if he had not already been told, deep in his heart, he knew.

He swore and raged and made offerings to every deity he had ever heard of. He prostrated himself in different temples and wept his fear into their floors while their incense clouded his throat, fighting for space with his increasing desperation. He pleaded for mercy and made promises, cajoled and threatened and bribed, until his voice sought to abandon him. And all the while his son followed him like a shadow every time he returned, worried and afraid, and perhaps thinking his father had gone mad. Sometimes, Saif thought perhaps he had.

The night before Oman crossed the threshold into adulthood, Saif barricaded the two of them in the house, sending all the servants away and refusing anyone else entry.

"Why do we have to hide?" Oman asked, twisting the sleeves of his sweater and watching his father lock the doors of the house with shaking hands.

"Don't worry," Saif muttered, his eyes wild, "we will be safe. You will be safe."

He led Oman to the attic, where the boy looked quietly at the two beds wedged into the small space, and perhaps catching on to his father's mood, merely got into one and pulled the sheets to his neck, eyes wide but fierce. He gave his father a somber smile.

"Whatever it is, Adda, it will be all right. We will face it together, and I will be brave. Have courage."

Saif stifled a sob. *Have courage.*

He sat on the floor between the two beds and watched Oman fall asleep, refusing to follow him into the land of dreams, just in case. But he was too tired from his endeavors of the past weeks, and his eyes slipped closed of their own free will.

He awoke to the smell of smoke and the heat of flames, and his son screaming in his ear.

They told him that Oman had pulled them both out, but had succumbed to the smoke that had infiltrated his lungs. That he had saved his father's life at the cost of his own. *He was so brave* they said, *so courageous*, and all Saif could feel was the memory of holding his infant son in his arms after he was born, and hoping with all that he was that he would get to see him grow up.

No one knew how the fire had started. There had been no

spark, no trigger that had set it in motion, but Saif, swaddled in bandages and burn ointments, listened to the police deliver their reports, and carried the burden of knowing. The spark had been lit eighteen years ago.

There was, it turned out, no compensation for his loss. Nothing to stem the bloodletting. Like a bucket of water thrown on a fire, Oman's loss had extinguished every joy, every hope. His world had collapsed around him like a telescope and he was now nothing but an animal, caught in the trap of his pain. All the prestige Saif's father had bestowed on him, all the success, had not done him any good in the end, and he had been forced to learn that unlike the life he had lived to this point, the things worth having, were bought at great costs.

Sunup Town

Town clock just struck five and that tinge of daylight is hitting the edge of Main Street to the east. I watch as the hands of the clock mark the moment like a moon dial, casting long dark shadows across the shaded face. The breeze brings up gooseflesh on my arms, the curly, now-gray strands reaching up as if grabbing at something on the wind. I hate that bad omen feeling.

It's quiet outside since rush hour is over and the day is already muggy. I always hope for a couple people to come pick up the last of the day's cookin, but I like it when it's a little slow.

I watch as the nude-colored sedan with the missing bumper pulls into the lot. That skinny dude, who shows all his teeth when he talks to Sheryleen about the menu, gets out and walks toward the door and to me, the creaking noise it makes sounds like old bones as he opens it. He's one of the few who wipes his boots on the mat before coming in: two wipes per boot like a ritual every time he stops past. It makes me nervous to see him this late. I woulda thought everybody like him had already left town before sunup.

He smiles with half his teeth showing as he comes through the door.

After a minute looking over the menu, he says, "Hello, sir. May I please have an order to go? I'd like a number two with collard greens, macaroni and cheese, and..." he pauses to scan the rows of meat options for the umpteenth time, then continues, "barbequed pig feet. I've never had those before. How are they?"

Damn.

I'm in no mood to fool with charming the latecomers. Never am. And where is Sheryleen? She's supposed to be on register at closing. Last I seen her, she said she was taking the trash out. More'n likely she's somewhere tucked in a corner, textin that no-good boyfriend of hers. I keep tellin her that I'mma make her clean the grill and this time, she's gonna, for real. He's still smilin that half-teeth grin at me.

"The pig's feet are like they are. C'mon now, cuz we closin."

You think I just gave him gold, a bag full. He shows almost all them teeth and I wonder if that means he likes me nearly as much as he likes Sheryleen.

"Thanks, I'll give them a try."

"You want a drink? Dessert?"

He scans the menu. Again. Still. "I'll take some rice pudding and," he squints at the drinks portion of the list, "what is that purple beverage?"

I roll my eyes. "Grape Kool-Aid. I heard Sheryleen tell you that last week."

"Oh, right! Yes, a large grape, please. With no ice."

"Be just a minute."

He looks around as if the place is bigger than a breadbox. "So, where is Sheryleen? I thought she worked the register at closing?"

I don't answer, and before he can say another word, I shove the curtain aside and walk into the kitchen. Sheryleen is already there, dishing up his plate. I bump her arm and she snickers.

"What the hell, Sheryleen? You 'posed to be on register. Instead, you been dilly-dallyin somewhere all this time. You back here gigglin' while I got to deal with this fool. Again. You gon' clean this whole kitchen after he leave, you hear me?" I point to the right. "That grill too."

She holds up her hands. "Hold up, Unk!"

When she wants to sweet talk me, she calls me Unk, knowin' good and doggonit well that we ain't no kin. I mean, her auntie and me get together sometimes but it ain't serious like that.

"I was just takin out the trash like you told me and what had happened was my girl texted me about plans for the weekend and I wanted to ask—"

I cut her off before she can finish.

"Look, girl. Just dip up his plate. And don't even think about asking for the weekend off."

A roll of the eyes and she's piling on the mac and cheese and greens.

This guy and his coworkers work at the plant on the far side of town. Our parents and grandparents built this town on their blood, sweat, tears, and dreams. My momma's sister was a scientist, and her design is still the base for operations over there. She started out designing what they call ergonomic workstations, then took it onto the plant floor so all the folks who had to stand for ten or more hours a day had some kind of hover pads to stand on, scheduled sitting breaks, all that. Story goes, she smelt herself a little bit, went to the top boss, said she had an idea for improving things more. In the end, she designed a quantum transport system. Don't understand the science, but how Momma explained it to me was that a tech pushes a button and a vat of chemicals over *here* turns into individual buckets of chemicals over *there*. Momma said her sister also wrote most of the equations for the automated mixing machines. Like Shirley Jackson, Otis Boykin, Dr. Emeagwali, and countless other Black folks, her name ain't showed up in a history book yet. Likely won't neither.

After while as times changed, the folks runnin the plant realized they needed to diversify the workforce. Not everyone was in favor, but for the past twenty-five years or so, we've watched the traffic flow in around dusk and roll out by dawn.

The men and women who drive in for work often stop past between shifts, one bunch in the afternoon, another in the evening, and the last at three and four in the morning after their shifts end, even if all we have is scraps. They can't get enough of our cooking.

He's lucky tonight we got more than scraps, even after the earlier shifts and a few call-in orders from workers who try not to be wastin time after they get off. I'm surprised we didn't have more food for Sheryleen to try and take, since it's the end of the month. Like folks say, more month than money and the locals ain't been comin in as often.

Problem with the end of the month is the cops tryna hit that quota. They in force just round the corner on the road outta town. Cousin Booby came through on his way home from his shift at the gas station and tole me he'd seen about five cars pulled to the side, drivers getting ticketed for who knows what.

Cops love to get them plant workers. They been up all night mixing chemicals, packing orders, and testing new mixtures. Only a few of them live here and they smart enough to get off work and home before light. For the rest, there's only one way in and one way out of town. Their only choice is to drive through here on their way back to wherever they live, which has been good for our business since before my momma and daddy gave up runnin the place.

The cops know the workers be tired and reckless sometimes on the roads. Sometimes not. Either way, they're perfect targets for our in-town officers who catch them right before they drive over the city line and into the unincorporated area that surrounds us on their way to those places where the people don't look like us.

Sheryleen shows me the bottom of the pig feet tray. There's two whole and a couple knuckles.

"Give it all to him."

I pour his Kool-Aid, put extra ice in it as payback for keeping me open later than I wanted to be.

Sheryleen gives him a healthy scoop of pudding and lids it, puts it in and ties the bag, and hands it all to me. I want to cuss her, but I'll save that for after I lock up.

I hear the bell and the old-bone creak of the front door as it swings open again.

Sheryleen and I freeze.

"A little late today, ain't we? Whatchoo doin here?"

That's Dubs, or Officer Dionte Jones.

I ease back the edge of the curtain to peep out and sho' nuff, he's got his fingers hooked in his gun belt and is looking at ol' boy like a wolf.

Dude is shook, but I give him props for standing tall.

"Hello, officer. I didn't mean to be here so early, I mean late, I mean ...well, I work at the plant and like to grab a meal on my way home. I believe my order is almost ready and I'll be out of here as soon as I settle my bill."

Dubs sucks his teeth. "Where you live at, man?"

"About 30 miles west, sir, in Stockton."

Dubs keys the mic on his shoulder. "Yo, Carletta. This is Jones. Send some backup to the restaurant."

Ten-four.

Dude puts up his hands. "Sir, I mean no trouble. I'll just get my food and be on my way."

Seems like seconds and three cars pull up, lights flashing. Sheryleen looks at me, her eyes wide.

I sigh, hand dude's order back to her, walk to the fridge, and pull out that half-tray of mac and cheese that she was going to take home. She seems to forget her fear and looks at me like she wants to fight.

"I'll make you a whole tray when they leave," I whisper.

Her shoulders relax and she nods. I point with my chin to the curtain, and she follows me out front.

"What's good, Dubs," I say.

Sheryleen takes position behind the register and rings in the order. Dude's hands are shaking as he hands over his cash and coins.

"Yo!" Dubs' eyes are on the tray. "Just doin the do, man."

I act like my customer isn't even there as I walk straight to Dubs and hand him the tray. "Thought I heard your voice out here. Figured y'all could use a lil snack." I lean close and speak low. "Ey man, this guy and the others from the plant who come here are good customers. He be comin in like two, three times a week. He ain't usually this late though. Any chance you could let him slide?"

Dubs takes the tray and sniffs the contents through the plastic wrap. "Got any banana puddin?"

"And you know this. Gimme a second." I try not to rush into the kitchen.

Once behind the curtain, I boogie to the fridge and pull out a full tray. Guess I won't be goin home this mornin since now I need to make three puddins and four trays of mac and cheese.

I toss a box of spoons on top and stroll back out front. "Here you go, partner."

I twerk my head toward the condiments area. The cabinet door is part-way open from when I was refilling the salt and pepper earlier. Dubs follows my gaze.

"Go over there and grab some of those plastic bowls from under there."

He does and comes back with a whole sleeve.

Damn.

"Lemme put all this in a box for easy carrying." I'm grateful I didn't toss the one from the oranges I had delivered yesterday. I put in the puddin, mac and cheese, spoons, bowls, and a stack of napkins. As I hand it over, I ask, "What up? We good?"

Dubs crooks a finger at me, wanting me to lean close again, and he lowers his voice to near a whisper. "Listen, I got the fellas outside and this—" he glances down into the box, "is appreciated, fo' real though. But I'mma need to scare this fool. We can't be havin any of his kind up in here after daybreak. Y'feel me?"

I remember my grandaddy talkin about The Green Book our folks had for findin places they could stop at overnight while they traveled. Makes me wonder if there's a new version for them folks, to tell them where they should and shouldn't go after daybreak these days.

"Yeah, I feel you. But Dubs, man, I need y'all not to scare off my customers."

He laughs. "Looka here. Y'all got enough customers every day from us, yo' own people. Whatchu need them for?"

I want to cuss him but keep the tone casual. I don't need any trouble from the brothas in blue. "Food is food and money is money."

Dubs looks me up and down. "Sho y'right. Aight so, I'mma

just give him a little warning, have my peeps, ah, escort him to the edge a'town." He looks at dude and sucks his teeth. "But if I catch him here after dawn again, it'll be different next time, fo' real."

I turn away and toward my customer without another word. I can't stand Dubs.

To dude I say, "Hey, lemme help you to your car." I take the bag from his trembling hands and walk with him out the front door. There are six officers, two per car, and they watch us until they see Dubs come out with his box. When me and dude are close to his car, I say, "Listen, I appreciate your business, but you gotta follow the rules."

He takes the bag and puts it on the floor behind the driver's seat, alongside a briefcase full of crinkled papers covered in carefully typed scientific equations, then climbs in. He's sweating, the day's humidity taking its toll on his resolve.

"I don't understand. I just wanted to grab some food. What's the harm?"

"Look, just get goin, okay? Keep about two miles below the speed limit. Use your turn signals all the time."

I turn around to walk back to the shop, stop, and turn back to him. "Hope you enjoy the food and that you'll be back again. Tell your friends at work too."

His smile is thin and there is new knowing in his eyes. "I always do enjoy the food. And I'll be sure to tell my friends." He leans over and looks at Dubs and the other officers. "All about it."

He drives off and Dubs and his crew are close behind.

The sun is well over the horizon now, making me sweat almost as much as dude was. When I get back inside and lock the door, I hear noises in the kitchen. I tip back there and find Sheryleen, already boiling water for the mac and cheese. I put some water on for the pudding, wipe out the inside of the big mixing bowl, and grab two bunches of bananas.

After a few moments of stirring our respective pots, we look at each other and say, "Damn."

Buyer's Remorse

Alvina drags her number into Job's forearm with a cheap pen. They were on the balcony so long, they didn't realize that the party had transformed into a drunken inn. Alvina calls a cab and waves goodbye. Job waves back and grins ridiculously on the walk home. She hums in the backseat which accidentally amplifies the good mood of her cab driver, but she lets it go. She likes that Job wore sweatpants and had a messy bun to a pajama party. Everyone else looked professionally styled to seem casual. As Job walks back, he smiles at the odds of meeting someone else on the telepathic spectrum. She didn't want to talk about her powers much, but the soothing sound of her telepathic output made that yellow flag more chartreuse. He looks at his arm to memorize her number, but the one he's been trying to forget for years keeps coming to mind.

***

When Job was six, he thought people were stars. The lights and sounds that radiated out of the very rare passing car was the stuff of magic. His mother, Diana, watched him run out of their trailer in his undies to see the car up close. His long black wavy hair flowed down his back like a stream. His powers were pre-pubescent so nothing made sense and everything was beautiful. His cinnamon face brightened as he smiled back at her. Moments like these made Diana realize that rural was the right choice.

Mornings were always hard for Diana. Telepathic senses woke up before the person did. So Job would make her a pot of coffee and light her a cigarette. He dug through her glam rocker pile of curls to find her face. He loved the feel of her curls wrapping around his knuckles. It was like his fingers were getting a hug. When he found her face, she'd smile and pinch his cheek. Job would play with her caramel spirals of hair as they had coffee and cigarettes together. The only things strong enough to turn down the volume on humanity. She would only give him half a cigarette though. He had to wait until he was fourteen to smoke a whole one.

Job dangled his feet in the sun and smoke yellowed trailer. Diana messed around in the kitchen. She put down a paper plate with a lump of nickel, star anise, and an umeboshi. She opened her slat window and juggled some apples while smoking. "Go ahead."

Job tossed the star anise in his mouth like a candy and coughed.

Diana chuckled. "Little bitch."

"Umm, sad."

"What kind?"

"I don't know."

Diana tossed an apple at him. It hit him in the nose. She made a buzzer sound.

"Isolated sad?"

Diana was about the toss another apple but went back to juggling.

Job licked the nickel nugget and successfully identified it as loss of stability, fear. And Job puckered till his eyes watered with the umeboshi. Diana laughed and ordered him to finish it because his face was too funny. Job got through it and admitted he didn't know. Diana bopped him on the head with an apple and said it's competitive anger. She told him he would have to get used to that one; he would run across it a lot. Job tried to relax his face as he nodded. Diana smiled and rubbed his head. Job had done really well at identifying emotion colors. She was worried preoccupation tastes would be too nebulous. Next was impulse smells.

***

At the end of their eleventh date, Job walks Alvina to the threshold of her blue bungalow. A cool night breeze passes between them. She looks at his perpetually preoccupied face. Despite the gray in his beard and hair, his face reveals how premature it all is. She tucks a stray hair coming out of his messy bun behind his ear. He holds her close. Her sepia face is dotted with pecan freckles. His arms feel like her bones are merely a suggestion. She invites him in. Job hesitates. Alvina lives in the suburbs. He worries that there aren't enough people in close proximity for their telepathic outputs to blend together. It is going to be like someone is playing five movies at different volumes, but he only cares about the quietest one.

Alvina smirks. "Don't like my decorations?"

"No, it is very you."

There are plants of varying sizes in every corner of this place. The walls are spice colored. The air is cleaner-smelling than it ought to be indoors. He takes off his coat and sits on the gingerbread love seat facing the TV. Alvina states that she is going to get more comfortable, but he can see if there is something to watch, and goes to the back of the darkly-lit house.

As Job scrolls through channels, he tastes the umeboshi vitriol of her neighbor. Her wall splashes with bronze rage. He smells burnt parsley insecurity. He takes a deep breath and counts backward from one hundred to get her neighbor's night of online gaming out of his head. A beautiful woman just left to get more comfortable. He wants to be ready. With breathing exercises, he is able to turn down the volume of her neighbor's signals. Alvina comes out in a pair of soft black sweatpants, a black tank top, and barefaced. Her freckles have multiplied with the removal of her makeup. Job palms her face and rubs his thumb across her cheek. His knuckles feel a familiar hug as he runs his hands through her curly auburn afro. He takes his hair out of its bun. It falls in a way reminiscent of eighties romance novels. Alvina bites her lip and they make out.

After a while, she stops and leans her head on his shoulder.

"I'm really glad I'm with you." She has not brought any man home since her ex. She looks at his face. It is not a happy one.

***

At fourteen, Job could successfully identify every telepathic sensation, so Diana moved them from the unclaimed fields of Indiana to downtown Indianapolis. She immediately went to a salon and got her hair straightened. It was never curly again. Job knew better than to say anything, but he understood that nothing was going to be the same. The city had sounds and signals everywhere, but because of that, the signals blended together. It was the fog equivalent of fruity cereal milk. In high school, he was incapable of making eye contact. He just shuffled around listening to brown noise on his headphones. The kids at his exclusive private school already thought he was weird because of his western Asian otherness. The shoe looking sealed his fate. Eye contact made signals more vibrant and clear. Job thought he might dry heave or inappropriately huff their signals. Over the four years, he would gain no friends but learn the importance of smoking, coffee and counting.

***

Job is trapped in a memory echo chamber: I wish you would go, don't do that, get away from me, I wish you would leave, I can't stand you, and fucking freak. Tears trickle down his face. "I like being with you too. That should have been my response. I am such a sad sack."

Alvina kisses his cheek, "And I love that about you."

Job tired smiles. Her neighbor's plum rage spikes again. It is like a sitcom character barging in but, due to her being on the telepathic spectrum, everything is quieter next to her. Her thoughts sound like a radio just out of range, her impulses taste like infused waters, and her feelings look like colorblind watercolors. He kisses Alvina and puts her curvy legs on his lap. His fingertips roam around the waistband of her soft pants. She is massaging his scalp and generally playing in his hair. Before she can get more involved, she feels someone brooding in the chair behind them. He loudly clinks the ice in his glass. She knows looking back will not show anything, but his disapproving glare singes her scalp. Job feels the sizzle and searches her face like a textbook.

Alvina grins like a doll. "You want tea? I don't have any coffee in the house, but I have some nutty black teas I can brew extra strong."

He shakes his head and nuzzles her neck.

She rubs his head. His hair smells like roasted rock because he smokes Stallion cigarettes. The singeing moves from her scalp to right below her left lung.

His mouth tastes like he licked a penny. He looks at her.

She squirms out of his arms. "I think I could use some tea actually. You sure you don't want any?"

"If you're making some, sure."

Alvina hops off of his lap and whirls into her southwestern style kitchen. She feels the glare dissipate as she puts the kettle on.

Job watches comfort descend on Alvina like a morning dew. "I didn't mean to force a mood."

"No no, you read the mood correctly. I'm just nervous." On her long dark oak counter, she pours out two cups of tea for them. Her lungs feel tender.

He walks up to the counter and puts his hand on hers. "You can change your mind."

She kisses him across the counter.

He smells fresh baked scones while kissing. He doesn't get too distracted but does smirk. This is why he has not been in a bakery since he hit puberty.

She feels him smile and grins too. Her arm feels yanked, she turns around and sees no one. She already knows that.

His skeleton vibrates. "We don't have to. I like seeing your place."

"I want to. But I..." Alvina points behind her.

He nods for her to continue.

"I haven't brought a man home since my ex." She scratches her head. "I used to think he put cameras in here. I demolished all the walls of my bathroom to find them. Then I realized with the kind of technology he has access to, I would never find them."

Job's bones throb as he comes around the counter and hugs her.

Alvina laughs. "I should probably move."

"Not if you don't want to."

"I'm sorry."

"Don't be."

***

Alvina teared up as she looked in the mirror. The drama built like a pressure front. Landon was on pins and needles for weeks working on his acceptance speech. This award would make his name as a tech lobbyist. He bought the dress for this event specifically. It was by his favorite designer. He believed it would bring him good luck. But the dress looked way more revealing on Alvina's shapely body then it did on the lean model. The backless nature of the dress meant there was no support for her chest. A night of painful amounts of breast tape was in her future. Also the crimson of the dress clashed with the auburn of her hair. She didn't know whether seeming rebellious or seeming slutty would cause less trouble. She put her hair in an elaborate updo and dabbed tears out of her heavily lined eyes. When she got into the car service with him, he snarled so hard his lip curled. "At least you tamed, that lion mane of yours."

Once Landon and Alvina got to the award ceremony, she escalated his confidence and lowered his anxiety slightly every fifteen minutes. She was on his arm the whole night to battle the emotional breakdown that threatened to occur. In the weeks leading up to the event, he had shattered about eight wine glasses. The dinner was all the pomp and glamour of a movie set in the roaring twenties. She spent the entire evening being equal parts trophy, sparkling companion, and sexual object. She swore this evening was shaving days off her life.

As Landon accepted his award, his speech had everyone nodding. Alvina saw that the approval of the crowd was creating a feedback loop that kept his confidence levels rising. The longer he spoke, the more his levels rose, and the more the crowd responded to his rising confidence. By the end of his speech, the applause at the end had him on a cloud, and Alvina knew she could take a break.

Hours later, Alvina's back was hurting from the breast tape, her head was spinning from using her powers so much, and she was nauseous from stress. Landon made a big deal about taking the little lady home for the night. Alvina assured him that she was fine with going alone so he could enjoy himself, but he was not having it. In the car, Landon joked about somehow being a bigger deal than her in that dress. "It took some doing," he laughed. He stared at his award like it saved him. A new tier of businessmen would be willing to talk to him now. Alvina smiled.

He said the speech was like driving a sports car, feeling it pull away, and forcing it into submission. Alvina nodded but closed her eyes for a moment. When she opened them, his face was tight and teeth exposed.

"You're not even listening."

He ranted that she was bored by his success and wanted to be the center of attention. Alvina wanted to remind him that he is the one that bought her this dress, but facts were not going to help this argument. She touched his leg to deescalate his fear a little. She spoke slowly about how proud she was of him. She joked about being an old lady who is usually in bed at this time. She used his car analogy to prove she was listening. This car ride was a practice in breathlessness.

Once they got to his house, Landon went to his study for a celebratory scotch and Alvina went to the bathroom. While washing her face in his slate contemporary bathroom, she wanted to be mad. But she had to remember that the comedown from that level of high could only be harsh. It wasn't all his fault. As she reveals her galaxy of freckles, she realized that she should have left his confidence alone. She didn't know that it would be compounded that much by the speech. That level of escalation could make anyone perceive actions differently.

In the middle of the night, she was having trouble breathing. She saw his weighted blanket on top of her. They had been very helpful for Landon over the years, but there was more than one on her right now. She couldn't move. She turned her head. Landon was kneeling on the floor next to her.

"I know I can be a bit much."

Alvina tried not to look afraid.

"You've awakened all these feelings in me, you know?"

Alvina wanted to respond but breathing was hard enough.

"You make me a better man."

Alvina smiled weakly. It was hard to feel her feet.

Landon smiled with watering eyes, "Please, never leave me."

"I'll never leave you."

***

A few months after Job visits her place, Alvina goes to a Parisian style cafe near her job. It is very full, but she snatches a small empty table in the back. She takes a deep breath of the bakery smell and chuckles to herself. She imagines teenage Job trying to keep from looking flush. Alvina puts an earbud in one ear of a lecture and listens to the din of the cafe. She meditates to blend the voices out, it takes her half of a large tea to even get close, and she has to keep her eyes closed. The occasional word or phrase jumps out from the lecture or a loud friend group at the cafe. She imagines never being able to turn that off. She feels bad that this is as close to quiet as Job gets. Then there is a plop of someone sitting at her table. She opens her eyes.

Landon still looks like a perfume ad. "Your little office is so adorable."

Alvina learned to sweat in her feet years ago. She is ruining her shoes.

Landon takes off his Burberry limited edition sunglasses. His ice blue eyes pierce right through the back of her head.

She smiles. "I wasn't expecting you."

Landon grabs her soft thigh under the table. "I am all for you exploring your interests, but a man has his limits."

She put her hand on top of his. "I don't mean to seem ungrateful." Her voice cracks.

Landon tucks in some of her less defined curls. "Someone has to keep you in order." When he finishes, he looks at her like an artist does their finished work. He reaches into his Tom Ford messenger bag and pulls out an art portfolio. "Out of the wedding planners I saw, Miss Dane's is the best match." He spreads out the portfolio and orders a waiter to take her tea away.

The weddings look more like gallery openings where one person wears white. The invitations have lettering so raised they cast shadows. Alvina has a flash of being in her backyard with a flower crown, simple chairs, barefoot, surrounded by friends and Job with flowers in his hair. She wells tears and uses them. "I love her."

Landon squeezes her leg and smiles.

Alvina kisses him on the cheek and rubs his hand until he lets go. "I have to go to the restroom, but I want to talk color palettes. I am thinking cucumber and ashes of rose?"

Landon wears a smile that would make the day of someone else. "You know I am partial to cucumber."

She smiles. "I'll be back."

Alvina has her knees up to her chest so the stall won't look occupied. Her legs vibrate, but she is ignoring that. She hangs up with the police. They will share this recent development with the prosecutor's office and pick him up momentarily. Restraining orders are not the strongest barriers to rich, angry white men, but it is the only tool she has. She can't risk using her powers. With his psychically damaged mental state, murder-suicide isn't unimaginable. She always thinks, *I wouldn't be in this mess if I didn't use my powers on him in the first place.* She puts her face in her knees and makes one more call.

Job's phone sends her to voicemail. She remembers he has a grant proposal meeting today. After the tone, she clears her voice: *Hey, I should have planned this better. In case I have to disappear, I have had a marvelous time with you. I felt both free and close. I didn't know that was a thing that could be. Thank you. I will send you a postcard of where I last was to let you know I am okay. If you don't get one in the next month? It was a pleasure to know you.*

Job spends the entire meeting reading the man's signals and seeming present. He wants to take a nap. He smiles when he sees that Alvina called. As he listens, he leans all the way forward in his chair. He covers his mouth. His palms sweat. He hits replay. His stomach constricts like a heartbeat. He hits replay.

Job pictures Landon self-flagellating to the point of shredding his immaculate blue suit jacket into ribbons of purple. He envisions Landon naked, chapped, and sunburned, whispering, "Forgive me." Job feels the bones of his jaw grind. He sees Alvina's house without her in it. Her walls demolished, her bags not even packed. An old number pops in his head from memory, 463 459...Job puts his hand over his face and drops his phone. "Not her."

***

Job hated the Indianapolis life. He hated the two story shale contemporary penthouse they lived in. He always tripped down the spiral staircase separating the bedrooms from the open concept living room. He hated the school he kept being called a rag head in, but what he hated most was Diana's job. A person would tell her a goal, and she would implant a phrase or sentence that would remove all psychological barriers. The person never knew what the phrase was, but Job could overhear the idea click. It was like the loudest record scratch. The person always accomplished their goal. They may have destroyed their relationships, harmed their employees, committed crimes, exploited the vulnerable, or completely changed their personality, but Diana did what she said and was rewarded handsomely for it.

Because of her abilities, wealth, and beauty, people often

knelt in the lobby for hours just to be hit with the scent of her perfume. They hoped some of her dream granting powers would rub off on them. Diana would often kick at these lobby disciples for amusement. Job swallowed when he saw this. She always had people in and out of the apartment. Parties that went until ten in the morning. Job mostly stayed in his room and waited them out. He could only take so many clusters of naked people looking for the bathroom. She would call him a prude and chuckle; he would smirk and learn something. It was fine when it was just the two of them. But something about the way other people looked at her, made him want to crawl out of his skin.

One night, Diana finally implanted someone after several failed attempts. Job overheard the implant reject in the previous weeks. It sounded like a VCR rewinding, but this time it took. She threw a party to celebrate. Job went to bed early. When he woke up, he felt like his marrow was made of ember, his heart raced, and he couldn't be sure if the screaming he heard was telepathic or not. He sneaked down the stairs. Diana had filled the place with some of her most ardent lobby disciples and people she knew who liked to abuse others. She put them in renaissance costumes and let them loose. Job thought he would vomit flames. As he shivered and crept down the stairs, the telepathic and literal screams got louder. There were twenty people begging her to stop what was happening, and twenty people who understood how much Diana liked this. Job crept close enough to see Diana sitting on a piano and eating.

Her hair was like glowing copper. Her eyes and the inside of her mouth were made of white light. Her laugh echoed with a metallic boom that shook the apartment. Her skin shone like gold plating. Her dress was made of melting silver. Job hyperventilated after getting a glimpse. He closed his eyes and swallowed whatever was trying to come out of his stomach. His bones felt like they would shatter from vibration. The more people begged for help the more majestic her form became. Job took the deepest breath of his life and all the shaking, sweat, and fire dissipated. It became quiet in his head and he thought one phrase as loud as he could. "Stop this and go home."

Everyone stopped including Diana. She looked up and saw him at the very top of the stairs. Job was so dizzy he crawled back to his room and shut the door. His head throbbed. His pulse got louder and louder until the last pulse knocked him unconscious. The next day, all of his neighbors' signals came through at maximum strength. He could hardly breathe with all he could smell. It sounded like he was at the Stock Exchange. He couldn't see anything but colored clouds with the outlines of real life behind them. He panted as he tried to find his bed. He felt firm hands guide him into it, feed him spoonfuls of hot liquid he assumed was coffee, and put a blanket on him.

When he finally woke up normally, his eyelids felt weighted and his stomach empty. Diana played in his hair. Some days had passed, her hair was starting to curl again. His lungs felt raw. His muscles felt like a newborn colt's. Diana shushed him and told him to rest.

"I thought you'd be mad."

Diana chuckled. "At that display of talent?" She kissed him on his forehead. "It won't always hurt this much. The more you do it. The easier it gets. Granted, if you implanted one person, you'd probably be fine."

Job smiled weakly.

"Rest up." Diana brushed her hair back. "When you're up and ready, we can talk more about this ability's many uses."

Job nodded.

The next day, when Diana went to the salon to get her hair done, Job left. He didn't leave a note. He pawned the Star of David necklace she had bought him for bus fare. On the tearful ride, he vowed to never speak to her again, but he never forgot her number.

***

Alvina texts Job saying that Landon was escorted out by the police. She will be at the station awhile to file formal charges, but she will see him at home. He turns off all the lights in the bathroom, plays some Smooth Jazz, and burns a bunch of sweet sage scented candles. They are her favorite.

He is adding rose water bath salts when Alvina walks in.

She smiles at the scene. "I should get traumatized more often."

"That's not funny."

She shrugs.

He gives her a bear hug and thanks her for the voicemail. Alvina muffles "You're welcome" into his chest.

He holds her face in his hands. It's like someone set her eyes to dim.

In the candlelit bath, Alvina keeps getting halfway through a joke but loses momentum right before the punchline. All of the jokes are about her violent demise. She rubs the salt between her palms.

Job sits cross-legged on the floor next to her. He adjusts his legs. "Is the macabre helping?"

She leans back and lets the tub water fill her ears. "It feels like putting an impossible video game on pause. You'll eat your sandwich, drink your soda pop, but eventually the game goes back on and you have to lose."

Job bites his cheek and holds her hand. No words conjure.

Her voluminous hair is wilted from the bath. It drips water on his Indiana University sweatshirt. He puts it in the dryer for her. She curls up next to him in bed. They watch an endless slog of vapid movies and neither laugh nor frown. After the fourth one, Alvina's eyelids click closed from dryness. Job sighs. He will never understand why Diana chases this sensation. When she is asleep, she doesn't produce a signal.

As he is about to doze, his bones wrinkle. Alvina grabs his arm. "In three months, I may be suffering every sexual pain a rich angry man can fathom. How am I supposed to care about what I eat? When this unpauses, I lose." She squeezes his arm hard enough to hurt him. She searches his face like a scared parent, "How can I do this?"

Job's bones shake. Tears race out of the corners of his eyes. He can barely think through what he is picking up and what he is feeling. Then all the vibrations shoot from his bones to his head and stop. "You are safe now."

Alvina sighs like she's deflating. A minute later, her eyes flutter close and she sleeps.

Job holds her tightly. He stares at the television. He prays that sound that he heard came from it. He needs that record scratch to be comic emphasis.

The next morning, Job's eyelashes feel glued shut. After manually separating his eyelids, the world is blanketed in a thick colored fog. He can't even see out of the window. The smells of vinegar ego and iron anxiety race up his nose and make his eyes water. He covers his mouth as it flushes with spit. Job can barely breathe, but it is a nostalgic sensation. Being completely overwhelmed by telepathic input is a reminder that he is merely a weak vessel for a strong force.

After an arduous routine of breathing exercises, his senses return to coloring his world rather than overtaking it. He wobbles out of bed and wanders toward the coffee smell that he is half sure is real.

"I bet you didn't even realize you were smoking."

Job's eyes widen as he takes a sizable drag from his cigarette, "I don't know how that got there."

Alvina chuckles. She is wearing a canary wrap dress. Her afro of curls is at maximum lion mane. She passes his teetering form a cup of coffee.

Job takes out his cigarette. "You look great."

"Denial mania, there's nothing like it. I want to redecorate my house, reorganize all of my session notes, and then go out dancing till 4 AM."

Job smokes.

Alvina grabs her stuff off of the counter. "I don't know how long this is going to last. A day, a week, two hours—but the crash will not be pretty, and I need to prepare for it."

Job nods.

90

Alvina puts her hands on his shoulders. "Thank you for being a man of few words."

Job opens his mouth then closes it.

"No really, thank you." Alvina kisses him and runs out.

As soon as she closes the door, Job frowns.

Job slumps into his dining room chair. His cigarette dissolves out of his peripheral vision. After the shock wears off, he wipes the ashes off of his shirt and scours the internet. He rummages through telepathic forums as well as chat rooms, medical journals, and finds nothing helpful. Job opens a new pack of cigarettes when he realizes he has to call his mother.

Job digs under his bed and pulls out a safe the size of a shoe box. Inside it has the usual: social security card, powered individual identification card, birth certificate, and a Polaroid. It is of him and Diana when he was six: she was tickling him. He wants to remember her real face before he calls. She doesn't pick up. He stumbles through his message. Coming to her like this, he feels ten again.

Five minutes later, she calls back. Diana's voice is high and maternal. "You never call."

Job smiles at the normalcy of that sentence as he sits up in bed.

"I just finished an orgy."

Job shakes his head.

"Once you have a different mouth on every erogenous zone there is no going back." Diana tightens her white silk robe and paces around her apartment. She looks over at her great view of downtown Indianapolis. "So you limp dick, what brings this call?"

Job looks out at his balcony facing another apartment building. "To feel the sting of your familiar insults, how else would I feel at home?"

"But they are just so accurate, you perpetual sad sack."

They both grin.

Job scratches his nose. "You know there is no information

online about implantation?"

Diana laughs with a couple of snorts.

He hasn't heard that in almost two decades. He enjoys the sound.

Diana wipes her eyes. "Boychik, you have no idea how much I needed that." She catches her breath. "Do you know how many great self-help gurus, politicians, and religious leaders would be exposed if implantation were common knowledge?"

Job wipes condensation off of his sliding glass door, "Good point."

"Why are you researching that?"

Job opens his mouth to answer when Diana squeals.

"You implanted that girl with the cum-on-me tits, didn't you?"

Job has always lived with the reality that his mom "checks up on him" from time to time. His life is like her secret favorite soap opera. But she doesn't mail the writers, so he doesn't complain. "Talk about her like that again and I will forget your number."

Diana rolls her eyes and leans her back on the window. "It took?"

"Yes."

Diana giggles. "You know how hard it is to implant someone on the spectrum? You try to bury your talent under all that sappiness but it always comes through."

Job rests his back on the cold glass and looks at the ceiling. His neighbors' orange envy and lavender boredom are fighting above him. He knows she is going to rescind all of this the moment he is honest, so he just sits with the sound.

"No signs of rejection? Ticks, sweating, spasms?"

"No."

"My special boy."

Job cringes at the memory of being fourteen and having to tell that many people to run without words. "Is there any way to undo implantation?"

"What?"

"It was an accident, Ma."

Diana doesn't say anything for a long while.

Job scratches his arm.

She rubs her arm. "Forget what I said." Job wouldn't and she knows that. "And of course not, you tit. The whole point is that their own thought processes break down the idea and makes it real to them regardless of whether it is true or not."

Job stands upright. "I have to tell her what happened."

Diana shoots up straight, "Like hell you will!"

Job doesn't respond.

"It took you almost two decades to find a place to plant your seed, you're not ruining my chances of a granddaughter."

"You were never promised grandchildren of any gender."

"Knowing won't help uproot it."

"I figured."

She leans her temple on the window. "You'll destroy the best relationship you've had to be honest about something you can't change?"

Job leans the back of his head on the cold window. "I think so."

Across town, Alvina smokes weed and lies on her back in her vegetable garden. She started cleaning her room, began organizing her closet, and proceeded to weed some of her vegetable garden. Her leg bones twitch while the leg remains still, but she isn't focusing on that. She hopes to complete at least one task. She tries to think about Landon. The more she pictures him; the more she wants to start another project. She knows if she moves one inch from that garden, she will reorganize her bookshelf according to color. The stability of this bout of denial mania baffles her. She knows having a supportive network helps but not this much.

Alvina remembers the force of the weighted blankets, the heavy smell of his musky cologne, his white knuckle anxiety. She swore Landon would banshee scream her out of existence at some point. She could acknowledge that these were bad times and objectively frightening, but she didn't want to run out of her skin. She didn't want to shave her head, change her name, and move to a rural town in the Caribbean. She didn't want to ask Job to call his mom. She only thought that once. As she ponders, she receives a message from Job.

Want to go for a drive?

Her thumbs type *yes* before she finishes reading.

In the car, she feels the air flee her lungs as she fills the car with words. Ranging from simple observations to befuddled musings, she talks with great speed. She bites her tongue to make herself stop and looks out the window instead. It is a gray day with periodic sunbeams slipping out of the clouds. There are plains with the occasional cow or horse on them. It is soothing to look at.

Job wants her to keep talking. Even though it hurts to listen.

"So. I can empathically see that you are distressed. I normally can't see anything. I thought I should tell you."

"I didn't know that." Job wishes they talked about her powers more.

She pokes at Job's side. "Is there some secret you're keeping from me?" She doesn't want the Landon stuff to bother him this much.

Job opens and closes his mouth without speaking.

Alvina returns to looking out of the window.

"Before I start," Job strangles the steering wheel, "it was a mistake and will not happen again."

She turns to face him. "Someone else?"

"What? No."

Alvina raises her hands in faux victory. "Woo hoo, our issues aren't trite."

A smile slips out of Job's jaw.

"It's only getting scarier the longer you don't tell me."

He swallows a ball of spit.

"Did you hurt Landon?"

Job focuses on the odometer. "I implanted the idea of you

being safe from him."

Alvina looks at the road ahead. It stretches out into more flat grasslands as far as the eye can see. She remembers talking to him about implantation.

"I'm so sorry, Alvina."

"Question. If you hadn't told me, would I have been able to figure it out?"

"Not once the mania wears off."

Tears sprint to her eyes, but she makes them stop there, "Stupid brain didn't even put up a fight, huh?" She giggles but doesn't look at him. The seat belt presses against her chest. The car's walls encase her. Its doors with locks keep her in. The buckle of the seat belt digs into her hip. Its glass rolled all the way up seals her in. The only reprieve is the stub of the door lock.

"Your brain was desperate for answers. I just gave it one."

"I slept so well that night."

Job winces.

"Hey." her voice cracks and she clears it.

"I didn't realize I did it until the next day. I'm so sorry."

"I got another question for you."

"Alv—"

"It is a quick one, I promise." She pushes and pulls up the door locking stick as a fidget. "If you implanted, 'never leave me' would I know?"

"I would never do that."

She fidgets with the lock more.

"Implanting a statement like that would fundamentally change you. Even if I was an evil man, I wouldn't. I like you too much as you are."

"Okay, answer the question."

"Please look at me."

Alvina unlocks the door, opens it, and yells louder than the wind. "Answer the question." She is a pair of raging eyes in a sea of flailing red hair.

Job stops the car. His heart stops too.

She leaves the door open.

"No, you wouldn't know."

Alvina closes the car door. "Take me back to your place."

Job drives. *She can choose to never speak to me again. She probably should.*

In the parking garage beneath his place, Job turns the car off. His hand bones hurt. Trauma throbs like nothing else.

Alvina takes a deep breath. "I'll be right back."

Job nods as she leaves. His bones stop hurting and he bites his steering wheel. His teeth sink into time-softened pleather and he feels the plastic give under the force of his bite. A stream of tears trickle out of his eyes.

About twenty minutes later, she comes down with a cardboard box of her stuff and wearing his sweatshirt. Job, who is sitting on the hood of his car, tosses his cigarette.

Alvina stands far away from him. "You can't implant Landon."

Job makes a sour defiant expression.

She gets a glimpse of the angsty teen Job must have been. On a normal day, it would have been cute.

"Okay."

"It's easy to blame him, but...he'll do something drastic."

"I won't. Don't worry."

"Don't call your mom on him either."

"I was tempted." He smiles at her, hoping she'd feel like smiling.

Alvina mimics his expression.

"I won't."

"I'm going to take a cab home."

Job doesn't recall putting a cigarette in his mouth, "All right."

Alvina checks her phone. "This is not a breakup."

I don't believe you. "Okay."

"I mean it."

At least I can't hear you lie. "I wish I could take it back."

"Me too."

In the Middle of Air

The baby's toes shocked Dr. Marcellus Sutton when he was feeling for a head. He pressed Marvette Lee Royster's thigh to the left, gesturing for a nurse to dab the downpour of sweat from her face, and gently coaxed a peculiar girl child into the world, feet first. She was onyx black, with hair the color of wet, red Mississippi Delta clay. She cooed instead of crying. Her skin appeared iridescent, highlighted by every nearby warm tone. *An accursed, unnatural birth*, the nurses said, standing in a cluster watching Pastor and First Lady Royster leave the hospital with their tightly swaddled baby girl. *A fierce, divine judgment for hidden sins*, the church mothers gossiped cutting their eyes at First Lady throughout services. *Had to be an outside child*, the Mount Moriah backsliders surmised during Friday night card parties.

None were particularly glad for Pastor Royster's marriage to a woman he left his own church to find. So, the birth of Savannah felt like a justice they couldn't have dreamed better.

***

Blood, fire, a baby, a gold tooth. These were the only words that First Lady Royster could make out as she ran down the center aisle of the sanctuary. The voice of her six-year-old daughter Savannah stopped abruptly just before First Lady pushed open the gargantuan red doors. Savannah was sprawled on the church step, holding her tiny dark face, tears glistening along the curves of her button nose. Mother Louise Seymour Sebastian stood erect, scowling at the girl, her hand raised in the air ready to come back down.

First Lady's hand shook. Just the right one. The one that had quickly yet fiercely connected with Mother Sebastian's rouged, slightly wrinkled face. She glanced down at her hands, then out to the sea of churchgoers frozen in place standing across the lawn and parking lot. Whatever progress she had made with the women of Mount Moriah Pentecostal Church disintegrated the second she slapped that beloved old woman on the church steps. First Lady's slim hand had landed so solidly on Mother Louise's plump, unsuspecting cheek that the old woman's pink and yellow flowered hat rocked to one side. It had been jolted almost completely loose from the sleek brass hat pin passed down three generations. First Lady could still feel Mother Louise's cheekbone along the length of her ring finger down to the center of her palm. She had done it without internal counsel. The specks of blood on her daughter's baby blue dress directed her. Protection is primal.

No words were exchanged between Mother Louise and First Lady. As she stooped to draw her crying daughter to her bosom, First Lady kept her eyes on the old woman. Little Savannah's right cheekbone offered up a gash bubbling with blood as red as her hair. First Lady's eyes fell on Mother Louise's hand resting limply at her side. Each finger donned a gaudy bauble, jagged with precious stones.

"Oh baby. Don't cry. Let's go inside, all right Savvy?" She gently rubbed her daughter's shoulders, stood, and walked her back inside the church.

A low din of accusatory conversation commenced as First Lady and little Savannah disappeared behind the big red doors.

Did you hear her? You heard what that gal said about Early Johnson?

No, but Mother Louise sure slapped the tar out of her.

That lil' gal is too grown for her own good. But you know she ain't been right since she was born.

Just look at her. Boot-black like that. And all that harlot-red hair!

"Here, let me help you, Mother."

Mother Louise used one lace-gloved hand to pull together

her sweater while the other pressed down into Deacon Sumner's palm. He walked her down the steps and out to her car. A parade of equal parts awe and embarrassment.

"That gal need to learn a child's place. Pastor Royster bet' git wit that uppity wife of his. Lettin' that little gal run around talkin' into folks' houses and doin's. She ain't no kind of prophetic."

The words slid from between teeth that clenched tighter with each venomous syllable. Mother Louise looked straight ahead to her shiny, new Cadillac with a determined ire. Deacon Sumner nodded his unwavering approval, barely hearing a word she said.

Inside the now-quiet church away from the commotion, First Lady nudged Savannah to slide into the second to last pew.

"I'll be right back, sweet girl. Stay right here."

Savannah nodded her head, still holding her cheek, weeping softly.

The tiny basement bathroom was eerie without the holy mayhem of shouting, dancing, and divers tongues permeating from the sanctuary overhead. First Lady leaned against the closed door. Behind her eyelids all she saw was red. No form. No person. No event. Just the deepest red she'd ever seen. Deeper red than the dirt roads she grew up walking. Deeper red than the blood that dripped from her daughter's cheek to her baby blue taffeta dress. Deeper red than the emerald cut ruby that decorated Mother Louise's backhand. She only heard glimpses and snatches of what Savannah had been screaming before Mother Louise shut her up, but First Lady had heard enough to understand. The way Early Johnson hightailed it to his car and peeled out of the parking lot leaving nothing but a cloud of guilty dust to dirty the air told First Lady all she needed to know. She pulled a cloth from the small rattan etagere in the corner and wet it under the rusty faucet's warm trickle.

How could God give this burden to a child? She counted the steps as she climbed back up to the sanctuary. First Lady Royster glanced over at Savannah as she slid into the pew next to her. With skin four shades darker than everybody in town and hair the color of anger, Savannah's appearance was already a spectacle without ever opening her mouth to speak. Her only baby's trials were piled high. She patted Savannah's knee. The day she had feared since she first married and began trying to conceive had come. The salt of Savannah's tears streaked her cheek and her mother's shame covered them both like a shroud.

"Savannah, you know that I love you, yes?"

With her eyes closed, First Lady's right hand found her daughter's left and held on, the pew's worn red cushion giving both their hands a soft place to land. "You do know that, don't you, Savvy?"

Savannah, frustrated that she could not form a single word through her crying, sobbed even harder and deeper, filling the church with an echo of lament it wasn't quite used to.

First Lady pulled the child to her and dabbed at the cut on her cheekbone. What kind of mothering could she do when God chose to offer no solution?

"Don't you worry about that ever happening again, you hear?" First Lady's breathy cries matched her daughter's as her eyes caught those of the brown-skinned Jesus hanging above the pulpit. Did Mary speak softly to Jesus when his divinity first started to show? First Lady searched every corner of her mind for something to offer this little girl whose gift now drooped like a leaf tossed about in a storm but still holding firm to its branch. Was her spirit irreparably shattered or were there shards large enough to meld back together?

"You know you're special, yes?" First Lady asked as she stroked the child's back, each stroke soothing hiccupping breaths to a relaxed cadence. She felt Savannah's head move up and down against her breast. She knew.

"How do you know?" First Lady asked.

"Because..." Savannah trailed off to catch her breath, "people don't believe me. Not at first. Even the good things." Savannah lifted herself from her mother's arms and wiped her face with the back of her hand. She sat forward, rested her forearms on the pew in front of her. "When they try, they see. And when they see what I saw, then they believe me." Savannah was now fidgeting, picking at the skin of her cuticles.

"Well you know what, Savannah? You don't have to tell them anymore. Let them find out on their own. I think you'll be much happier that way. Can you try doing that for Mama?"

Savannah looked up at her mother, her tears drying now. She craved this moment, to live here in this softness. No mention of what she'd seen or done. She just wanted the softness of her mama and her own vision clear of anyone else's life but her own.

***

First Lady Marvette Lee Royster's bloodline was rife with women forced to bear babies not much darker than the color of ancient, chiseled alabaster. Her husband, the good pastor Royster's family line, boasted the same jagged horrors smoothed into sharp points of condescension and privilege. Baby Savannah's peculiar looks raised questions through the pews of Mount Moriah's congregation like the dead to the Rapture. Guests stopped accepting First Lady's tea invitations, afraid to enter the house where the infant they deemed cursed lived.

One moment alone recovered First Lady's honor from the wreckage of church gossip and scrutiny. The day of baby Savannah's christening. The dark, fire-haired baby girl hadn't flailed when the anointing oil touched her forehead. She hadn't foamed at the mouth when the holy water drizzled down her scalp. Instead of transforming into the demon they all wanted to believe she was, little Savannah cooed sweetly just as she had at her birth. An indelible company of sun rays streamed through each of the church's East-facing stained glass windows as the ceremony came to its close. An unexpected reprieve from a week of torrential downpour. Was God smiling on *this* moment, for *this* peculiar child?

Just after the ceremony ended, a trail of family, friends, and busybodies snaked from the church to the Royster household a few hundred feet away. Some were hungry for the spread they'd contributed to. Others were starving for a morsel of scuttlebutt to spread since the christening had been uneventful. All anticipated a feast.

As the stream of guests entered the house, they greeted Pastor Royster's grandmother, a woman called Sweeter. Formerly enslaved and mother to fifteen children, Sweeter was sepia-skinned, with a shock of white hair braided into a long, skinny rope, the crinkled ends grazing her lap. She was small but statuesque in her way. Deeply ensconced in an old handmade wicker chair in the sitting room, Sweeter slowly twisted the lid back onto a small can of chewing tobacco. Her mouth moved involuntarily with age as she watched the trail of people milling about, kissing her cheek or her hand and uttering a, "Good to see you, Sweeter" or "Afternoon, M'Sweet" or "God bless you, Mama Sweeter."

A duck feather pillow at her back propped her soft body upright and her small feet sat atop a mahogany footstool. Though coaxed for months, Sweeter did not attend the christening. She marveled at Mount Moriah's stained glass whenever she rode past her son's church now in the hands of her grandson, but refused ever to enter. Any relationship with Jesus she needed was right in her heart and not in "Nothing built up and burned down by man's hands." No. Sweeter swore never to set foot in another church since that night when she was only nine years old. But she kept her God with her everywhere she was since she said God was everywhere He wanted to be.

First Lady rushed toward Sweeter as the guests moved on to serving themselves from the community-prepared buffet of fried chicken, ham, mustard greens, yams, fried tomatoes, turkey necks and gravy, dirty rice, string beans, crab cakes, honey-o biscuits and buttermilk pie. The town could talk about a woman like a dog, but never would they dare let her celebration go without food.

"Mama Sweeter, you want to hold your great-grandbaby?"

First Lady twisted her mouth into something resembling a smile, doing her best not to melt into a fit of nervous tears as she handed over the baby who looked nothing like her.

Sweeter's eyes were closed but her wrinkled fingers, the color of turmeric skin, set the can of chewing tobacco onto the table next to her and reached up for the drowsy infant. She drew little Savannah close to her sunken chest covered by a soft, white cotton camisole.

"Oh this child," the old woman mumbled with eyes closed. "She know me all. From the beginnin' she know me and I knows her." Both Sweeter and baby Savannah's eyes opened at the same time. The gaze between them paused the whole world for First Lady as she looked on through tears. Sweeter claimed Savannah as her kin and said so where everyone could hear! Tears navigated the wrinkles on Sweeter's face as she lifted the baby, kissed the top of her head right in the middle of her red hair and handed her back to First Lady Royster.

"My God, that baby know me all. And I know her," Sweeter said again as she settled back into her chair, tears finding resting places here and there in the ancient wrinkles along her cheeks.

There could be no mistaking it now. An acknowledgement of lineage, a blessing from the eldest elder. And though no one completely understood her meaning, they were satisfied that Pastor Royster's grandmother believed the baby was her kith and kin. Their disdain for First Lady and her unusual child melted under the warmth of Sweeter's declaration.

First Lady turned to walk away but Sweeter whispered to her with soft authority.

"Marvette. Come."

Startled, she turned on her heel and slowly drifted down to her knees next to Sweeter, still cradling the drooling, cooing baby.

"She gon' need you. When she gets up seven years, she'll need you to speak for her in a mighty way. She's just like you and she'll do just like you done. Do you hear what I say?"

She heard, understood and nodded vigorously. She felt

Sweeter's command massage itself a space between her ribcage. It rippled beneath her shoulder blades and traveled her marrow down to her ankles.

Satisfied that her prophecy had not fallen on closed ears, Sweeter leaned her head back against the chair, folding her hands one on top of the other and closed her eyes.

First Lady stood, looked down at Savannah and felt heart-exploding love gaining on her fear.

***

The saints found their way back to loving First Lady and her daughter after Sweeter's blessing. If they voiced their opinions of Savannah's dark skin and red hair, they did it behind the closed and locked doors of their individual abodes. And when the girl became old enough to speak and began prophesying blessings that came to pass mere days, sometimes hours later, they all lived devotedly toward her. Pastor and First Lady Royster's home overflowed with company throughout the week. And it seemed the entire congregation would follow them home on Sundays, awaiting little Savannah's morsels of good fortune.

She was six when her prophecies and visions became as un-predictable in their tenor as the spring air in its warmth. Warnings and secrets flowed just as freely from the child's lips as blessings. And the saints once again found their distance from the child and the woman who birthed her. They decided to recuse themselves from fellowship and the possibility of an agreeable prophecy rather than to risk their secrets being laid open.

***

Four months after the incident on the church steps, Mother Louise Seymour Sebastian forced an invitation to tea from First Lady Royster.

"That child of yourn. How she? She done had a birthday since...since the last time I saw her, ain't she?" Mother Louise adjusted one of the many rings on her right hand and tried to peer around the corner of the large sitting room, looking for some trace of the red-haired girl.

"She turned seven last week. Had a lovely party. I'm so sorry Minnie and Eliza couldn't make it. We would have loved to have them." First Lady nodded toward Mother Louise, her teacup obscuring the slight upward curve of her lips.

"Well, you know how forgetful them girls are. Ain't tell me till the last minute."

First Lady nodded again as if she understood. And she did all right. Minnie and Eliza had been two of Savannah's closest friends despite their grandmother's God-awful treatment of the girl. No way in the world they had forgotten Savannah's birthday or her party.

Mother Louise laughed a boisterous and hearty laugh. Her seat on the front pew of Mount Moriah typically reserved for church leadership spoke to the fact that she was the church's most notable benefactor. Her chubby, gaudily adorned hands in nearly every church decision said more.

"Good gracious 'a life! And all that red hair. I can never get over it!" Mother Louise was holding up the Royster family portrait that sat to her right on a mahogany end table. The photo was taken just one year prior. Savannah's skin even photographed iridescent and her carmine hair flowed over her shoulder into a braid as thick as fisherman's rope, the crinkled end grazing her waist. Mother Louise's faux amazement did not fool First Lady. Savannah had told her about the times Mother Louise would find any reason to comb her hair when she went to her house for play dates with her granddaughters.

"Is my hair a vulgar color?" Savannah once asked her mother. A tidbit learned from Mother Louise Seymour Sebastian during a summer play date. Red was reserved for nightwalkers. The only people who laid claim to the color were women who forced bad things on good men under the cover of dark nights.

"And here you are with this putrid red hair. I don't know why your mama don't slap some dye in it. That's what I'd do. Keep ya from the life'a sin you's bound for."

Mother Louise had watched Savannah with a disgust that surpassed the girl's vocabulary. And she made it a point to remind Savannah of all her differences. Her skin was anomaly enough in a family, a congregation, a town that prided itself on skin not much darker than the color of light itself. But paired with her long, blazing red hair, Mother Louise seemed to breathe fire in Savannah's direction any time she caught the girl in her line of sight. She never had to play too hard for her soft, thick plaits to come undone. So, Mother Louise didn't have to search very hard for a reason to get her hands in the girl's hair. She always returned Savannah to her mother with a new hairstyle no matter how hard Savannah declined. She had learned how not to wince when the comb dug into her scalp or tore through a knot so viciously she checked for blood when she was safely out of the angry old woman's reach. And she prayed no blood surfaced. Mother Louise would probably pop her on the head with the comb for bleeding the color of harlots.

"She still call herself havin' The Sight, do she?" Mother Louise asked, leaning so far forward, her ample bosom sent a bit of raspberry leaf tea into her saucer.

"Well, excuse my frankness but *she* never claimed to have anything, Mother Louise." First Lady Royster turned to the delicately flowered teapot to pour more into her cup, giving her hands something to do before they pulled her up and across the room to slap the old woman again.

"Well, now that we're discussing it, I do remember some months back Savannah made quite the ruckus outside Mount Moriah. My, my."

First Lady Royster pursed her lips the way she did during testimony service when an overeager parishioner told a little too much of their business no one else needed to know.

"She didn't know what she saw or didn't see. Children and

their imaginations would run amok..."

Mother Louise, refusing to take the hint, set her cup and saucer on the side table. "Didn't she see fire all around Early's feet and Genevieve Babineaux near dead?"

"Mother Louise, I've got more tea sandwiches in the kitchen if you'd like." First Lady Royster stood hurriedly.

Mother Louise continued, eyeing First Lady's uninterested disposition with little care. "She screamed, 'What did you do to Ms. Genevieve?'" She stirred her tea matter-of-factly with ever the slightest smirk. Then she looked up. "And Early ran off, didn't he? First Lady, ain't that what happened?"

First Lady Royster sat back down, breathing shallowly. "Yes. She was screaming and crying. It wasn't her fault, what she saw." She felt both caught for a crime she hadn't committed and ready to fight for a cause she thought she'd long given up.

"Wasn't it? The whole town knows the police found Genevieve half conscious, a bloody mess. Early's trial was so quick. And his wife, poor fool, ended up in the nuthouse after trying to burn down their home with herself in it. Real interestin' who God chooses to see things, ain't it?"

First Lady's head snapped upward.

"God didn't choose Savannah for anything. It was a coincidence at best." First Lady guzzled some of her tea, now cold and offering no real comfort for the nerves and anger stirring inside her. And then, she caught a glimpse of herself in the mirror hanging on the wall just behind Mother Louise. The moment Sweeter held Savannah shone itself in the mirror in a circular haze of light. She saw herself kneeling beside Sweeter and remembered the old woman's voice as if it all happened that morning. *"When she gets up seven years, she'll need you to speak for her in a mighty way. She's like you. She got what you got and she'll do just like you..."*

Mother Louise's voice cut into First Lady's remembrance.

"You say God ain't choose her? Why don't you let me be the judge of that? Tell her to come here."

First Lady looked toward the stairs where Savannah was playing and then back to Mother Louise. Surely Mother Louise wouldn't try to harm her daughter right in front of her?

"Call her here, Marvette." Her voice was calm but took on a depth that only obsession with absolute authority could bring forth.

First Lady bristled but called toward the stairs. "Savvy? Come say hello."

Savannah rocked backward from her knees to her tiptoes, caught her balance and stood carefully. Her white eyelet dress was wrinkled and one of her ponytails had come undone while she was playing with her dolls on the stairs. All the different shades of her fiery hair glistened as she stepped into a wide stream of sunlight piercing through the tall sitting room windows. She stood still in the light, her head turned slightly to the right as she took in Mother Louise's full frame almost as if for the first time. Savannah could feel the warmth of the sun all over but most notably on her scalp. She remembered Mother Louise's comb and the horrible things she'd told her.

Mother Louise's face hardened at Savannah's peculiar presence. She hadn't touched the child's hair in months, since First Lady had stopped all her play dates. And here it was flowing like a warm bloody river, falling rivulets in stark contrast with her white dress and her black skin. The sunlight loved on the child. Savannah was illuminated in an unnatural way that at first drew forth a holy reverence. But depending on the heart and past of the beholder, that reverence could quickly descend into contempt.

"Oh, come here, child." Mrs. Louise Seymour Sebastian clutched the head of her cane and commandingly jabbed the floor twice.

Savannah did not move. She was staring at the top of the cane, fashioned into the head of a jaguar with green gems for eyes and a mouth primed for gnashing.

"It's all right, Savvy." First Lady nodded toward Mother Louise.

Savannah took three steps toward the old woman and averted her eyes. Not for fear but to avoid the scene that was willing itself from the jaguar eyes in the middle of the air between them. Savannah, with all her might, tried to resist the vision rolling out before her. She hadn't seen anything of anyone's life since that Sunday on the steps of Mount Moriah.

"So you've got The Sight, huh child? Tell me what you see of me. Go on, tell me." Mother Louise Seymour Sebastian shifted her weight in the chair to the tune of creaking wood. She sat like royalty awaiting a jester's entertainment while Savannah stared down at a scuff on her left shoe. She bent to look closer. The scuff looked vaguely like a crown.

"I said stand up and tell me what you see, child!" Mother Louise rammed her cane down to the floor so thunderously the sideboard rattled.

But Savannah did not rattle. Nor did she immediately stand up straight. She turned her head upward slightly while still bent at the waist.

"Will you tempt God?" The words sailed from her tiny frame and sailed from her lips like a ship moving confidently toward shore. "Will you, Mother Louise?"

Now Savannah stood up straight and moved forward at a pace that caused the old woman to gasp and her tea cup to clatter against the saucer.

"If the money you control the church with was rightfully yours, you would have peace. But it's not, is it? So you don't, do you?" Savannah moved closer to a sputtering Mother Louise. The old woman's hands began to shake violently. Tea spilled onto her lap.

Savannah took the cup and saucer from her hands and placed them on the side table.

"How did Mr. Sebastian die, Mother Louise? What else was in *his* teacup that day?"

Mother Louise Seymour Sebastian jolted up out of her chair, stepped forward toward Savannah and raised her cane toward the ceiling. Her small plump lips curved inward toward her teeth. Her intention was as clear as the rage that traveled every line in her face.

Savannah, small in the shadow of the 5'9" woman, flung her arms open wide, lifted her face, closed her eyes and leaned forward. The sun shone through the windows with a fervency so blinding that all that was visible were the two women and one child standing there. Savannah's hair sparkled in the sunlight as she waited, made peace with the impact of Mother Louise's cane. But the cane did not come down.

When she opened her eyes, her mother's left hand held the cane by the jaguar head above Mother Louise's head. Eyeing Savannah like a ravenous wildcat, Mother Louise's chest heaved.

"The river didn't carry that vial as far as you thought it would, Louise," First Lady said in a firm tone just above a whisper.

Savannah looked up at her mother, her mouth slightly agape. She saw.

"It's okay. You can go, Savannah," First Lady spoke softly to her daughter while staring intently at Louise.

Savannah backed away a few paces. Then turned and disappeared up the stairs to her room, waiting for a scolding that would never come, nursing a mixture of feelings she did not yet have language for.

Healer of Herself

Mama always said love was all you needed. She said it on those cold winter nights when the freezing wind would blow through the wooden boards of their shotgun house, making Cora and her five brothers and sisters shiver and clutch the tattered cotton sheets sewn from Mama's wrinkled, indigo-stained hands.

But love never warmed Cora. Not when she huddled together with her siblings on that one bed. Not when Daddy walked her down the aisle to marry a man the same age as him, all the while saying she was blessed that a man with a steady paycheck during this Depression wanted her for a wife. Not when she fled in the cool, Fall night with Tim, leaving their hometown of Lafourche, Louisiana and all their sins behind.

And it certainly warmed nothing now with a week's worth of groceries in front of her, and Mr. Boudreaux telling her he wouldn't give her any more store credit.

"Please," Cora whispered. She hated how desperate she sounded. Out of breath and out of options. "You can't give me just five more dollars, Mr. Boudreaux? Just enough for this week. I'll get it back to you. I'm good for it. You know I am."

"I know you is, but that man of yours ain't. Bastard done got so many packs of cigarettes and bottles of liquor from me! And ain't paid for none 'em yet!" His voice rose, and his sand colored skin turned a light shade of red. He must've noticed Cora flinch because the scowl quickly left his face, his lips settling from a puckered frown to a straight line. He unclenched his fists and flattened his palms against the counter. "Look, I'm sorry, but I can't. I run a business, not a soup kitchen. Tell Tim to start walking them streets lookin' for a job, not a bottle and a pair of open legs."

A customer snickered behind Cora. The sound hurt her ears, striking a chord that had long since been plucked until it no longer played in tune. She forced a step forward, willing herself to hold her head high. Her legs wobbled in the battered heels and she almost tripped coming down the store's front steps. The embarrassment used to warm her. A constant furnace that burned low in her gut and eventually flamed its way to her face, burning her cheeks and the tips of her ears. But as Cora made her way down the dusty sprawl of the town's main street—the old maids whispering behind their gloved hands, the men, both old and young, acknowledging her with head shakes of pity, the young gals not bothering to hide their laughs—she felt no warmth.

Only a frigid grip in the place where Tim used to have her whole heart.

***

Two dollars and ninety-four cents.

That was all Cora needed to hop on the bus bound for New Orleans and start a new life. Well, start a *third* life. The life she had with Tim was her second. And the life before him—the life with Earnest—had never really been her own.

She fingered the beads of Mama's wedding necklace. The only thing of worth she left Lafourche with. Something old that Mama had gifted her when she had married Earnest. The thing Cora clutched every time Earnest pounded away at her into the night. And now, it served as a rosary of sorts. On the nights Tim didn't come home, she clutched the white beads close to her chest, praying to a God who probably wasn't listenin'...at least not to her—an adulterer, a sinner. But she did it anyway, praying for Tim to come back. Why? She wasn't sure. Common sense would say to pray that he never came back. That he would get into a fight after a bad gambling match and be found with a bullet in his head in some pissy alley.

But she didn't have much of that. Sense. Daddy always told her that, always said he hoped she would find a good man to take care of her because girls like Cora couldn't take care of themselves. And for a while, she had believed it. Believed that she could look past the gray hairs in Earnest's ears and the patch above his privates, believed that she could survive in their marriage despite how empty and starved as it made her feel. Until the day Tim came along, knocking on the door saying he was there to fix that leak under the kitchen sink. She had watched him from the table, pretending to eat her breakfast and sneaking looks at him as he hammered away at the pipes. She had watched the muscles strain in his upper arms, listening to him grunt, and soon enough started wondering just how much those muscles would stretch if his hands were on her hips, pulling on her hair and grabbing at the back of her shoulders. The thought had swelled inside her and made her feel things that Earnest never did and stirred up a courage in Cora that willed her to get up and go squat down beside Tim. She had asked if he wanted to take a break. At first, he had looked confused, saying he was almost done. But then Cora had asked again, taking his hand, placing it on top of her bare thigh. Tim had cocked a brow and nodded, following her to the bed. The sink had gotten fixed and something in Cora had been fixed too.

But like those sink pipes, it didn't stay fixed for long. Every passing year since they fled, the cracks grew deeper, a rushing force threatening to burst through and wash away what was between them. Yet Cora remained waiting and waiting. Back to believing, just like she had with Earnest.

But believing in something didn't make it true.

"Tomorrow, tomorrow. I'll go tomorrow," Cora whispered to herself, sinking to her knees and bending over the small wooden-frame bed. She would take Mama's necklace to Mr. Jarreau's pawn shop tomorrow morning. Choke back any tears and thank Mama for the gift. She figured it would cash in enough to afford her a board for a week and few meals, too. Whatever the necklace got her, it'd be enough to last until she got a job.

Cora stood, walked around the bed to the window and pulled back the thin strip of white sheets. The evening sun had disappeared, replaced by a blackish-blue night sky. She peered further in the distance, gazing at the outline of the swamp. A twinkle caught her eye, and she blinked. A star? No stars sat in the sky, not in the low murkiness of a swamp. It was probably just some fireflies. Or maybe some Feu Follet. That thought made her shake her head. Feu Follet were bedtime stories. Mama had spun the tale to Cora and her siblings. *Stay away from the lights in the swamp. That's the Feu Follet and them witches ain't got nothing you want.*

The memory made her shiver, and she plodded back to the bed. Usually, she didn't go to sleep before fixing a plate of food and leaving it in the oven for Tim. It sat uneaten until the next morning when he stumbled in, knocking everything about and searching for something to coat his liquor stained stomach.

But not tonight. Tim could fix his own meal.

Cora crawled into the bed and pulled up the threadbare calico covers, and rested her head against the flattened pillow. The scent of Tim washed over her: a piney scent mixed with mouthwash and tobacco, and a hint of cinnamon whisky.

She turned over the pillow, falling into the deep, peaceful slumber.

***

Cora felt Tim before she saw him. He gripped her waist, locking her against his chest, his hot, rancid breath blowing down her neck.

"I missed you, baby," he slurred, hand slithering down her thigh and his dark brown finger pushing back the edge of her nightgown, revealing dimpled amber-colored skin. His fingers, once a tool that gave her so much pleasure, felt more like sharpened talons readying to carve up flesh. His claws reached her hip and pulled at the top of her underwear, followed by a more forceful tug.

"Not tonight, Tim." Cora grabbed his hand, pushing it away, and scooted closer to the edge of the bed.

"What you mean?" He was back against her again, sliding wet, slick lips across the inside of her neck. "I ain't seen you all day."

"You so full of shit, Tim!" Cora jerked away, getting out of the bed and standing beside it. The moonlight shined down on him through the window. He looked awful. A torn shirt and a busted lip. She touched her neck and squinted at her fingers. A metallic, coppery smell confirmed the dark liquid was blood. *What has he done now? Probably got caught with someone's wife or didn't pay for whatever whore he rented at the gentleman's house down the way.* Cora stood still, staring down at Tim with blood dripping from her hand, wishing it was his. She had half a mind to wrap her crimson-coated fingertips around his neck and draw more blood, to take back the life he owed her.

"I said where you been, Tim? You been gone for two days! Just leavin' me here with nothing! I went down to Boudreaux's today and you know what he told me? You done ran up all the damn credit!"

"That bastard lyin'." Tim laughed. A loud belly laugh that filled the room. He had no right to be this happy. To have such joy. Not when Cora suffered and sniffled in this house and walked the town's streets like a lost child, looking for him. Like a fool.

Cora slipped her hands down on the bed, staining the sheets red with the print of her palms.

"I can't take this no more, Tim. Look at you. Nothing but a drunk. All you do is drink and leave. I can't do this! I don't deserve this!" Hot, fat, salty tears streamed down her face. She hated herself for crying. She knew Tim found an odd comfort in her cries. For him, it meant he still could make her *feel*. He liked his role as puppet master, pulling her heart on a string. He could make her laugh, cry, scream, with the tiniest pluck. He liked the power to pull her this way and that. Loved how much she loved him.

But love wasn't swaying and pulling her strings anymore. This was a rage. Not the kind that made you want to kill or thrash about, but the rage that gave you strength. The strength to—

"I'm leaving."

Cora turned around, walking toward her drawer. A silence settled over the room. The only sound came from the buzz of the cicadas outside. She grabbed a handful of clothes, not bothering to count the pairs of drawers or how many socks. She was leaving, and that was that. Tim could drink himself away in whatever whorehouse until Jesus himself came back, but she wouldn't wait. Not anymore.

Hands seized her by the waist, turning her around. His square jaw jutted toward her, hot spittle spraying her in the face. "You what?"

"Get off me, Tim!" She tried to wiggle from his grasp, but he only clutched harder. He crossed his arms around her and dragged her back to the bed.

"You what?"

"I'm leaving, I said!"

"And where you gonna go?"

"Somewhere! Away from you!"

"How you just gonna leave me? After all I done for you?"

"You ain't done nothing for me, Tim! Nothing but give me misery! I don't want you no more!"

Their tussle stopped. Tim's hands dropped to his sides. He looked down on her, lips in a straight line, and his thick brows relaxed. Almost as if he had sobered right back up.

"That's a lie. You know it is. You can't leave me." His tone was flat. Cold. Unfeeling.

"I can, Tim, I can." Cora forced, but even she heard how weak she sounded. She didn't sound like a woman about to leave at all.

Tim's mouth turned up in a sneer.

"I'm tied to you, and you tied to me. We made that bond in blood, Cora."

She shut her eyes when his mouth covered hers. It came back to her. That day.

Earnest was supposed to be working. He worked every day from five to four except on Sunday. And every Monday and Wednesday mid-afternoon was when she and Tim tumbled in the starched sheets, a conjoining of tangled limbs, swollen lips, and shuddering moans and sighs.

Until the day Earnest came home from work early and busted into the bedroom, hollering about what he had heard. And when he cocked his gun, aiming for Tim's head, Cora grabbed the sewing shears by the bedside and plunged it right into Earnest's neck.

The life had left Earnest's eyes slowly, like molasses being poured from the bottom of a jar. But his blood had squirted out in rapid, quick bursts, going everywhere and covering everything: the front of her naked chest, the crumpled pile of Tim's clothes by the bedside, across Tim's face.

And covered in Earnest's blood, Tim and Cora had made their decision.

To run. To never look back. She was no longer Inez but Cora. He was no longer Leon but Tim. Two new names. Two new lives.

"Five years, Inez. You been with me for five years." Tim pulled back, whiskey breath lingering inside her mouth. "I ain't the one that stabbed that man. That was all you. But guess what? I ran with you. I kept you safe. Still do. Ain't nobody come looking for you yet, huh?"

Cora hugged herself, teeth knocking together. Where had it gone? The strength. The will.

He pointed an accusatory finger at her, flicking the end of her nose. "I-I-I keep you safe. As much as I should, I don't ever leave. I don't go running to no sheriff to set myself free. I *stay*, and I keep you safe. Ain't that right?"

Cora bit her trembling lip, fighting back the words she always said.

Tim dropped his hand to her shoulder and stroked her

shoulder, his face softening into a fallen, sorrowful look that made Cora uncross her arms and relax her stance.

"I may drink. I may fool around here and there. But I always come back. You know I do." His whispered words soothed the storm within her, soaking up the tears that threatened to fall.

It was true. That was a promise he still kept. Even if it was days later, he always came back.

And in that truth, Cora surrendered as she always did time and time again, screaming his name—his real name, Leon—into the night.

***

When Cora awoke, Tim was gone again. His side of the bed was still a little warm. That familiar sense of loss crept up within her. She had fallen for it again. His sticky little trap that she could never escape.

Cora sighed and threw off the cover, fanning herself. The house was already muggy from the humid summer morning. A cold bath would do. A cleanse from what Tim had left on her. After he had rolled off of her, she made a promise to herself: this would be the last time. She would stick with her plan. Run again, but this time without Tim.

Cora stopped by the door. The neat line up of knick-knacks on her dresser were crooked., and the lid on the small, white porcelain jewelry box laid in shattered pieces on the floor. Cora's heart sank. *No.*

She took small steps. Swallowing, she looked down into the box.

Empty. No string of white pearls.

"No, no," she muttered.

But her search produced nothing. No necklace. Nothing to take the pawn and buy that bus ticket to New Orleans.

Cora's face twisted and she let out a cry—a hollow whoosh that sounded more like a gasp for air. No tears this time. Only a dry, stinging feeling in her eyes.

Tim had finally taken everything.

The chance for a third life.

***

When the cicadas strung their nightly melody, Cora sat on the back porch, staring off at the low hanging Spanish moss trees. Tim hadn't returned, and he probably wouldn't, with the price Mama's necklace had gotten him. At most, it would probably last him for three or four days and then he'd come back drunk as skunk, falling down in their bed, sinking into Cora, then waking up and doing it all over again.

But Cora was tired. Of the rage, the cycle, the see-saw of this thing called love.

Beyond the trees, a bright yellow luminescence caught her eye. A small, floating mass of dotted lights. She stepped off the porch, slippers padding against the soft grass. She had never ventured very far in their backyard, certainly never off to the swamps. Partly because she feared the water moccasins and gators that lurked below the water's surface, but mostly because there was nothing there to see. Just muck and water.

Nothing to see... a place nobody would look.

The perfect place to disappear.

Forever.

Cora imagined ducking her head into the murky water, holding her breath until everything went black. Or even wading into the swamp's sinking, deeper middle until the waters went above her head, burying her underneath the green-coated surface. The thoughts delved deeper, plunging to the growing darkness in her mind. And as she thought, she walked closer and closer toward the swamp, keeping sight of that dotted mass of lights, thinking of all the ways. It gave her a strange sense of relief. Like the years of hiding had been thrown off of her, and she was Inez again: the wide-eyed, French-braid wearing amber-skinned girl who had never been beyond the town limits of Lafourche. The girl who never married a man twenty years her senior, never lost herself in the throes of lust, never killed, never lost herself to a man who probably wouldn't even try to find her.

Come ma chérie. Come to the light. Give up the fight. Come to the light.

Cora stopped a few feet from the edge of the woods. She looked around. Who was singing? Had she even heard it? That beautiful, soft angelic voice that had touched her soul? Or was she finally losing her mind?

Feu Follet? Cora thought. *Did Mama ever say something about them singing? But how could such a beautiful sound be something to stay away from?*

The singing started again. Louder but harmonious, insistent yet coaxing, demanding while gentle.

Come ma chérie. Come to the light. Give up the fight. Come to the light.

The lullaby was coming from the glow. A glow that was beautiful now. Cora wondered if the stars in heaven looked like that. A soft, but bright, guiding light into a place that promised freedom. A place to cleanse her soul and leave this disappointing thing called life.

She was past the outhouse now, but the glow was further away. Had it moved? It didn't seem that far away when she was on the porch.

Come ma chérie. Come to the light. Give up the fight. Come to the light.

A force, warm and comforting, prodded her forward. The feelings of danger and Mama's stories emptied from her mind, replaced with a strange sense of surety.

Cora walked again, breezing past the drooping trees. She could see the swamp now. That still pool of water. And just above it was the light. But it kept moving. Kept itself just out of reach.

She had to keep walking. Keep going. Keep walking. Keep going.

Come ma chérie. Come to the light. Give up the fight. Come to the light.

Water seeped through Cora's slippers, covering her ankles.

She was in the swamp's waters now, but that light had moved again just beyond the other side of the swamp's banks. Cora had the sudden urge for it to be the last thing she saw or touched before she left this Earth. She took a few more steps. The water was up to her knees now, lapping at her thighs, dampening the edge of her night dress. Just a bit further. She was almost in the middle of the swamp now—it wasn't so deep. She could make it to the other side and see the light up close...touch it, admire it, then return to the swamp and finish what she came here for.

But first, she had to get closer to the light.

A few inches away, the fat, triangular head of a cottonmouth peaked above the water slithering its way toward her, its forked tongue peeking out of its white-coated mouth. But Cora didn't stop. Fear wasn't stronger than what moved her to the light.

Come ma chérie. Come to the light. Give up the fight. Come to the light.

Her foot got stuck. Something was wrapped around her ankle. The cotton mouth was only a strike away, rearing back and showing her its fangs. But Cora didn't scream or swim away. She ducked down deep, hearing the snake's hiss just before the water filled her ears. She watched it slither away above her, then reached down, twisting and turning the vine wrapped around her ankle. It wouldn't let her go. She pulled and tug to no avail. A fiery sting burned inside her lungs, and black spots blurred her vision.

No, no, no.

She couldn't stay trapped in the muck. No, she had to see the light one last time before—

Cora jerked her ankle. Hard and quick. A pounding pain shot from her foot up to her leg, making her scream underwater. The salty swamp water rushing in.

But the vine had broken. And she was free.

Cora shut her mouth and raised her arms, fighting back to the surface, fighting for a chance to see the light. She emerged from the waters with a deep gasp, her ankle throbbing. She flipped on her side and waded through the middle. When the water turned shallow, she put her weight on her good ankle and hobbled to the soft, moistened ground of the bank, coughing out mud and murky water.

Ma chérie, look up!

Cora's head shot up. The light was no longer small dots but blazing orbs as big as a balled fist.

Then they moved. Toward Cora.

Cora stumbled back. Half of her screaming to go back to the swamp, to get away from the orbs that were moving faster and growing bigger. Now, it looked as if they almost had legs and arms and carried by whirring wings. Laughter filled the swamp. A shrill, almost cruel sound. But Cora stayed stuck in place; rooted to the ground in awe.

The orbs had legs now. And arms and a head. The burning balls were now bodies belonging to the most beautiful women Cora had ever seen. Skin ranging from a dark ebony to a light, silken maple. Hair praising the sky in tight coils, lean muscular legs and arms and full breasts. In normal conditions, Cora would've turned away from their nakedness, but their bare skin didn't bring shame. She stared at them open-mouthed, taking in the circle of bodies, suddenly feeling unfit to stand before them.

"You all are so beautiful," Cora whispered, kneeling on the ground, ignoring the sharp pain in her ankle.

"So, are you, ma chérie." A reddish-brown skinned one floated closer. Her eyes had no pupils, only blackened pits. And her smile revealed a row of sharpened teeth. Was this monstrous mouth the one that had sung the heavenly hum?

"So pretty." The light-skinned one with honey colored hair gilded next to her sister, grinning at Cora. She sniffed, long and deep, her eyes rolling in the back of her head. "Her essence? So sad. Such misery. Come, ma chérie. We'll take it away."

They were hungry for her. Ravenous to suck for her misery, her weakness. But even imagining those sharp teeth tearing her to bits, Cora didn't move. She held their gaze, heart pounding, and a slow-moving trail of sweat going down her already soaked back. She saw her face reflected in those wide, black pits for eyes. But she didn't see what they saw. She didn't see the sadness or the misery. Only the determination. The hard set of her jaw, the cross of her eyebrows. And she felt it down to her bones, down to her soul.

"Jolie, stop," one of them hissed. The one with the glistening skin that matched the night sky. She appeared beside the one named Jolie and eyed Cora with dark pupils that nearly covered the white. In it, Cora could see herself. Desperate, broken down, and with a face full of longing.

The rest of them halted in their steps, forming a tight circle around Cora.

"This one didn't die." Their leader pointed a finger at Cora. She was like a tall obsidian statue. Formidable. Beautiful. Devastating. Nothing would break her. Certainly no man. Never a man like Tim.

"She lived," Jolie exclaimed, pacing around the circle. "She lived!"

"She lived! She lived! She lived!" The rest of the Feu Follet joined, rising into an angelic chorus that shook the trees.

"Yes, I lived," Cora stood. She lifted her nightgown, tossing the soaked rag aside. She stepped out of her drawers and lifted her arms. "I lived!"

***

Tim came back home four days later to an empty house, an empty bed, and no wife.

Truth be told, he was too drunk to notice, but when he woke up that morning, he reached his arm over, only to find a cold spot. He had searched through the house, yelling and throwing open doors. But no Cora.

So he went into town.

He wandered the streets, stopping at Boudreaux's, where he was promptly told to get the fuck out. From there he had gone to the saloon meaning to ask the patron if they had seen his missing wife, but when ol' Jimbo invited him to play a game of spades his day long search found itself delayed by a round table full of cussing men slanging worn, bent up cards sticky with spilled cinnamon whiskey.

But the next day, Tim resumed his search. He fell into the same pattern, but kept searching and searching. Soon enough, the days turned into a full month and then the month slid into another and another.

A year passed and still no Cora.

Until the day Tim stumbled from the outhouse after taking a long piss, and heard someone call his name.

"Cora?"

Tim watched his wife walk out of the woods as naked as the day she'd been born. And though he had seen her like that before, many, many times. He had never seen her like this.

Glowing, shining, beaming, and...

Smiling?

"Cora, what the fuck you doin' out here? Where you comin' from?" Tim stepped toward, gawking open-mouthed at his wife. Or who looked like his wife. She had the same face, those round cheeks that reminded him of pumpkin and wide, puppy dog eyes, but her body was different. No longer fleshy and full but long and lithe, and she prowled through the yard like a beast prowling for prey.

"Cora, I said what you doin?" Tim shouted.

But she didn't answer. She only kept up that slow, gliding walk and held that smile that almost showed all her teeth. The last time he had seen her smile like that had been back when he fixed that broke sink when she was with Earnest, and she had asked him if he was thirsty and put his hands in between her legs. He had kissed her, slowly and softly, then once he dropped the hammer in his other hand, she kissed him back, harder and more urgent, both of them burning as they made their way to the bed.

But what he saw now didn't excite him deep down in the groin. This almost terrified him to see her like this.

Head held high
Neck up.
Free and confident.

Before Tim could take another step, Cora was standing in front of him. How had she moved so fast? Or had he just been standing still?

"Co—" His plead was hushed when Cora placed her mouth over his, wrapping her arms around his neck. Her kiss wasn't the timid slowness he was used to. Her lips swallowed his, her tongue forced its way into his mouth, going in deep, touching the back of his throat as if she wanted him to choke. She moved her arms and dug her finger into his shoulder, pushing against him and making him tumble backward in the wet, dewy grass. The sound of the cicadas grew louder and louder and he dug his hands into the dirt, feeling like a prisoner, both willing and unwilling.

Cora sat up. Her face had changed. She looked older. More like a woman. Her cheeks were more angular and jaw more set. And her eyes, no longer a soft brown but two wide pits of black.

This wasn't Cora. Not anymore. This was—

"Get off me!" Tim sputtered, trying to wiggle free from underneath her. But it didn't work. Cora only clenched her thighs, locking him in place. She titled back her neck and let out a cry. A shriek that almost seemed to rumble the ground. Fear struck Tim. A sudden, icy fear. Trapped. Stuck with this...person...no, this thing... that was now glowing. The face of Cora but not Cora.

He thrashed and raised his arm, trying to strike it in the face, but she snatched both his arms and pinned them to his sides. He saw nothing in her eyes...not love, not even a thrill from what was going on. Only emptiness, a bottomless pit. A pit that he had dug and filled in with pain. He felt it now. All the lonely nights, the betrayal. Each memory stabbed into him, lingering with searing vengeance. His whole body felt on fire. Like a shot of moonshine on a cold winter night.

"Do you see Tim?" Cora hissed.

It was her voice, but it wasn't her voice. It no longer carried that soft, pretty tune, but something hard and rough. "Do you see what you've done? What you did to me?"

"I'm sorry, Cora. I'm sorry!"

"Too late for that," she smirked and screeched again. The cicada went silent and a swarming light floated from the woods. *Fireflies? That many of them?* Tim thought. *Why so many?* As the mass came close, it evolved. Got bigger and transformed into glowing bulbs and then the bulbs turned into women. All with those same black pits for eyes and skin shining like they dropped from the sun. They formed a circle around him and Cora, holding hands, silent and unmoving, as if waiting for Cora to give the command.

Cora straddled him and brushed her lips along his neck, tracing her finger down his chest. "I don't need you to keep me safe anymore, Tim. I've got my sisters—and myself."

`Her fist plunged into his chest, gripping his heart, pulling and pulling until Cora beheld a bloody pulp, still beating in her hands.

Mama Said

"Only three times a lady's gotta wear a dress," Mama dropped her patchwork and syllabically pounded the table as she spoke. "Three times."

Her bloodshot eyes surveyed the two empty, mismatched chairs at our wobbly, splintered table; hiked across my bowl of bland, lumpy grits and pitched a tent at the peak of my large, brown nose. A fly buzzed around my ears and landed on Mama's forehead. It made a game of dodging the beads of sweat that broke free from her kinky scalp. Lost its footing more than once, but never gave up.

"Three times," I said.

"For your wedding," she said. She waved her hand in an attempt to dismiss the fly. It returned, weaving in and out of her wrinkles. "When you're dead and—"

She smacked her forehead. The fly crawled out from under her palm like a wounded soldier from 'Nam. A bit of its blood stained her purpling skin. Mama prepared for a second strike as the little critter struggled to get its wings going. *Smack!*

"And to please the Lord," she said.

"What 'bout college?"

The little war hero made it. He zigzagged a few inches above the table, slowly gaining altitude. If he could only reach the open door or at least camouflage himself with the dust from our busted ceiling fan, he could radio for support. A medic, even. He'd be home in time for Judy's dinner. Steak. No. Filet mignon. Medium rare with garlic mashed potatoes, glazed carrots, and gravy. But first, Judy'd meet him at the door. Newspaper in hand. Red lips on his cheek. All of them, Judy and the kids, Johnny and Julie, their blonde locks swaying in unison as they praised him. He'd rub Johnny's scalps. Call him champ. Give Julie piggyback rides through every room of the house.

That's my boy!

Look at my little lady.

Everything smells great, dear!

They'd say grace and, between bites of food, make plans for catch and teatime and dollies and movies and ice cream. Definitely ice cream. And that hour between bedtime and waking when he and Judy would chat. And between all of that they'd compliment Judy's cooking. Hand over her heart. Glistening blue eyes reflecting the pride of those around her.

Clap! Mama opened her palms, searching for his remains. He was still flying, but took heavy damage. His wings malfunctioned. He went into a tailspin. Round and round. *Plop!* Right into my grits.

"Got that tiny, black-assed bastard," she said and fell back into her seat. "And no!"

The chair wobbled. She grabbed the table to steady herself. I picked up my spoon and moved around the goopy mess beneath the fly. His leg twitched and stiffened.

"How 'bout other people's funerals?" I heaped a spoonful of grits over his lifeless body and gave a quick salute. That horn, the one from the military funerals on TV, played in my head.

"Three times," she held up three ashy fingers. "That's it, that's all."

My forehead was hot. As if caught in a sniper's laser beam. I looked up. Mama's glare ran a chill up my spine. She couldn't deflate her puffy red and black lips into a flat line. She simply tightened them the best she could whenever anything or anyone displeased her.

"And ladies always finish their meals," she said.

She stared silently at my bowl. I grazed the spoon. One finger. Two. I slowly stirred it around. Felt the different vibrations in my hand as the spoon moved through multiple textures. Mama bit her bottom lip and leaned forward, hands clasped on the table. I snatched up a spoonful of my cold hot cereal and sipped from the edge of the spoon. Lips tight. Only small bits at a time. As the granules receded, his mangled black body appeared.

Shaking, I lowered his body. Tried to return him to his resting place, but Mama saw.

"Go on," she said. "Finish it."

Mama took back up her needlework. She was always making or patching clothes. Especially when hand-me-downs were running dry.

"But...there's a fly in it."

"Good." She ran her eyes over my lanky body. "Little protein'll do you good."

I raised my little buddy up to my lips. I imagined the horror on Judy and Johnny and Julie's flawless faces as an officer gave them the news. He was a great soldier. A hero. Here's your folded flag. It'll keep your dinner warm and play with your kids and take them out for ice cream and console Judy.

Bolts and crushed metal wedged between my teeth. I wondered if the black box was really indestructible.

That night, I spun the old, squeaky globe that Mrs. Jamison gave me when she discovered that she didn't quite like teaching sugared up third graders as much as she had hoped. It spun and squealed until I dug the tip of my finger into the sands of Cuba.

That's where Daddy was. Dropping care packages from his plane for the needy.

The week before, he was in Nigeria. Made the front page. Headline: Man Builds Schools and Hope for Poor Village Children. Underneath a black and white photo of little Black boys and girls clustered around his legs looking up and basking in his smile. Goggles high on his head. Red scarf flowing in the wind. Hands on his waist. His captioned quote: "Every child has the potential to succeed if given the opportunity." Then, he shoveled the souvenirs he picked up for me into the plane and headed for Cuba. I figured his cockpit was getting pretty crowded. He never left without a souvenir or two or three.

Eventually, he'd land his plane out front under the oak tree and shower me with dolls and jewels and stories of all his adventures.

I crawled into bed and gazed out the window. A plane drew white, chalky lines across the night sky. A commercial plane. Too big to be Daddy's, but the hum of the engine lulled me to sleep just the same.

Mama's snoring clawed up my walls and into bed with me. I shielded my ears with my blanket, but it pried away my fingers like orange slices and performed a drum solo in my ear. I tiptoed to the door, trying to avoid the tell-tale creaks whose locations I'd nearly memorized in the wooden floor. I slowly turned the knob and guided the door forward with my open palm. It slipped and squealed. The snoring stopped. I held my breath. Mama's bed stretched and yawned and eventually fell back into snoring. I closed the door, released the handle, followed the charted path back to my tiny bed and plopped on the floor.

I lifted my thin, dingy blanket and pulled out several books from under the bed. I wiped the covers clean with my sleeves. A flurry of dust and lint floated like stardust in the moonlight beaming through my open bedroom window.

Peter Pan.

Alice's Adventures in Wonderland.

The People Could Fly.

The sole survivors of Mama's this-is-the-only-book-you'll-ever-need recycling project. Only, it wasn't recycling. As my books burned in the front yard, Mama told me my imagination was too wonky at times. She turned to me, her cheeks red hot from the fire, and explained that I needed to root myself, my mind, to the ground like the great oak tree out front.

My shelf was full of different editions of the only book I would ever need. The New International Version and New American English and New Living Translation. The King James Version and the New King James Version because I guess he got God to copyedit the second one. They stood perfectly erect, side-by-side even though my bookshelf leaned slightly to the right as if on crooked ground. I'd never touched them, but somehow they remained dust free.

I decided on *The People Could Fly* and slid the other two back to the monster under my bed for safekeeping. Snug in my blanket, I flipped to the page I dog-eared and gazed at the picture of a group of former slaves as they flew through the air. Just like Daddy, but without a plane. Up and over fields that were being worked by others who didn't have the power to leave. Over my shoulder, Daddy's portrait looked on as I ran my fingers over their faces. A couple of years before, I emerged from the dumpster out back with an armful of old magazines. I thumbed through them. Looking for traces of Daddy. His understanding, brown eyes stared out at me from an article on *The Cosby Show*. Mama said I wasn't coordinated enough for scissors--though I was able to tie my shoes well enough. So, I slowly tore out Dr. Huxtable's eyes and set them aside. I taped the jagged edged eyes, crooked Dr. Doolittle smile, and perfect Uncle Jessie hair on top of Denzel's flawless face and tacked it to my wall.

A voice whispered to me.

Why don't you just fly?

I looked up from my book. A dark shadow flitted across the corners of my eyes. I tried to track it, but it evaded my gaze.

Why don't you just fly away?

I turned toward the window in time to see dark specks falling in the moonlight. I shut my eyes and covered my ears.

Rooted like a tree.

***

On my twelfth birthday, Mama sat on the deflated burgundy couch that Aunt Minnie the mousey, crimson-lipped jezebel gave her before she found L'Oréal and the Calvin Klein ads that drove her out of "our simple life" and into "ungodly pursuits" such as fame and "gyrating Chippendales crotches." Mama threw away Aunt Minnie but held on to the couch, even though she thought it too colorful for the black rug and coffee table and yellowing walls. Her toes tapped the giant rusty bucket in front of her. Sleeves cuffed above her elbows and skin glistening from submerging her arms in the bucket's soapy water. I couldn't sneak by.

"I already took a bath," I said.

Mama's eyes honed in on me as I ambled by. Her clammy hands cuffed my wrist, spun me around and cuffed the other. Clouds passed back and forth across the sun as it shone through the window. Its rays pulsated on the empty walls like a flickering interrogation room light. Mama leaned in real close and took a whiff. Her nostrils flared and whirred. Sucked my shirt in like a vacuum.

"Girl," Mama said between sniffs, "You too old to smell like that. Get out them clothes."

Mama was already unbuttoning my pajama top. I grasped the final button and held it firm.

"I'm old enough to bathe myself."

Mama flicked my hand away, dropped my pants and pushed me into the bucket.

"Did you hear me, Mama?" I said.

Mama scrubbed my arms and neck and armpits. She rubbed words of wisdom into my open pores. It's rude for a lady to smell. You're too old for pajamas with footies and cartoon characters, but too young for a nightgown. Mrs. Jamison's daughter just started high school, she may have something in your size. Don't forget to clean behind your eyes. That's where the devil's hiding. Your Sunday school outfit's on...

I hear you.

Mama ran her fingers along my back. When she reached my shoulder blades, she hovered there like a miner with a faulty metal detector. Afraid to waste her energy on the first blow.

Just fly fly fly fly fly ha haha!

Black shapes flickered in and out of my vision. Wings hummed past my ear. Mama sprung up with so much force she capsized the bucket. Black bits of carpet clung to my moist skin. Mama towered over me. The laughter faded. Her eyes bounced back-and-forth over the walls and eventually locked onto mine. She tried to silence her beating heart with her hands.

"G-get some clothes on," she said.

"Mama," I said as I picked carpet from my skin, "did you—"

"I said get dressed." Mama flung open several drawers in the kitchen. "You'll be late for Sunday school."

A pair of khakis rested on my bed, patched up with fabric a few shades too light and a shirt that intimately hugged my waist. I felt naked. I slid my finger over my stomach and found a small bump beside my belly button. It reminded me of the dead soldier I swallowed. Maybe he was alive and this was morse code or an SOS. Down in the dark with a single light. Surviving off the scraps that I ate. Keeping me thin as a sewing needle and—I grazed the nubs on my chest—flat. I'd better stop skipping breakfast.

Mama's footsteps shook the floorboards and roused my goosebumps from their hiding place. I covered my nakedness with a long, somewhat white jacket and cuffed the ends of my sleeves just in time to free my hands for Mama's grasp.

Mama dragged me out the front door and around to the back of the house. In a folding chair, under the canopy that he jimmy rigged out of an old sheet and clothespins, sat Deacon Joseph. He insisted we call him "deacon" though Delilah said that no one *ever* elected Joseph to be deacon and that he didn't have half the character, brains, or teeth of the deacons back home in her city church, but when I told Mama she said Joseph earned himself the honorary title of deacon for all that he'd done for the church and the children over the decades and that we should be grateful to have a man that was *so* close to God personally paving us a path to heaven through his blood, sweat and tears.

Deacon Joseph fanned his bald spots and swatted at flies as his stomach gushed out from under his shirt like water from a broken pipe. The tall, dry grass hid the gap between the hem of his church pants and his sandal bands. The other kids raced over to the makeshift wooden board and bucket benches to get a good seat next to their friends. Jeremiah's dark drown hand jutted out and waved at me from within the group. I wiggled a few fingers back at him. Mama's hands clamped my shoulders before the heel of my foot could hit the dirt.

"Here," Mama said.

I looked up. All the way up to Mama's furrowed brow and narrowed eyes. Her wide-brimmed, straw hat eclipsed the sun. A string of light outlined her usually ashen, puce skin. She shook her head and dropped the Bible into my open hand. The weight of it nearly brought me to my knees. I hunched over like a lanky sunflower left in the shade too long. Mama straightened me up and I realized how dark and puny my hand was compared to hers. Mama always wore her skin with pride as if it were a steal at a vintage thrift store. Mine felt unnatural like a discount coat from the bargain bin. A few sizes too small. Itchy and sweaty. One you can't wait to throw off once you hit the door.

I turned away from Mama just in time to see Delilah saunter over to Jeremiah. She lifted his jacket from the seat beside him, placed it in his lap and sat down. Her relaxed Shirley Temple locks swung as she tapped Jeremiah's shoulder and shot whispers into his ear out of painted lips. He locked eyes with her and their chuckles bobbed their heads about and the whole time Delilah cut me with her eyes and woven between it all I heard Mama telling me something about errands and flies and God and she coughed between every word and every step I took away from her and there I sat three rows behind Jeremiah and Delilah as she twirled her raven hair around her fingers and mine got tangled in the dry Brillo pad mess on top of my head just as Jeremiah turned to me, shrugged and raised the corners of his chapped lips in a way that seemed to beg forgiveness, but set my leg shaking so bad that I focused on trying to draw perfect squares with the tip of my shoe even as we all stood and sang *My Hope Is Built on Nothing Less* and we got to the part about sinking sand and I felt the ground swallow my foot and my leg and I raised my hands high above me and called for help until I couldn't breathe anymore and gave up hope and through the darkness I heard a voice and the voice grabbed my hand and pulled me out and when I opened my eyes—

—*Fly away.*

My hands were still in the air and everyone was laughing at me. Even bucktoothed Christine and Ricky the four-eyed Inhaler and especially caramel-kissed Delilah in her Sears catalog summer dress.

"She's nuts," Delilah said, "She thinks she's just going to take off like a butterfly or a bird or a—"

"A fly," Ricky took a puff from his inhaler. "A big ol' nasty fly."

Christine ran around with outstretched arms. Buzzing. The chorus of laughter reached new heights. Christine circled around me. I raised my hands to the heavens and brought my open palms down on top of her head. One after the other. Her barrettes stung my palm, but I kept swinging my arms over and over again like a windmill. Soon, I was screaming and I didn't know why. Just screaming and swinging and striking until Deacon Joseph grabbed my wrist and shook the devil out of me and Christine as he tried to disarm the circle that grew around me. Only Delilah's squeals survived.

"But she thinks she can fly, Joseph," Delilah said, as she hopped about. "Back home we had special places for people like her."

"Cut it!" Deacon Joseph said. "If God wanted us t' fly, he'd a given us wings."

"I never—" I started.

—*But you can fly, can't you?*

I wriggled free and tracked the sound of the voice. Jeremiah watched me. Tight-lipped. A shadow ran across his face.

"M-maybe I will fly away," I said, returning his gaze.

"Go on then," Delilah waved her dainty hand as if she could set me in motion herself.

"And I'll leave you all behind."

A plane whirred overhead. A small plane.

"Aint nothin' but the devil workin' thru all ya," Deacon Joseph spun in a circle pointing fingers as he spoke.

I looked for a change in Jeremiah. His face was blank. Delilah elbowed him in the ribs. He frowned and opened his mouth to speak but my legs carried me away before he could utter a word. I stopped short of the front door and looked to the sky. The plane was gone. I tried to dry my cheeks with my sleeve between rapid, involuntary breaths. Mama always made me breathe into a paper bag whenever it happened. Then she'd have me exhale one final time, tie a string around the opening and crush the evil spirits inside with her bare hands. I grabbed the doorknob, but couldn't find the strength to turn it.

"Sorry," someone said behind me.

The shadow of a much taller man crawled up the front door. Hope tugged at the corner of my lips. It let go when I found myself face-to-face with Jeremiah. A trail of glistening snot ran from his right nostril and moistened his parched lips. He wiped it away with the back of his hand, but some of it was already crusted over and gave shape to a shimmery moustache. Much better than the milk chocolate ones he wore before. Back when we would play safari in the backyard. Before we hit "puberty" and Mama still allowed me to have guy friends. I cracked a Mona Lisa smile. He pulled me close to him. His shirt was wet and he smelled like a musty bottle of cologne, but I didn't move even though I was allergic and couldn't stop sneezing and when he let go I squinted at him through my itchy, watery eyes as he stroked my arm and I saw the glitter reflecting off his lips and I thought about how much I wanted mine to glitter also and before I knew it I dabbed my lips on his like a sponge and when I pulled away he snorted and wiped the snot away.

"Jeremiah!" Delilah said.

His brown eyes went from soft to searching to sharpened, accusing points. I reached for his hand, but it was already gone.

"Jeremiah!"

I stepped toward him. He squeezed my arms.

Too tightly.

I felt his burning, shaking palms through my jacket. He looked away. I followed his eyes down to his feet.

He had nice shoes.

"Sorry," he said.

My butt hit the ground first. Then my back and my head. The great oak tree stared down at me. Its twisted branches pierced the sky and its serrated leaves scratched the gray clouds forming overhead and cast me in shadows. The fall's impact shook some of the glitter off my lips and into my mouth.

Salty.

***

"It's so hot out," Mama pinned another fly trap to the ceiling, "the flies tryna come shack up with us now."

She swatted several times at empty air while gasping for breath as if in a marathon. The table bowed under her feet. She pointed at the garbage bag on the floor. It was full of flypaper, venus flytraps, zappers, sprays, swatters and trappers. I reached inside and handed her a tube of fly paper. She unrolled the tube and hung it beside the trap she'd just installed.

"Just too hot," she said as I handed her another. "Can't always close the door."

"What if we got air conditioning?"

Mama dropped the fly paper. I tried to peel it off the table. No use. I handed her another roll.

"Then you could close the door," I said.

"No no no can't trust 'em," Mama struggled with the pushpin. "They'll sneak right in. Crawl right under the door or up the drains."

Mama climbed down from the table and dragged the bag into the living room. My stomach growled. The sink was empty and the stove clean. Mama stomped around the living room like an exterminator on a carpet made of ants. She kept smacking and popping her legs, but nothing was there. I buttered two slices of bread, sprinkled them with sugar and sandwiched them together. Mama alternated between stomping fits and collapsing on the couch from exhaustion until I went to bed.

***

The pages of my book fluttered me awake. The wind was dead, but the pages kept flipping on their own. Black specks quivered in the moonlight. Shadows flickered across the wall and skirted past my eyes.

You ready?

"Ready for what?" I drew the blanket up to my eyes as I struggled to keep track of the flitting shadows.

You know what.

In the moonlight, I saw the outline of a clear, webbed wing. I buried myself in the blanket.

"Are you a fallen angel?"

No.

The blanket blew off the bed, flew around the room and landed on the floor. I curled into a ball. My shaky knees rocked my chest.

"A fairy?"

No such thing.

"Then what?" my head was spinning.

I'm just like you, only fully bloomed.

The figure stopped in front of my crossed eyes. It was a he. Tall and thin in a worn tuxedo jacket and slacks. His top hat tipped to the side, casting his face in shadow. I tried to gaze directly at him, but he disappeared and reappeared in the corner of my eye. I rubbed my eyes and there he was again in front of me, but out of focus. Almost as if someone tried to remove his face with a dirty eraser.

Can't see what you don't understand.

"So help me."

Nah. First things first, baby. You gotta fly.

"But how?" I turned to face him. He threw himself on my bed. "People can't fly."

I'm flying. He flew in circles around my room. *Just clear your mind.*

"Like Wendy in Peter Pan?" I stood on the bed, closed my eyes and thought happy little thoughts. A cool breeze tickled my cheek. I looked down. Disappointed to find my feet right where I left them. The figure was blowing his breath on my face.

"Oh, so you've come to make fun of me too you...um..."

Amadaius. Just Amadaius.

"You didn't bring no pixie dust?"

Not when y'got something better. Check your back.

I ran my fingers up my spine. Everything felt normal until I got to my shoulder blades. Between my fingers I felt two sheet-like stubs budding from my back. My face lit up. Were those wings? I had wings! I jumped up and down until my toes dug deep into the mattress and I sprung off the bed like Superman.

Wind ran over my limbs and gave way as I fell flat on the floor. Amadaius laughed and slapped his thigh and laughed, laughed, laughed.

They need a bit of cultivating.

The floor quaked. I grabbed my blanket. The door swung open and Mama found me upright in bed. I couldn't see Amadaius.

"I heard something," Mama stood at the foot of my bed. "What you up to?"

"Nothing."

Mama sniffed around my room on all fours like a bloodhound, licked her finger and held it up to the air. She swatted her face a few times and shut the window. Said it was cold out. She was in the doorway on the verge of leaving when she suddenly froze like a cartoon dog that finally caught a scent.

"Little girl," a single step and she was beside my ear, "What are you hiding?"

"Nothing, Mama."

Mama's nose crept up my blanket. I felt dizzy. My mouth dried out. She gripped the edge. I tried to hold it down, but the blanket slid out of my sweaty palms. Every muscle in my body tightened as her arm snaked behind my back and snatched my breath before I could catch it.

"What is," Mama ran her fingers down my spine, "this?"

The People Could Fly dangled in front of my face. I touched my shoulder blades. They were still there.

"I'll burn it in the morning," Mama said as she hobbled out the door. "Keep your head out the clouds."

I called out to Amadaius. He didn't answer.

***

The next morning after breakfast, I asked Mama if I could straighten my hair.

"What's wrong with the hair God gave you?" Mama handed me a wet plate from the sink.

I dried and buffed the plate until it reflected the thorny bush on top of my head. Tiny birds poked out their beaks and wove nests out of my kinky strands. "Delilah said I look like Kunta Kinte" bounced on the tip of my tongue, but I swallowed the words before they reached Mama's ears. I touched my hair. The little birds nipped at my fingers.

"I thought it might be easier to manage," I said.

"It's best to manage what's left alone," Mama said.

I grabbed at the little birds. They kept ducking in and out like a Whack-A-Mole game while Mama went on about my hair being like hers and if her hair was good enough for God, which it was because he chose it, then so was mine.

But little birds didn't live in Mama's hair or nip at her fingers. Her nests were empty.

My little birds started chirping. I squeezed and pulled at my hair, tried to drive them out. They got louder. Like they were scared. Like they were calling their Mama. If only He had come down and sat next to me on Sunday and told the other kids how great my hair was, maybe then I would've believed Mama. But He didn't and I didn't want to be alone.

I didn't want to be Mama.

***

Delilah snatched my hat off at Sunday school and everyone laughed at my bald head. I left the relaxer in too long. It burned and smelled like rotten eggs. I imagined it would smooth out my wrinkled locks like a liquid hot iron, leaving my hair just as shiny as the girl's on the box--and easy to curl or to whip into a ponytail. Instead, it sucked up all the moisture and my brittle hair snapped between my fingers like burnt bacon. Clumps sizzled in the sink water and disappeared down the drain along with tiny, chirpless birds. Mama found me behind a curtain of screams. Promised to fix me up. Fixin' me up meant clippers and a shaved head and a lecture on starting from scratch and repenting for turning away from God's plan. She forced me to go to Sunday School where everyone was laughing at me.

Except for Jeremiah.

He read quietly in his seat as Deacon Joseph chased the kids around. They scattered across the back yard. Each time someone ran by he lunged toward them, missed and reached for another. He ended up out of breath right where he started. Threats of God's eventual wrath didn't frighten them, but the threat of their parents' wrath did. As they calmed down, I saw Delilah giggling in Jeremiah's ear. He stopped reading and looked over his shoulder toward me.

"I don't know," Jeremiah said. "It doesn't look that bad."

Delilah didn't say another word.

***

I stacked all my bibles up into a pyramid beside the couch while Mama was out running errands or taking care of Mrs. Jamison's new surprise twins for extra money. I'd climb to the top, jump, plummet to the ground and spit out mouthfuls of carpet. My scraped knees always carried me back to the top to do it all over again. Each time, Amadaius hooted and hollered louder than before. And each Sunday, Delilah and Jeremiah seemed to sit closer and closer. Especially when her breasts swelled up and begged for air at the top of her dress. Even Deacon Joseph stole a peek or two when he thought all of our eyes were closed for prayer. But I stopped being upset a long time ago, really. Too focused on flying. I spent more and more time in the air, but it was still falling all the same.

***

Two summers later, the day finally came. I hovered a full five minutes until I heard the front door creak open. I lost my concentration and my knee crashed into the floor. A sharp pain ran up my leg. I grabbed my knee. I was bleeding. Red stained my fingers. Someone picked me up by my arms. I gasped when I saw a much taller and stronger Jeremiah. My face burned crimson hot as I tried to free myself. I pounded him the best I could with my fists, but he kept going.

"Let me go," my arms weakened. "Just get outta here."

He wrapped his arms around mine. The more I struggled, the tighter he held me. He led me to the couch and helped me sit down. A cloud of dust enveloped him as he plopped down next to me. Glares shot out over our heaving chests and drenched faces.

"You're strong for a beanpole," he chuckled.

I didn't blink. He bit his lip. Squirmed in his seat like a fish on dry land.

"I, uh," he reached in his back pocket, "I've held on to this for—"

"You must be lost," my eyes slid down my flat chest. "If you're looking for Delilah, she's obviously not here." I turned my back toward him.

"Look, about before—"

"There is no before." My body quaked. "Only now and right now you should go."

My rapid breathing knotted my stomach. My skin was on fire and only then did I realize how mad I really was. How much pain I was in. He dropped to his knees in front of me and I wanted to bruise his face so Delilah wouldn't love him anymore and he'd be free to live a disfigured life with me up in the tower of Notre Dame helping me to ring the bells for Sunday Mass. Then I was ashamed for allowing him access to my fantasies and immediately cursed myself for living in a dream.

He placed a tiny, cool book on my lap. The King James Version. From that day. So long ago. It was much heavier before. A lot smaller now in my thin hands.

"Boy!" Mama shouted from the doorway.

I dropped the Bible. We were too close. Too sweaty. I could only imagine what she'd thought, what I wished, had happened.

"Get the hell away from my daughter and out my house."

Jeremiah sprung to his feet and bowed and uttered, "ma'am" between apologies as he scurried out the door. Mama slammed it behind him. She gave me the once over. Said I was just like Aunt Minnie as she grabbed the old rusty bucket and filled it on up with water and insults like hussy and harlot and ripped my clothes off and--why are all these Bibles on the floor--pushed me into the bucket. Only this time my legs dangled over the sides while she scrubbed my mouth with a frayed sponge and scraped my skin until the outer layer of sin was gone and only then did she notice I was bleeding, asked me if Jeremiah caused it and when I said no she hugged me and shrunk in my arms, told me to wrap a towel around myself and wait on the couch while she grabbed the Campho-Phenique.

Mama swore Campho-Phenique could cure anything. Even broken legs. Though it was really only for insect bites and scrapes. Mama dabbed some on my knee and ooooooh it burned. I looked on as she extinguished the fire with her breath. Kept blowing even though she was winded. I hadn't noticed how tiny she'd gotten. A plump grape shriveled into a raisin by the sun.

"Boys are only after one thing," Mama coughed into her arm. "One thing and then they gone. Fly away just like your daddy."

I wonder why he flew away.

"Why did he fly away?" I asked. I searched the walls for signs of Amadaius.

"I told you," she dabbed my other, uninjured knee, "he was a pilot."

Amadaius stood behind her.

She's lyin', darlin'.

"How do you know?" I asked him. "You've never seen him."

Mama slapped my cheek, her pupils drowning in fiery pools.

She stuffed the Campho-Phenique and used cotton balls into her pockets. Amadaius placed his hands on her shoulders. She didn't flinch.

Now why do you think she's so mad? He rested his chin on Mama's shoulder. *Go on. Ask her.*

I rolled down my pants legs and got to my feet.

"What did you do?" I whispered.

"What?" Mama's eyes widened, then narrowed. "You ungrateful little—"

"You're why Daddy flew away." I felt Amadaius' hand on my back, pushing me forward. "What did you do, Mama?"

"He left us," Mama beat her chest as she spoke. "It doesn't matter why he left. It doesn't fucking matter."

Our noses met. For once, we inhaled and exhaled the same air.

"You don't even know who he is," I said.

I caught Mama by the wrist. Her open palm inches from my face. Eyes searching for a new strategy. A way to triumph. They failed like Mama's feeble attempt to slam her bedroom door behind her.

My back spasmed and beat me into submission. My vision tripled. I writhed on the floor. Head pounding. It felt like a couple of samurais decided to slice their way out my back. Everything went black.

You're ready.

When I came to, Amadaius stood over me. I think he was smiling. He handed me a wad of blue fabric. I threw it over my head and he led me outside. Said he wanted to show me something. He flew up to the roof and waited on me to find a way up. It's hard to gain your footing in the dark. The windowsill gave way and I nearly slipped, but he caught me. Helped me up. Told me to hold on tight. The tips of my toes grazed the roof and kissed it goodbye.

We flew over the oak tree, hand in hand. Clouds wrapped around my fingers like celestial rings. Amadaius' wings glimmered under the moon's gaze and scored the sky with streaks of light that rivaled the stars. They clasped, bangle-like, around my wrists and exploded into an iridescent dust storm. I chased after them. Grasped them with my hands. Pressed them to my chest. Released them and they disappeared and new ones were born and I was chasing those and soon I realized I was flying, flying all on my own and laughing at how beautiful everything looked from up here, the way the dried grass burned under the fire of porch lights and how the tops of trees sparkled like diamonds, it was like running across land and looking up and really seeing the sky for the first time.

I followed Amadaius through trees and around mountains and to the lake hidden within mountains where the fireflies danced to a cricket concerto. He landed at its mossy edge and when I arrived he told me to look in the water. My eyes reflected a glow that hugged the curves of my cheeks and illuminated my lips. On each side of my head were the tops of two thin, full-sized, shimmery wings. I poked them. Ran my fingers over them as Amadaius pointed out his home behind Orion's belt. Said he couldn't wait to show me. My fingers glowed. The surprise got me to my feet. I shook my hand and it rained glitter. When it cleared, burned out on the lake's clear surface, I saw myself in a dress haphazardly patched together in varying shades of blue that mimicked the ocean or at least what it looked like on TV. I turned to the side, ran my hands over my body, turned to Amadaius with twinkling eyes and asked where he got it.

It was always yours.

***

The dress disappeared the night I found Mama unconscious on the floor.

I thought she was sleeping. The paramedics said otherwise and tossed her in the ambulance like an old, dirty couch. Doctor said she had a growth. That it was malignant. That it was in her bones. Mama wouldn't let them give her anything for it. Bit the nurse when she tried. Said she didn't need the devil's ointment.

She'd fight on faith and Campho-Phenique alone. The doctors and nurses shook their heads and let her go.

I saw Deacon Joseph more than anyone ever should or like to. He came over every night to tend to Mama in the same dirty Dickies and frayed striped sweater. To pray with her and around her and over her. His words swaddled her to sleep. Soothed her soul. Yet, he always emerged from the room hunchbacked. Head hung low like a man without faith.

At night, when Mama was asleep and the dishes washed and the Deacon gone, I'd fly around with Amadaius or we'd sit on the roof and he'd point and plead, but I always told him I wasn't ready. Needed more time. More practice. He said I wasn't getting no younger. Seventeen was just around the corner.

Jeremiah came to visit from time-to-time. He'd lock himself in the bedroom with Mama and Deacon Joseph and they'd all pray. Sometimes, he brought Delilah. Other times, he didn't. It was those times that he found a reason to talk to me. Asking after Mama's health was his usual way in.

Was she eating? Did she sit up today? She seemed a lot better this time around.

Then he focused his periscope on me.

How was *I* doing?

Was *I* eating?

Would *I* at least eat the apples he brought me?

What was *I* watching? He heard it was a good movie.

He chipped away at my one-word responses until I came to expect him to sit next to me on the couch long into the night. We'd eat popcorn. Throw popcorn. Tell stories that we both knew the end to. Like how we refused to exchange cards on Valentine's Day because Christine said your first Valentine is the person you're going to marry and neither one of us found living with cooties 'til death do we part appealing. Or, how on my eighth birthday, when I heard a low flying plane, I snuck away. Jeremiah followed me. Lifted me up onto his shoulders so that I could climb the oak tree and look out for Daddy. I swung my legs too hard and kicked him over like a step ladder. He brushed off his sniffles and climbed to the top of the tree. We waited as the sun fell behind the mountains and our parents called our names and then, eventually, the sheriff. Eyes searching the sky. They found us in the morning. We couldn't sit for weeks. Daddy didn't make it that year.

He was probably refueling in Mexico.

We told stories where the end was yet to be determined. Like how Daddy would take the day off from fixing the world just to walk me down the aisle. Or the time I saw Jeremiah and Delilah kiss under the oak tree and when he saw me he smiled and hugged her close and she waved and I smiled back and closed the curtains. How Jeremiah meant to leave for the city. To go to college. To make something of himself.

***

Jeremiah came by every week with a different book. Most were test prep books. All of them were run-down. You had to squeeze them to keep loose pages from slipping out. Jeremiah said if he scored high enough and kept up his grades, people would pay him to go to college. I timed him and graded his practice exams so much that he thought I oughta take one myself. I scored a 1630. Ten points higher than Jeremiah.

Deacon Joseph, fresh from heartfelt prayer over Mama, would loom over us and shake his head as we studied. One day he couldn't take it anymore.

"Haven't seen t'ya at Sunday School fer a while."

"Sundays are for studying now," said Jeremiah without looking up from his book.

"Fawse ambition severs restfel sleep." Deacon Joseph locked eyes with me, but spoke to Jeremiah. "You'd a made gud preacha if not fer that."

Jeremiah winked at me over his book.

"Wisdom preserves the life of him who has it," he recited from memory.

"Nothin' but the devil," Deacon Joseph muttered on his way out the door.

After that, he left us to our own devices. Couldn't say the same for Amadaius. He didn't care much for Jeremiah. He tried to annoy him by flipping the pages in whatever book Jeremiah happened to be reading. Jeremiah fixed that by firmly pressing his finger on the page until it finally submitted to his will.

When Jeremiah wasn't around Amadaius would flick books out of my hands or hide them throughout the house.

You ain't spendin' enough time flyin'.

Sometimes, he'd kick up such a dust storm in the house that it became impossible to read. Those days I gave in and flew around with Amadaius.

***

One evening, Jeremiah shut his book. Between sips of black tea, words poured from his mouth praising city life. There was a club for everything. A job for everybody. Even for people whose only skill was handing out towels in public restrooms. He exhaled and stared out the window as if a portal to a better life would open up before him.

I told him I intended to fly away.

"People only fly in books," he said, grasping my hands, "but you can soar if you study hard enough."

"But, I can show you," I said

He stopped me from rising, stared into the centers of my eyes.

"You're too old for fairy tales," he said. "Too old."

***

Amadaius stood behind me as I pushed aside the mosquito netting over Mama's bed. I stroked the bones beneath Mama's sagging cheeks. Told her I had to go. She squinted past me. Right past me. Her eyelids sprung open like a window shade. She shook her head. Coughed. Don't go don't go don't go. Can't trust 'em. Coughed. Don't go don't go. Coughed and coughed herself to sleep.

***

On the roof, Amadaius took my hand and lifted me into the air. A splinter snagged my finger on top of the oak tree. I tried to suck it out as I looked back at the house. At the little window leading to Mama's room. I looked away. Up at Amadaius. The sun smoothed his face and revealed his eyes. Two burning coals reflected off his chiseled, onyx face. They split, cracked and shattered. As he faded into dust, his laugh hung over me.

And I thought I knew him.

My hand was empty and suddenly I'd forgotten how to fly and I was hitting every branch while his laughter shredded my clothes and cut my face and I thought of Mama withering away in her bed and how, if I wanted to please God, I needed that dress and maybe if I just had it I'd transform and become some-one new like Wendy or Alice, golden locks twirling in the wind after slipping off the hands of Big Ben and falling down the rab-bit hole into Wonderland and before I could sit down to tea.

The last branch knocked the wind out of me.

My knees buckled and my head hit the ground. Everything shook and swayed. Something crawled out of my mouth and took flight. My little war hero survived. Zigzagged in and out of my vision. He'd finally make it home. Find Judy behind the doorbell. Right where he left her. She wouldn't see through his beard, but would recognize his eyes, gasp and look back inside. He'd grab his wife, smell the roast in her hair and follow it over her shoulders. He'd drop his arms. Observe the man teaching Johnny how to tie a tie and telling Julie he wouldn't miss her ballet recital for the world. Julie's lips find his cheek and Johnny shakes his hand. They'd join their mother at the door. Who is this strange man? The other man'll come to the door. Reach into his pocket and give the fly a few crumpled dollar bills. Closing the door and thanking him for his service the whole time.

***

Jeremiah took care of Mama and me up until I could walk on my own without support. Then, he sat me down and told me, without blinking, that he was leaving. He had dreams and one day he was off living those dreams with Delilah somewhere in the city and I was glad. I helped Deacon Joseph take care of Mama. I learned to cook and bathed her and brought her her sewing kit when she asked for it. Some days she'd be better than others. On those days, I'd get her dressed and help her out to the great oak tree, let her feel the air on her scalp. We'd sit in the shade, eat peanut butter sandwiches and watch as the sun splashed the grass and mountaintops and ourselves with purple and orange. Sometimes, she'd get quiet and I could see a question clogging her throat, but she never managed to cough it up. We'd water the grass and I'd point out the new green patches sprouting beneath the dry, brown blades.

Most days she was terrible. Coughing and heaving and wheezing. Deacon Joseph installed a commode in her room because her frail legs couldn't carry her to the bathroom anymore, even when both of us held her up. Each time I saw her, she sunk deeper and deeper into her bed until she became a part of it. Once, when she'd gotten particularly bad, Deacon Joseph got the idea in his head to exorcise the demon out of her.

We didn't have Holy Water lying around or a priest, but Deacon Joseph reckoned he could make some himself. He filled a bowl up with tap water and waved his right hand over the bowl while reading the notes scribbled on his left hand. Halfway through he wiped his brow and smeared the ink across his forehead. His lips kept moving, but the words jammed in his throat. He mined his brain for wisdom, but was only able to dig up half-truths and cryptic mutterings.

Several ill-placed amens later, I held out a bowl of Holy Water as he flicked drops over Mama's forehead, invoked the name of Christ and waved his cross all over the room. Her sheets were wet, but she didn't get any better. Afterwards, I asked if there was a certain way to dispose of Holy Water and Deacon Joseph told me to dump it out back as if it were no more special than a 40oz. Said I'd have made a good deacon if I weren't a girl and that was the end of that.

***

One hazy morning, I carried a small bowl of tomato soup to Mama's door. I tried the handle. It was locked from the inside. I knocked. I heard shuffling and muffled whispers on the other side. I knocked again--louder and longer. Finally, someone unlatched the door. Deacon Joseph stood on the other side. Crosses were haphazardly nailed all over the walls. Big, obtrusive wooden ones and polished, slippery metal ones and tiny silver ones that were typically reserved for personal use. Only a few were upright. Most were slanted at odd angles to fill as much empty space as possible. Even still, Deacon Joseph shook his head as if it still weren't enough. Each cross was an emergency call that ended with a busy signal. I hung my head. There was no call waiting in heaven. The room reeked of Campho-Phenique and piss and I thought to myself this must be what death smells like and the man in the fancy black suit praying ceaselessly in the corner must be its soundtrack.

I placed the bowl on the nightstand beside the bed. The spoon clinked against the rim. Mama raised her hand and pointed to a box in the corner. I grabbed it, placed it on her bed tray and helped her up. Her thin, bony fingers fumbled with the flaps and flexed until she pried them open. She reached inside, waved me close and brought her lips to my ears.

"The Lord's coming fo' me," Mama said.

I felt a ball of cloth in my hands. I let it fall open. *The People Could Fly* tumbled out and banged against the tray. I picked it up and hugged it close. Mama waved a hand at the cloth. I spread it out and my jaw dropped. Mama chuckled. It seemed duller in such a dark room, but it was the dress. My eyes searched Mama's for answers.

"He's coming," she closed her eyes. "Y'need to be ready."

I nodded and grabbed her ghostly hand. Listened as Deacon Joseph joined the well-dressed pastor in prayer. Mama's hand disintegrated and slipped from my palm like sand. She gave me a final nod as her voice rose in unison with the others. The words soft. Distant. As if from a foreign land.

"I will fear no evil: for thou art with me..."

I stepped out onto the porch. The sun pushed the clouds aside, reached out and blinded me. I shielded my eyes and, book in hand, sought shelter under the old oak tree. The green grass tickled my legs as the earth seeped into my dress and anchored it to the ground. A cool wind skated up my arms, caressed my ebony face and flipped the pages of my book.

I sat there.

And waited.

Two Halves Of A Whole

Lucille had never grown accustomed to the extravagant state balls hosted by the Sauvage clan. Ostentatious displays of witch magic paraded before her as levitating trays of dark chocolate truffles with gooey cruor centers, and tumblers of blood soup flavored with exotic seasonal spices. Indulgences imported from the colonies they'd stolen her people from. Dramatic frescoes depicted battle scenes and historical events in scintillating animation. Bronze statues wept champagne and blood with a purl echoing across the gold-veined ballroom floor.

Lucille helped herself to a coupe of champagne to settle her nerves. Her shoes clacked on burnished marble as she blazed a trail through the blood-drinking elite. She tried to ignore how they gazed upon her neck, frail and exposed from the lowered neckline of her gown.

She was surrounded in a room of sinners. But she was no sinner. She was the sin.

Her eyes sifted through the crowd to locate one of the vampires she sought. Camille Sauvage was slurping vigorously from a glass of blood soup and lapping his tongue over the grisly stain on his thin lips.

Lucille wrinkled her nose in distaste and pointedly cleared her throat. "Monsieur Sauvage, if I might have a word?"

"Hmph?" The vampire glimpsed her up and down as though she was a smudge upon his sleeve.

"My name is Lucille Bonnaire. You may remember me from my visit to the Ivory Senate." She kept her eyes downcast to show her place to him. A vampire didn't like it when you looked them in the eye. It indicated a challenge for dominance. "I was hoping you might have received the schematics I sent to your offices. Along with my letters to appeal for the witch research facility."

"Ah, those." His vague indifference dissolved into understanding. "Yes, those went straight into the fire, girl."

"I...beg your pardon?" She gulped down the fury scorching the back of her throat. She'd penned those letters and designs with painstaking care and he had used them up as kindling.

"Your request was denied, Miss Bonnaire." Camille turned on his heel in dismissal. "There shall be no such facility for you witches."

Lucille clenched her glass as she watched him leave. A pyre had ignited in the pit of her stomach and filled her with a boldness that might have whipped any fangless gentleman into shape. Such was not her luck.

"If you'd please listen, if you'd just—"

The vampire pivoted on his foot with a sneer, all canines bared in warning. "You've overtired my patience, mortal. Relent now, or I'll have your throat."

Lucille tapped her foot before she turned away. Her chest sagged in defeat. Groveling to the head of the clan had been her final hope.

"You look as though you could use a sympathetic ear?"

Her heart stilled at the familiar voice.

Prince Ilya Likhanov stared down at her, his tow-colored hair so luminescent he looked like he'd eaten the moon. His lithe figure was poured into the pristine cut of a black suit with a fitted red shirt.

"Prince Likhanov!" Lucille fiddled with the ends of her gloves. "I didn't expect I would see you tonight."

"These are boastful affairs, but I am required to make an appearance." He brandished his half-empty glass for her perusal. "Your coupe is empty. May I interest you in another drink?"

Lucille arched her brow at the blood wine. "I hope that is a jest on your part."

Prince Likhanov chuckled. It was a whiskey-rich sound that replaced the fire in her belly with something softer. "Of course."

He procured a coupe of champagne from one of the many floating trays surrounding them.

Lucille eyed it hesitantly before succumbing, downing it in one go.

"May I ask what has Camille Sauvage in such a fury?"

"I only intended to continue our discussion from before. Regarding my facility." She huffed in defeat and swept a hand through her hair. Her spiral curls were bound into two separate buns, a singular cornrow running up the center that hung her magic amulet.

Prince Likhanov disposed of their empty glasses. "Dance with me." He bent at the waist, one hand extended with the other behind his back. "Please."

Her face softened an increment as she took his hand, allowing herself to be drawn in by the waist. She picked up her skirts in her hand, resting the other on his shoulder.

"You should know better than to appeal to fools like Camille Sauvage."

"I just don't understand it." Lucille shook her head. "The Sauvages benefit most of all from witch magic. Going back to the very conquest of the colonies. We resurrect the corpse hordes of their armies. We manipulate the aerodynamics of their rifle bullets. Our magic powers the convenience of their every whim...how can they not see that?"

"Perhaps the problem is they do see it." Prince Likhanov spun her with ease around the floor. The fluidity of his movements made her feel like they were gliding. "They see it very well. And they fear it. They fear what might happen if you realize how necessary you are."

She glanced up at him. "It's not as if much can be done with such knowledge when they hold control over our magic. I only wish for the autonomy to practice as I will."

His chest rumbled in response in a way that made her shiver. When she looked up, she could see Prince Likhanov's glacial blue eyes were upon her neck. She couldn't tell whether he wanted to kiss it or bite into it.

"I did offer to help, you know," he reminded her. "Why didn't you accept?"

"Because vampires of your stock only desire witches for eating or torturing," she said, "and that means you may want either from me. I can't figure out which it is but until I do, I cannot trust your benevolence."

This was no platinum-haired prince from a storybook—the reputation the Likhanovs held was a brutal and blood-soaked one. Lucille couldn't afford to be a fool. No matter how prettily presented such illusions came.

He dipped her low.

"What if I told you that what I wanted was far less nefarious than you might envision? And far simpler to conclude?"

She searched his face in confusion before realization dawned. "You couldn't possibly mean—?"

"I may desire your body and blood—but all I require is your mind." He stroked his hand down the curve of her face. "You give me that, I vow to leave everything else intact."

Lucille dimpled her bottom lip between her teeth as he lifted her back up. She had ended up looking into his eyes and sought to break contact. "Why is it me you want so badly?"

He took a step closer to tilt her chin up to face him. She felt the whorl of his cold breath on her lips as he leaned in.

"Because you are a bright spark, Miss Bonnaire. Something that only kindles once in a generation. I want to lay my claim before anyone else does."

She swallowed, her lips parting in speechlessness. "Well you should know I won't be easily obtained."

He chuckled enough to bare his fangs. "Oh, I'm counting on it."

***

Lucille lay in her garden pond, gliding like a lily in water and pushing her foot against the edges.

She had always loved to float. She loved the way even her bones seemed weightless. She'd often pretend she was still in the tropical heat of her homeland. Home. Her chest pulsed over that one syllable.

If only she and her witch mother hadn't been shipped off to vampire territory, perhaps she'd still be there now sitting cross-legged before the spiced, potent fumes of smoking fish with her toes curled into the sand.

"Lucille," her mother's voice rang through her teeth like a clank of dull metal. "You have a guest."

She rolled into the water with a groan. Her dark curls billowed around her face as she sank, obscuring her vision. A trail of air bubbles danced from her nostrils to help her reach that dizzying place of airlessness where everything felt so euphoric.

She wasn't sure how long it took before she resurfaced but when she did, she was being approached by the narrow, forceful footsteps of her mother.

"Honestly, Lucille!" The woman sounded her displeasure with a purposeful cluck of her tongue, her brown eyes burning even from beneath her straw hat. "We're entertaining gentleman company. Get dressed."

The inflection of her voice and what it implied was all too clear.

Lucille swiveled round and lifted herself out of the pond in one brisk gesture. Her mother quickly handed her a towel which she used to envelop her body.

"What kind of gentleman?" she asked as she milked her hair free of moisture.

"The blood-sucking kind," her mother replied. "Prince Ilya Likhanov."

Lucille flinched in surprise. "I'll be a moment."

She ran upstairs to her room to enter the shower, the water hot and soothing. Lucille rinsed herself of the earthy-smelling pond, replacing it with a fragrant, lavender-scented soap. She emerged from the bathroom in a cloud of vapor and approached her wardrobe, creaking open the doors to seek her white lace tea dress. It had seen some wear, and some of the ends had started to fray, but it was the nicest casual item she owned.

"You're not wearing that, are you?" her mother asked from the doorway, distaste evident in a way that burrowed beneath Lucille's skin.

"What's wrong with it?" Lucille resigned herself to her mother's unwarranted critique.

"Come now, darling, you know better than to wear lace on your neck in the presence of a vampire," she scolded. "We don't want you giving off the wrong impression."

"And what impression would that be, Mama?" Lucille's responses had grown mechanical as she reached for her cocoa butter, slathering it on her now dried skin.

"A little advice for you, Lucille. Vampires of Prince Likhanov's caliber tend to prefer a little subtlety."

That had her pausing mid-rub, damp hair now flung across her shoulder. "What makes you think I care what vampires of his caliber think? Or any caliber for that matter?"

"Lucille." Her mother gave a disgruntled chortle. "You know very well the world we live in. If you want to make your way, a vampire master is how you do it."

Lucille puffed her chest in her annoyance. Yet she knew her mother was right. Her mother's master had kept them fed and housed but even he only had so much to offer. If Lucille wanted more space to roam then she would need to net a bigger fish.

"Mama, this is the only dress I have fit for greeting a prince and you know it." Lucille's voice strained, almost a plea. She did despise each time she was forced to humble herself.

"Fine," her mother conceded, tonelessly, mercifully, until finally the gravity of her presence was lifted from the room.

***

When Lucille arrived downstairs, her mother had brunch served on the patio atop a wrought iron table.

"Nice of you to join us at last." Her mother poured her a cup of chamomile tea.

"My apologies." Lucille dipped her chin, her feigned humility laid on thick as a treacle. "Did I miss anything vital in your conversation about me?"

Her mother stirred honey into her chamomile tea in perfect circles. Not a single clink of porcelain or squeal of metal to be heard. "Prince Likhanov and I were just discussing how you two met."

Prince Likhanov was settled into one cushioned seat, conservatively sipping at a monogrammed flask of blood. She noticed his jaw twitch when he saw her. Was lace over skin truly so enticing to a vampire?

"Oh, of course." Lucille laughed, helping herself to fried toast. Then she reached to pour raspberry coulis onto it. "I didn't think our last encounter would endear you much toward me."

"On the contrary, Miss Bonnaire." The corner of his mouth lifted in amusement. "You left quite the impression."

She glanced up at him in bewilderment. "I assume you're here to...reinstate your offer?"

"I don't intend to force you into anything." Though he could. He always could. And that threat would always linger between them. "However, I believe you and I could be of immense benefit to one another. I even have a suggestion that might be more... persuasive."

Her mother's eyes glazed over. "Oh? And what might that be?"

"I would like to request your daughter's hand in marriage."

Lucille's hand lurched as she lifted the toast to her mouth. A light drizzle of coulis slithered off and left a thin red trail along her collar. "Oh no."

"Oh, Lucille," her mother sighed. "Not your dress."

"I'll fix it!" Lucille scraped her nail over the sauce, clearing it with magic, and sucked the residue off her finger.

She noticed Prince Likhanov glance away very quickly as she did so. His jaw tightened in strain. Slowly, she retracted her finger and looked down at the faint red impression still present. Was this to be her fate?

"Marriage between a vampire and a witch..."

"Of course." Prince Likhanov had turned back to her again. His eyes twinkled with sincerity. "I can think of no one more fitting to become my bride."

To embark on a lovelorn affair between the races alone would be the height of scandal. Though certainly many cases had been whispered of in the past. To officiate such an abominable union was another matter entirely.

"Well, I can't see why you'd have much to consider with that." Her mother stabbed a raspberry neatly lined around her thick brioche, causing a light translucent spatter to ooze onto her plate.

"Of course there is!" Lucille protested. "I have nothing I could possibly offer you. Not wealth. Not my womb—"

"That's where you're wrong, Miss Bonnaire." Prince Likhanov held up a hand to stop her. "There is something most valuable you can offer. Something a vampire can never attain. Your magic."

A flicker of dread inflamed her stomach. "You wouldn't desire to turn me then?"

"Goodness, no," Prince Likhanov scoffed. "I would never dream of robbing you from the connection to nature's magic. I merely want to siphon some of it for my own use. Become my bride and everything I have I will give to you. And everything you have will be on offer to me. We'll be united as one."

It seemed a romantic notion and yet she couldn't escape the words unsaid. Everything she had would be his. Every idea. Every invention. Her every accomplishment would be inextricably bound to his name.

"I can see I've given you a lot to consider." Prince Likhanov withdrew from his chair. "If you need, I can return again—"

"No." Lucille swallowed and bit her lip. To accept his offer would mean wealth and security beyond her wildest dreams. More so than the tenuous comfort her mother's vampire master brought them. "I... I accept."

Vivienne clutched her chest in surprise and delight.

He blurred too fast for Lucille to see him. Before she knew it he had descended to one knee before her. He clutched her hand in his and lifted it to his lips.

"I hope you know I intend to keep you for a long, long time, Miss Bonnaire."

***

A black carriage arrived by the end of the week to escort Lucille to Prince Likhanov's manor in the city. She couldn't help noticing how its long shape mirrored a hearse and wondered if that was some form of inside joke among their kind.

She boarded with her two brown suitcases after a strained kiss to her mother's cheek. Then she was off to the city central where a wrought iron gate kept a ring of palatial houses cordoned from humans. Lucille imagined it would appear a high-nosed snub from their perspective. To her, it seemed to be a pen where all the grandest beasts were kept. The rose bushes hemming the area had been savagely trimmed; not a single petal was allowed to blossom out of place.

Her arrival was met by an animated corpse-valet with cross-stitched eyes. Though she had long come to expect it, a shudder rippled through her the moment he extended his hand for her luggage. She passed it over with little resistance.

The valet led her inside the manor and she was treated more to its cultivated opulence. Her chest tightened at the thought that this and the estate he had in the country would come to be her home.

They ascended two flights up a wide staircase flanked by a bannister engraved with grapevines and figured maidens on each pillar. Colored shadows filtered in from a stained glass window on the first landing, dressed with drapes of asphyxiating velvet.

The valet drew the curtains along their journey and pointed a knobbled finger toward the door Lucille must enter.

The prince had a regal office—huge mahogany shelves full of old books and antique leather furniture. The gentleman himself was lounging in a smoking jacket, sitting at a massive desk with gold accessories and blood in a crystal decanter. Scents of sweet tobacco leaf, leather and wood polish composed a smooth symphony in Lucille's nostrils. Yet she could also catch the undertone of formaldehyde, which was enough to set her on edge.

"Good afternoon, Miss Bonnaire," Prince Likhanov greeted her with a genial smile. "Please sit. I hope you had a pleasant journey."

"It went quite well, thank you." Lucille approached the empty seat across from him and sat, fretting on how to position her hands and legs. The effortless repose of his folded legs unnerved her. He looked more marmoreal than man.

"Wonderful." Prince Likhanov leaned forward to steeple his fingers. "May I interest you in some tea? Some cakes perhaps? It's been a while since I've entertained a mortal so I had the house stocked specifically."

She found something about that almost touching. "I would love some."

He lifted the bone handle of a bronze repoussé bell and gave it a ring. A low, vibrating clang sounded. Moments after, the door creaked to signal the arrival of a corpse-servant.

"Some tea and cakes for Miss Bonnaire."

The servant made a haggard sound from his chewed-out vocals before leaving.

Prince Likhanov returned his stare to her. "Now, shall we discuss the matter of your research?"

"Yes." Lucille rummaged through her satchel to retrieve her sketchbook. She swallowed once she held it in her hands, realizing how quaint it must look with its fraying clothbound cover and faded gold foil.

Prince Likhanov took it from her, saying nothing of its condition. He flipped through diagrams of her original conceptions or recreated historical inventions with her own magical flair, littered with labels and arrows. There were various drawings showing the devices in operation, capturing its changes at various states.

Lucille took a moment to study him as he studied her mind. His face had an old world quality to it—the gaunt, weather-beaten features of the callous north. High brow, hooded eyes and sharp facial bones. The Likhanovs were perceived to be the original vampire line in existence. Perceived, for confirmation would never be had either way.

"There is a well of untapped potential here, Miss Bonnaire. I am most intrigued." He glanced up to smile at her. "I would like to nurture this potential any way I can. Upon our marriage, you may receive funding from me to put toward the crafting of these inventions, up to and including your own facility and personal hiring of staff."

"That's very generous of you, Prince Likhanov." Lucille was unable to fathom her fortune. "Thank you."

"The pleasure is all mine," he said, holding out the sketch-book.

Their fingers brushed when she reached to retrieve it and she lunged back with a start. She found herself blushing as she thought of the more liberal touches a marriage would allow between them. Would it feel pleasant to kiss those rosy lips? To feel light caresses from his long, graceful fingers?

Thankfully, her tea and cakes were wheeled in on a tray to distract her from her tangent. Plumes of steam exhaled from a porcelain teapot paired with dainty pastries adorned with edible flowers.

Lucille poured herself tea into one of the matching cups, stirring in lemon and sugar. She realized it was chamomile, same as when he visited.

Prince Likhanov's eyes were on her all the while, immensely fascinated by this mortal ritual. "I would also like to introduce you to my clan one night."

Lucille struggled to keep from dropping the pot. "I beg your pardon?"

"Nothing extraneous." He shrugged with his elbows. "Only a small family gathering over a dinner party."

The thought of being the only warm-blooded guest present

at a vampire dinner party held little appeal.

"I don't believe I'd have anything to wear—"

"I'd fetch you dresses, of course," Prince Likhanov assured her. "And jewels. Whatever you require."

Seeing he would not relent, she found herself nodding.

***

The morning preceding the dinner party had seen Lucille swarmed by corpse-servants marching in couture dresses and exquisite jewels. All befitting of a vampire princess.

Lucille had nearly choked on a breath when met with the fine fabrics, the innumerable spray of gemstones dangling from one parure. These garments looked nothing like her wardrobe of before, but she ought to have expected that. If he was to erase her name and title and supplant it with his, then why not her clothing?

"Due to the short notice I was unable to tailor the dresses to your measurements." Prince Likhanov leaned furtively against the wall with arms folded. "No matter, your magic should take care of that. Though I am sure you will fill them in quite nicely as they are."

Some part of her couldn't help but feel abashed by such a comment. Even though she was sure that it was just a flippant remark. With the prince, it was near impossible to tell. His heavy accent gave a smoker's husk to his voice that made everything he said seem somewhat tawdry.

Lucille retired behind the silk folding screen and let a servant lace her into her first gown. It was buttercup yellow taffeta and had sunflower appliqués on the bodice. She smoothed her hands over the luxurious fabric before stepping out.

"What do you think?"

She stiffened as ice blue eyes traced over the curves of her body. His gaze pierced through the gown and she almost felt as though she was presenting herself to him utterly naked.

Slowly, she did a full spin show off every view when a pair of hands clamped down on her waist, stilling her in front of a full-length mirror.

"Hmnn." He lightly ran his fingers down to her hips. Though his touch was cool she could feel his fingers burning her skin. "It seems rather innocent."

"Innocent?"

"You don't want to waltz in tonight looking like a lamb dressed for slaughter."

Lucille stoppered her tongue to prevent from responding unfavorably. She wasn't sure why his words cut her so deeply but she felt compelled to seek his approval. The prince had such a commanding presence, he exuded worldliness in every aspect. As his future bride she would be a reflection upon his character. Their attire should complement.

"So...I should choose another one?"

"Do you want to?"

She couldn't say she didn't. Despite its beauty, it felt more like the dress was wearing her. "I am not sure."

"Your image is a vital weapon, Miss Bonnaire. If you are not confident in your image, they will sniff it out and they will strike." His breath cooled the nape of her neck. "How you present yourself tonight to the others and how you allow them to see you will determine your power over them."

His words made sense but the notion of a simple garment holding so much authority over how she would be perceived by others was daunting. She decided to try a white silk dress next with a black netting overlay of beaded peacock feathers, red velvet tied into ribbons on the shoulders and capped sleeves.

Hurrying once more behind the folding screen, she had the servant peel off the dress until she was down to her undergarments. She risked a few glances over her shoulder to locate Likhanov.

"There is no need to worry for your virtue, Miss Bonnaire." His tone was wry, almost mocking.

"I know," was her immediate reply, oddly defensive.

As she slipped into the material of the second dress, a sudden sprout of defiance bloomed within her chest. She emerged to show him her back.

"I think the laces could be a little tighter?" She glanced demurely over her shoulder to see his pupils had widened.

He tightened the bodice in swift movements. His fingers ghosted over her skin, causing a chill to slither down the column of her spine.

Looking upon her reflection she understood what Likhanov meant about power in appearance. She most certainly felt powerful wearing this dress. Vampiric. She could almost fit in with the sultry styles of the other vampire ladies she knew.

"I think this is much better." She swiveled her hips, causing the beads to tinkle. "Don't you agree?"

"That depends on you, Miss Bonnaire. The choice is entirely yours to make."

"I like this one," she said, more firmly, "I think this is the one."

He smirked. "Then it shall be yours."

She made a note of the alterations she would need to make as she changed back into her regular attire.

"Well then, I suppose that leaves only one question." Prince Likhanov strolled toward the parure displays with a fist beneath his chin. "Rubies or black diamonds?"

***

That night, Prince Likhanov took her down to the cellars in order to select a few choice blood wines to welcome his clan.

Lucille had heard of these wines, for their infamy was well-spread throughout witch channels. The bottles held pristine human blood preserved through the centuries with magic, infused with fruit and spices.

What was particularly gruesome about this blood was where it originated. For it was drawn from a human that had undergone immense suffering before being fermented. Something about the stress added invigorating flavor to a vampire's palate and bottles like this were most coveted among the clans.

They wandered through the wine racks before Likhanov

gestured to rows the servants should take bottles from. A hollow clink of glass resounded through the cavern as they followed his directives.

"A word of warning about my sister, Tanya," he murmured, once they were heading back upstairs. "She has a rather...insatiable appetite."

"Insatiable?" Lucille echoed. She fiddled with the ends of her lace gloves.

"Nothing to worry about. I have measures in place to protect you." He gave her a soothing smile. "These bottles will mainly be for her."

Outside, the tread of a horse and carriage could be heard drawing at the entrance. Prince Likhanov straightened his cufflinks and smoothed the lapels of his jacket in preparation to greet his ancient relations.

"Ilyusha!" A female vampire pounced on him when he entered the reception room, her diamond earrings jingling with expense. She had the same moon-pale hair as him styled into ribbon curls.

Lucille lingered behind the door to observe them. Her heart warmed at the sight of the prince embracing his sister with unbridled fondness.

"Hello, Tanya." Prince Likhanov kissed the top of her head. "It's wonderful to see you."

Behind her, another female vampire remained in a dignified pose. "I smell human on you." She stepped forward to flex her dainty nostrils. "A witch, to be precise."

"Ooh! Has our Ilyusha brought us a little delicacy for our long travels?" The first sister squealed in delight.

Lucille stiffened. She daren't even breathe lest they hear it.

"I'm afraid this witch isn't for eating, Tanya."

She pouted in disappointment. "Then what *is* she good for?"

"You'll see in a moment." Prince Likhanov poked his head out to usher Lucille inside. "And here she is now."

Lucille straightened her spine as she entered the room for their appraisal. She sensed the atmosphere shift in her presence as his sisters looked upon her in greed. She wondered if the rubies had been a poor choice in the end. The way they glittered on her throat like pear drops of blood must look practically indecent rather than playfully suggestive. Not to mention the lustrous rouge she'd applied to her lips and cheeks to enhance the natural vibrancy of her brown skin.

"My dear sisters, I would like for you to meet Miss Lucille Bonnaire." Prince Likhanov extended his hand for her presentation. "Miss Bonnaire, may I introduce you to Princess Nadezhda and Tatiana Vasilevna Likhanova."

Lucille gathered her skirts to curtsey. "Good evening, Your Highnesses."

Nadezhda acknowledged her with a dismissive peer down her nose.

"What a delectable little caramel you are!" Tatiana crooned in appreciation as she grasped Lucille's wrist and groped the emerald veins there. Her white fingers looked cadaverous wrapped around her arm. "Such rich, dark skin!"

Lucille kept herself from recoiling at her touch. Unwanted petting from vampires was something she'd long known to endure.

"Tanya," Prince Likhanov tore his sister's hand free and held it gently within his own, "do kindly keep your hands to yourself."

Tatiana protruded her bottom lip. "Fine. Be greedy."

"Though I think it's time we feast."

He ushered them all into the dining room to be settled.

There, corpse-servants cracked open aged bottles of blood wine that suffused the area with their charged copper aroma. Like the scent of air before a thunderstorm.

As the sole human guest, Lucille had been served a sacrificial lamb rack paired with fig and prosciutto salad. The ribs arched upward like a man in prayer, drizzled with decadent red wine sauce underneath a glass dome. The meat was newborn, tender, and browned with sugar, a recipe taken from ancient cookbooks used during the Likhanovs' human lives. Regular wine warmed beside it in a decanter.

"Do tell us, bratishka." Nadezhda swirled her glass with refined insouciance. "Why have you chosen to take on this witch as your newest pet?"

"Yes, Ilyusha, please explain why you deign to waste such a mouth-watering truffle." Tatiana chimed in, draining her glass with a loud smack of her lips. She'd already gone through two bottles and was starting her third. "Witch blood is a taste like no other, you're missing out."

Lucille shifted uncomfortably in her seat, cutting her lamb chops into smaller portions.

"Miss Bonnaire is hardly my pet, Nadya. She is to be my bride."

Tatiana slammed her glass down until it shattered. "Your *what?*"

Nadezhda rubbed at her temples. "Why do you persist on these silly antics, bratishka? Witches are our tools. Useful tools, indeed, but tools all the same. Hardly a suitable companion for our kind."

"Truly, Ilyusha, this is obscene!" Tatiana had gone shrill with disgust. "It was as if you'd gone to the stables to marry one of the horses."

Lucille's cheeks burned from the slight. How foolish she was to think she could dress her way into camouflaging among these predators. She would never be a wolf among them. It was time she stopped intending to try.

"Miss Bonnaire is no horse, Tanya," Prince Likhanov replied sternly. "And I demand you refrain from making such vulgar comments."

Tatiana's upper lip curled in affront.

"And I would have to disagree strongly with your assertion, Princess Likhanova." Lucille placed down her cutlery, unable to refrain from reacting any longer. "I think you are greatly underestimating the contribution of witches. We are more than tools. We are the grease that has kept the Sauvage wheel turning for centuries. Without which they would never have seen a sunrise, never have the unparalleled martial success that they have. Magic elevated them to imperial might and it could do the same for you."

"Miss Bonnaire in particular has demonstrated a rare gift." Prince Likhanov took over. "She has designs on how to harness sunlight and use it to power machinery. Or vaporize a vampire within a blink. How to make carriages self-propel without the aid of horses. And make contraptions that can communicate waves of one's thoughts long distances without the precarious nature of letters. Think of all we could accomplish with this knowledge. It could mean our family being restored to its superior rank."

"How you blather, Ilyusha." Tatiana rolled her eyes. "Even if such things were true, she'll be withered and rotting within a fair few decades or so before she'll make half of these things. If that. Waste of good blood if you ask me."

"Which is precisely why I believe a true union between vampire and witch to be the key to the future!" He gesticulated in a display of fervor. "Think of my longevity paired with her magic. Or vice versa. A marriage of bodies and minds. We could dominate the world with that."

"You would turn her then?" Nadezhda arched an elegant brow.

"I would find a solution," Prince Likhanov replied through gritted teeth. "Magic always has one."

"Your sermon bores me, Ilyusha." Tatiana stood from the table. "Clearly spending too much time around this mortal has muddled your mind. No matter. I shall soon remedy that."

Her true monstrous face burst through the seams of her porcelain visage. Reflective eyes and saber fangs. Then she launched herself toward Lucille.

Lucille was rooted in her seat. Her legs went numb from fear. Any notion of defense besides simple prey instinct was lost to her.

Prince Likhanov acted with almost predetermined efficiency. He snapped free a wooden stake from beneath the table and used it to skewer his sister by her throat.

"I warned you, sestrichka." Prince Likhanov murmured softly as he stroked a few ruffled curls from her silken cheek. "Why did you have to go and ruin an otherwise pleasant supper?"

Tatiana hacked and gurgled in agony. Putrid black blood spewed a puddle from her neck. It wasn't a lethal stab through the heart, but she surely wouldn't be moving for a while.

Nadezhda rolled her eyes and sighed. "Truly, Tanya. You never fail to make a scene."

He left her pinned and turned toward a startled Lucille. She flinched as he neared her, sidling toward the edge of the seat until she was near stumbling.

"It's all right, Miss Bonnaire." He pulled up the chair next to her and took her hand. "You can continue your meal."

She did not relax, her eyes trained upon the moaning Tatiana. How could he expect her to eat with his sister spilling her open throat onto the table?

"Here, I'll help you." He used her cutlery to cut a fine portion of lamb and lifted it to her lips.

Lucille's eyes widened that much more in disbelief at his actions. She stared at the piece of meat as it hovered before her lips, her stomach turning. Without thinking or knowing why, she obediently parted her lips to receive the lamb he fed her.

***

After all that excitement, Lucille approached the idea of sleep with trepidation rather than eagerness. She applied her night cream with still trembling hands before parting the gossamer drapes to her four-poster bed. Tatiana's gnashing teeth and glowing eyes still permeated her brain and so she was grateful for the knock on the door when it came.

"Miss Bonnaire."

Prince Likhanov's rasp was unmistakable.

"You can come in."

He stood at the doorway with one arm positioned against the

frame above his head. Lucille imagined it was to allow her space, for she only wore a flimsy nightgown of filet lace. A laughable barrier between her skin and his teeth.

"I wanted to apologize for my family's conduct this evening."

"There is no need, Prince Likhanov," Lucille said, fluffing the pillows and smoothing out her bed's silk sheets. She hadn't been privy to the aftermath of their family dispute and she hadn't wanted to be. "A predator will only act within its nature."

His lips crooked at one corner. "Still I had hoped they would've been better behaved."

"Well, I can certainly say I was grateful for your chivalry." It seemed an insane notion, to regard his violent assault as an act of valiance. But he had saved her life, and for that she owed him thanks.

"There was no chivalry on my part, I can assure you of that." His expression grew inscrutable. "I simply couldn't allow myself to lose something so indispensable."

Her breath hitched as she turned to look at him. His bright eyes were like beacons in the lambency of the room, she felt magnetized toward them.

She bridged the gap between them until her neck was straining to meet his face. "Regardless, an act like that deserves a show of gratitude I should think."

His eyes bored down into hers. "What did you have in mind?" He brushed her curls behind her shoulder to trace a path along her collarbone.

She leaned in to rest her hands on his shoulders. "Perhaps a kiss." She pushed herself up on her toes to brush their lips together.

"Miss Bonnaire." He spoke her name with longing but did not envelop her into the passionate embrace she envisioned.

"I apologize." Lucille pulled back in an instant. Her cheeks flushed in shame. "I misread you."

"Not at all," he said, voice still thick. He cupped her cheek. "There is nothing more I want than to have you. All of you. For you to yield to me mind, body and soul and for us to meld together as one."

Her stomach fluttered at the notion behind his words. "Then have me." She captured his hand and pressed it to her heart. "If we are to be man and wife then it is only right we allow ourselves to experience such a blissful union."

"Then come with me." He took her by the hand and led her out of the bedroom.

She followed him into the darkened hallway with nerves building in her chest. This was not how she imagined the night would go. She had never been intimate with another outside of her own imaginings and there was a tinge of fear and exhilaration at what to expect.

Lucille tried to catch a glimpse of Likhanov's face over his shoulder to guess at his thoughts. He was so unreadable to her even now but she hoped that he was feeling even half what she was. That this was an emotional turbulence they could both share.

When they stopped before an empty passage in the hall, her brow furrowed in confusion.

"It's only a ruse," he explained, "the true door is hidden by magic."

She understood the intent behind his words and cast away the enchantment to reveal a heavy vaulted door.

Prince Likhanov inserted a crow-shaped key into the elaborate lock, causing the bolts to slither away in retraction and the seal to break with a gasp. "Step inside, please."

Lucille glanced at him once more before she entered. The room was dimly lit with lanterns and she strained to make sense of the silhouettes inside. When the door closed behind them the lights intensified and brought everything into clarity.

Within an instant Lucille's heart was thumping from another source. In front of her was a filthy cot smeared in blood and viscera. A tray of stained surgical instruments was laid out alongside it.

"What?" Lucille pressed a hand to her mouth to stifle her nausea from the stench. Her heart leapt into her throat as she discovered more scientific apparatus, the makeshift confines of a laboratory. She spun round, frantic, seeing newspaper clippings of several witch killings pinned in a gruesome collage to one corkboard.

Their smiling faces beamed at her.

White teeth against dark skin.

He'd been experimenting on witches. For all his noble posturing, in the end this was how he truly saw them. Saw her. Mere specimens to cleave into and examine as she might have with dead mice. How many had come here before her only to lose their lives at the end of his scalpel?

"What is all of this?" Lucille's chest heaved as she clutched at her stomach. She stumbled back until she met the stone stillness of Likhanov's chest.

"The path to our future." His hands came to rest upon her shoulders. "We can bind ourselves to each other, you and I. My eternity in exchange for your magic. A symbiosis between our bodies and minds. A *true* marriage. Far superior to any paltry transactions of wealth that came before it."

"You are a madman." She turned in disgust to struggle from his grip. He didn't budge an inch.

"Oh, Miss Bonnaire," he spoke her name with such tenderness. "Can't you see? I've been waiting a very long time for you. I went through so many witches and vampires to ensure the process was refined to perfection. All this, for you and me."

Lucille fought and flailed but it was no use. She may as well have been a butterfly trying to break through a boulder. She was so foolish, thinking that his ardent speeches on union between a vampire and a witch had been a romantic overture toward her. When what he truly had in mind was far more perverse.

"I will never yield my magic to you!" Lucille sneered. "Any eternity you will give me is an eternity I will spend trying to thwart you at every turn."

"Oh, Miss Bonnaire." Prince Likhanov sighed. "I so hoped you would answer differently. Rest assured, we'll have all the time in the world to set your mind right."

Spanish Moss

It was said that Spanish moss could not grow where innocent blood had been shed. And yet, according to Glenn, Savannah's classmate and their high school's resident ghost historian, the most haunted road in the county was a quarter-mile section of Georgia State Route 99 on the outskirts of Ridgeville, where the Spanish moss draped from thick oak branches extending over the road like fingers.

Savannah had been traumatized enough by the ghost stories her grandmother mumbled in Geechee on still Saturday afternoons after her mind turned to mush—too many haunting tales of strange fruit swaying in the breeze, of slaves taking vengeance upon their masters and White lynchers stringing them up and setting them ablaze. Any chance she could find to get out of their two-bedroom mobile home she took it, even if it meant going alone to a deserted town off an abandoned road with two boys she barely knew outside of sharing U.S. History.

"Pop said I gotta get the truck back by seven for his shift," said Darien, the only one in their trio with a license.

Glenn, who sat in the passenger seat, pointed to the clock on the dashboard displaying 5:53. "That ain't givin' us a lotta time."

"If this road's as haunted as you say, we won't need it."

The drive was silent at first. Savannah sat in the back seat and watched the backs of Darien and Glenn's heads as they quietly talked between themselves, forgetting she was even in the car.

They weren't friends.

Darien was the star wide receiver of their high school football team. He was the only reason people had even heard of Eulonia, Georgia. Bigger schools all over the state were vying for his attention, but if he really wanted to get noticed by scouts at a big name university, such as UGA, he'd have to transfer out to a school with a truly challenging football schedule.

Glenn was a huge history buff, always telling little-known facts about the town's past, whether people wanted to hear them or not, and most of those facts he got from Savannah's grandmother, as he lived just three doors down. It was during one of his regular interruptions of soft-spoken Mr. Stallworth's class that he suggested a group of them go look for the ghost said to stalk the highway near the old historic district.

Savannah and Darien were the only ones who volunteered.

As the tiny homes along the sides of the road were slowly replaced by large, billowing trees, Savannah wondered if it was a good idea to leave her grandmother at home alone. Of course, Ms. Edna, at the grown-up age of ninety-seven, would fuss and complain that she "Don't need no damn babysitter," but the truth was they were all they had left after her mother's accident and Grandma wouldn't admit that her dementia was getting worse. More and more days she lingered in a past life that few people in town remembered. And each day, her stories got scarier.

"Do y'all know the legend of the Ridgeville ghost?" Glenn asked, interrupting Savannah's thoughts.

"Nope, but I'm sure you're gonna tell us," Darien said.

"It was prom night."

"Why is it always prom night—" Savannah cut in, thinking of her grandmother.

The only difference between hers and Glenn's ghost stories was that at least Savannah could stomach Glenn's. His were always about a white girl whose boyfriend left her or a young Union solider missing half his face desperate to get home. Never anything that felt real, personal, as if it could happen as easily now as one hundred and fifty years ago.

"We still second-class citizens in dis here country. And ever since Trump, dem Whites ain't scared to call you a nigga to your face," Grandma would say.

Savannah once made the mistake of talking back. "It's the 21st century. People aren't overtly racist like that anymore, and besides, there are laws. It's not so easy to get away with that kind of stuff now."

"So how come that drunk bastard that hit yo mama still runnin' round here free?"

That, Savannah didn't have a rebuttal for, because it made no sense that even a year later, the police still hadn't found him. In a town of less than four hundred, someone had to have seen a car with a dent the size of a human body on the hood, blood splatter on the paint.

All of it was wishful thinking, Grandma would tell her. And deep down, Savannah knew she was right, because all she had to do was turn on the news and see another Black man murdered by overzealous cops, and the "not all police officers are innately racist" utopia she built in her head came crumbling down.

"Some guys have said they've seen her," Glenn was saying as Savannah tried to pull herself out of the dreadful memory of her mother's accident, the knock on the door, the officers solemn faces downcast, the lonely ride to the hospital in the back of the cruiser to identify the body because Grandma's gout had flared up and she couldn't walk.

"She was dressed in white, blood all over the front of her dress. She would ask for a ride to the police station, but by the time they got there, she would be gone."

Silence invaded the car when he finished. Darien had apparently been tuning him out too, but Savannah also noticed that the sky had gotten considerably darker.

"I think we're here," Darien said. He pulled to a stop and turned off the engine.

Savannah leaned forward and peered through the windshield. The trees on either side of the one-lane highway appeared to be closing in, and at the center of the road, above the solid double lines, the sinuous tendrils of thick Spanish moss hung low.

Swaying in the breeze.

Like strange fruit.

"Y'all do know the legend about Spanish moss, right?"

A chill raced down Savannah's spine, like a cold hand gliding down her back. "I don't want to hear it!" she shrieked.

Suddenly, she couldn't breathe, as if all the air had been sucked out of the car. She quickly pressed the button on the door to roll down the window before Darien could remove the key from the ignition, but that was a mistake, because he had parked further off the road, with half the car in the grass and the Spanish moss from the nearest tree inches from her door, flooded inside, tickling her chin, curling around her neck.

Savannah imagined the ghosts of angry white men with torches and nooses dragging her out of the car through the window and stringing her up. The lump in her throat grew. She felt a spark of heat start at her toes and rise fast. Gasping for air, she scurried to the opposite side of the car, yanked back the handle, and tumbled onto the asphalt, gagging and heaving.

Darien followed. "Girl, you good?"

"It's too fucking hot," she said, panting. She was still on all fours when Glenn came jogging around the back of the '99 Ford Explorer.

"Did I scare you? The Spanish moss is actually a good sign. It means no one died here."

But that's not what her grandmother said, and even his own ghost story of the dead prom queen haunting this Spanish moss-infested highway contradicted that statement.

Savannah planted one hand on his creased Reeboks, dug her fingers into his jean pockets, and pulled herself to her feet.

"Whoa there," he said, grabbing for his waistband. "Don't pants me."

"You good?" Darien asked again, sounding more like a scratched CD skipping on a track than a friend showing genuine concern.

Embarrassed about her minor panic attack, Savannah nodded and tried to shift the attention back onto him. "Did you have to park so close to that tree?" she demanded, pointing to the blanket of Spanish moss pouring into the back window.

"Well, I didn't have many options. This place is like a tent."

Savannah glanced up at the sky—or what would have been the sky if not for the Spanish moss. Darien was right, it felt like a tent. The branches were the skeletal framing and the leaves a canvas draped over like a covering, keeping them inside.

The road was silent. Not even the echo of a distant I-95 could be heard. As far as she could see, all that surrounded them were trees, asphalt, and Spanish moss. And they stood in the center of the ring, the only living beings in a quarter-mile radius, yet Savannah felt crowded, as if there were more than just two pairs of eyes watching her, analyzing her.

"Legend goes that after he date raped her, she took the hem of her dress, torn during the assault, and hung herself from a branch hanging low over the Fancy Bluff Creek bridge. The limb snapped under her weight. They found her in the water the next morning."

"Strange fruit," Savannah mumbled as the image of the lifeless body swaying, of pale blue toes grazing her forehead invaded her thinking. She had never been claustrophobic, but in that moment, her only desire was to be in an open field under an open sky—not a cloud to be found, not a tree in sight, no looming shadows of spirits forgotten, of screaming ghosts from a distant plane.

"Let's get out of here," she said quickly.

"We still got thirty minutes," Darien said.

"No, I'm done."

"All those ghost stories your grandma be telling, and you freaking out like this?" Glenn teased.

Savannah rolled her eyes. She'd had enough. This trip made her grandmother's stories feel too real, too close. She still felt the tightness in her neck. The intense Georgia heat burned her chest, stifling the air. Her ears rang like someone screaming.

"Yo, do you hear that?" Darien asked.

"No. Let's go," Savannah said, with more urgency. She was already back in the car, on the street side, away from the Spanish moss billowing inside through the opposite window.

"Oooh, it's the ghost," Glenn sang, fluttering his fingers in her face.

Frustrated, she slapped them away. "I said—" she began, then froze. She couldn't ignore that the ringing in her ears had grown into a hollow echo that reverberated from the car door, to the branches overhead, to ricochet from trunk to trunk, back and forth across the road like a zigzag, vibrating through her head, making her dizzy, bringing on a splitting headache the louder it got until she could start to make out the words.

"Help! Help! Help!"

Just ahead, where the road dipped into a hill, a pale figure started to manifest, rising inch by inch, until a human shape took form.

A woman. Completely white, head to toe, save for the blood splatter on the front of her dress.

"Shit!" Darien and Glenn shouted in unison.

Darien jumped into the driver's seat, and Glenn strongarmed Savannah to join her in the back. She frantically swiped at the Spanish moss, pushing it outside and away from her as Darien cranked the engine and it stalled.

"C'mon, c'mon, c'mon!"

"Dude, let's go!" Glenn shouted.

"I'm trying!"

The high-pitched shrill startled both Glenn and Savannah. It didn't sound like Darien's usual deep voice. Was it the ghost or Darien who had made the noise? But there wasn't time to investigate further.

Finally, the engine turned over. Savannah slammed her hand down on the power button to roll up the window, slapping away the dregs of the vine as the window rose and sealed them off.

For a brief moment, she believed she was safe, that she'd avoided the worst of it. She never thought she'd say it, but she was happy to be going back home to Grandma, to stories that sent chills but stopped just short of taking her to her own grave.

But when the three of them looked at the road ahead, there she stood at the hood of the car—her face as translucent as the thin damp dress clinging to her body. Her stringy blonde hair forming a web-like frame around her oval faces. Her lips were a deep magenta, and they expanded as wide as a boxer's glove as she screeched.

Please!

Savannah screamed.

"Fuck! Fuck! Fuck!" Glenn shielded his eyes behind the driver's seat head rest.

Darien floored the gas, catapulting the woman into the tree behind her.

The hard crush of metal echoed in the silence that followed, and as the smoke from the dying engine cleared, they discovered that the girl's body did not dissipate with the smoke, but remained still, pinned between bark and bumper.

"Oh no," Glenn whispered.

"I didn't—" Darien started. "I thought she was—" but he couldn't bring himself to say it.

And Savannah couldn't say anything at all, as her gaze traveled upward and she watched the Spanish moss on the oak tree in front of them recede, replaced with the bodies of three charred Black teens with bent necks, swaying in the breeze.

Bleeding Marble

The first full moon after Charlotte was sent away in disgrace, the third-years who slept beneath the annex all claimed they could hear her birthing the beast above them. First the waters broke, they said—and they could *hear* it, like a rushing river, the one that Moses turned to blood. Then she screamed and panted and writhed like the devil was breaking out of her, until he did, scuttling on all fours. The Beast curled into the walls of the Academy like a rat, and Charlotte ran staggering after him with her legs still smeared by her mess.

It didn't make sense for him to be born here, Charlotte had left the school as soon as she'd started showing, but nobody cared about that. The whole school was captivated in horror at Charlotte; everyone seemed to have seen the beast. No one could agree, exactly, on what he looked like, and accounts could not be verified. We had no information on the father. What, exactly, we all wondered, had Charlotte invited into her bed?

"A boy, of course," June said, although we were not supposed to. It had been a boy from Ashwood; everyone knew that. But a good boy, a nice boy, a bright young lad that went to Ashwood wouldn't dream of leaving the appropriately supervised co-ed Christmas festivities for a quick fuck. And, certainly, no girl from Lady Hawk would let him. So, the father was a snake-man; the father was a wolf. And that meant the babe was too.

They said that it crawled on hands that had eight fingers each, fat fleshy spiders; that its hair was black and wiry and covered its skinny scaly body; that it galloped on all fours through the night with blood and milk dripping from its teeth. Those, of course, were fangs or tusks—one girl claimed that she had seen them born, bursting all at once from its rotting gums.

The rumors never once ceased, not even when Charlotte had returned, even though she never replied. She strode through the school on her marble feet, a picture of mute defiance; an ancient statue, pale and cold, erected to remind us just how easily one could fall. She was much quieter than she had been, reed-like in her thinness. You'd never have thought that she'd had a baby, no matter what Deirdre whispered, but she had lost lots of hair. What was left was soft and strange, very unlike the pretty thick curls that she'd had before.

They put her back in our dorm, like nothing had happened, like she hadn't been missing for all of last year. Ellie's mother, furious, said that she would write to the Academy. Ellie begged her not to make a fuss, but she sent it anyway. And once the school had received the letter, they moved Charlotte on her own into the annex.

"It was my mother that asked," Ellie said that night, voice wet with impending tears. "Not me."

I didn't roll my eyes, because I knew that she was waiting for me to do it.

The lights went out at ten o'clock—some things never changed—but the room stayed spotted with the sickly yellow glow of the thin cream candles the nurse quietly distributed to us older girls. Although the light was dim, I could see the movement of Deirdre lifting her chin. Deirdre loved to lift, her hands, her eyes, and she even stood on her tip-toes in Mass, as if waiting for her wings to curl out of her so she could ascend even higher than everybody else. "We're not upset with you," she said firmly. "Or at least, *I'm* not."

Still, I said nothing.

"I feel like you are. I feel like I've done something wrong."

That was Ellie. I could tell she was looking at me directly, now, so I kept my eyes trained on the barely illuminated page of Proverbs. It read, *Like snow in summer or rain in harvest, honor is not fitting for a fool.*

"Well, you shouldn't," said Deirdre. "It wouldn't feel right for her to be here, after all of sixth year without her." She looked around for someone to challenge her, and June finally took the bait, putting her own book to the side with a louder clatter than necessary.

"I mean, I did miss her."

Deirdre's face pulled together at the mouth. "I didn't say that I didn't miss her. Just that it wouldn't feel right." She paused. "Besides, she was Precious' friend more than mine or yours."

I felt the paper wrinkle between my pursed fingers. *Like a fluttering sparrow or darting swallow, an underserved curse does not come to rest.*

"Precious?" Ellie, again. Her voice was small and I felt like hitting her. "You're not mad at me, are you?"

Do not answer a fool according to his folly, or you yourself will be just like him. Followed by, *Answer a fool according to his folly, or he will be wise in his own eyes.*

I marked the page and then closed the Bible.

"No. Just go to sleep, Ellie."

There was silence after that. The other girls drifted off. Deirdre first, then Ellie, and at last a tossing June, like always; but I did not rest with them. Charlotte was not here. Charlotte Flint, who had given me my first ever cigarette; who tutored me in French when I fell behind, who had snapped at the other girls for teasing me about my bonnet. She was sent out of Physics for red lipstick when we were thirteen, and it felt deeply special that she'd borrowed it from my drawer. Ever since I had met her, she had been at once the room, and the only thing that made it not a stranger to me. I'd never known the Academy without her; in fact, to me, she *was* the Academy. Charlotte Flint who was on the lacrosse team and always wore a ribbon and looked like a painting. Charlotte. Charlotte Flint. *Pregnant.* It was not just her presence that was lost, but her picture. Where was the girl that they put on all the brochures?

Not here at Lady Hawk, that was for sure; not in the neighboring bed, as she had always been and always should be. No, she was far away, nursing some monstrous babe with goat horns and rotten teeth and flowers woven into his limp and dirty hair. The thought of him made me sick. All that night, I kept seeing his wicked face, whether I closed or opened my eyes. So it was not a surprise to me when Ellie screamed.

The room, however, stirred.

"*Christ*, Ellie." That was June. Her voice was even rougher than usual with sleep, and the sound of it brought me to the real world again.

The beast-man vanished at the tell-tale click of her lighter. It was a horrible, inappropriate lighter, one that my father would use. And then her candle was burning. Ellie screamed again.

I scrambled for matches and then lit my own. I could see her silhouette wringing its shadowy hands like Lady Macbeth, cast across the wall and, when I stumbled across to her bed, I could see even in the pale light that the color had been cast out of her face. It was damp with tears. Her lips quivered, shuddered, but I could no longer see anything else.

The beast boy's gone, can't you see? I wanted to ask her.

Instead, I voiced a much less absurd, "Ellie? Have you hurt yourself?"

"Is she all right?" June leapt across the room, clasped a large, rough hand across her forehead.

Ellie screamed and flailed, nearly catching her face, and June jumped back in alarm.

"I think she must be dreaming."

"Should we get Matron?"

"But if she's just dreaming—"

"What on Earth's going on?" Deirdre finally consented to wake. She wore a floor-length nightdress like she was already a mother, an old-fashioned ghost holding her sickly candle aloft. "Ellie?"

"We think she's dreaming."

"She was quite upset." Her face was curled up in worry for Ellie, but her eyes looked cold even in the candlelight. I met them solidly as they came to rest on me, unwilling to bear responsibility for Ellie's bad dreams.

Deirdre grasped Ellie's arm with a singular, bony hand; it looked, in the damp light, like an evil witch's claw. Ellie started to sob, and it sounded oddly pained. I'd heard her cry by then a hundred times, but never like this.

"I think we should get Matron," I said again.

"She's going to wake the others," Deirdre hissed, casting a glance back as if she could see the rest of the corridor through the wall. "Ellie? Ellie!"

June crossed the room and switched on the light. Deirdre and I both stepped back, scandalized. It was the rule of the Academy that lights went out at ten o'clock. But the decision was pragmatic, just like June. Ellie always woke early in the summer months, could never sleep when the world was bright. As soon as the lights flickered on, she jolted awake, rabbit-like, all damp soft cheeks and wide bright eyes.

"For heaven's sake, Ellie. Were you dreaming?"

"It was him," she whispered. "I saw Charlotte. I saw *him*."

June frowned. Deirdre put down her candle.

I, unable to help myself, snapped, "Well, she hardly brought the baby back with her."

In the silence of the room my reason sounded stupid. Ellie was still staring at the wall, but she whispered, "She did."

"Ellie—"

"She *did*," she insisted, voice still hoarse and quiet. "I saw him. He had the sharpest teeth. He was biting me."

"It was just a dream, Ellie," responded Deirdre, in her best impression of Matron. "Do you want a cup of tea? I'm sure in the circumstances—"

"It wasn't a dream." Ellie curled her arms around herself protectively. "I'll never be like Charlotte. He was biting me. He bit all through my stomach."

And that was that: she refused all offers of tea, of blankets, of relighting the candles. We checked her stomach, but there were no bite-marks and no blood. So we all went off to bed, to the sound of her crying, despite her best efforts to be quiet. I could still see her shadow, hunched and curled up, as if trying to prevent Charlotte from getting under the covers.

"Are you all right, Ellie?" I murmured into the darkness, suddenly feeling guilty that I had been unkind to her. Although the sobs were silly for a girl of almost seventeen, it seemed to be written into Ellie's bones that she simply could not help it. She was the last to conquer homesickness when we first moved in and the first to cry out if there was a spider in the shower. It was how she had always been.

"I don't want to be here anymore," she said to the room.

We all flinched in our beds. I burrowed into the darkness, warm and insular, in the hopes that the sound would not be able to mark me.

"I don't want to be here."

Nobody answered her, unable to interact with such an absurd statement.

I might have, had I known that I would never see Ellie again.

Nobody could work out when, exactly, it happened. Deirdre, as always, was the earliest of us to rise; Ellie, uncharacteristically, was already in the shower, but Deirdre thought nothing of that since she knew Ellie had struggled to sleep, so she lit her candle and read in the relative darkness for forty-five minutes. It was then that she decided to check on her.

June and I woke at her scream.

Ellie was no longer in the shower, although it was still running. Rather, she was in bed, and the blankets entangled around her middle were torn through and stained bright with blood. She was white against the pale sheets, aside from her cheeks, which were pink as if she had smeared them with it. Her eyes, open, were glazed and unseeing, but we could thankfully still hear strange, rattling intakes of breath.

"The beast," said Deirdre, staring at me with wet, outraged eyes. "She said the beast was biting her stomach."

"Don't be stupid," said June, wetting dry lips. "I'm going to get the nurse. It must be...it must be her time of the month."

"When has Ellie ever bled like that?" I was shocked to hear

my own voice, and the others were too; neither of them replied. I looked back at Ellie, mauled, and before I knew it I was out the door. Up the stairs, up the stairs; into a staff bathroom, secreted away at the very top of the Academy where actual staff were unlikely to use it. That bathroom was a necessary place, a good place, a private place. Private in a way that our communal bathroom and crowded dorm, noisy eating hall, and busy classrooms, were not and would never be.

It all clawed out of me, tearing like tissue, ragged little bites of quiet pain. Tears, breath, sounds, all terribly undignified. I looked up at the mirror and saw myself, still dressed for bed and sleepy-eyed and my face damp like poor stupid Ellie's. I hated it and despised Charlotte and loathed the Academy. I never wanted to see or smell blood again.

And then, suddenly, there it was, leaking out the left tap and staining the sink a murky red. I jumped back with a cry.

The monster shoved open the mirror to follow me.

He'd grown up now. He must have been four or five years old, with a tattered cloth hanging round his bony hips. I could see sinew and vein shining in his wiry arms—and the blood was dripping from him, not the tap. It was his arm, all ripped open; I could see between the exposed muscle that he was all iron inside like the Nemean lion. He smiled mockingly as if he could hear my thoughts and then leaned forward, stretching out, palms opening and shutting like snapping jaws.

He wanted me to hold him.

I stepped back with a gasp. He snarled at the rejection. His teeth were just as sharp as Ellie had said. I could see scraps of pale flesh and loose hair hanging from them. And yet, still, he hungered. An unannounced kind of vehemence rose in me like vomit, and before I knew it, I had charged the mirror.

When the glass broke, so did he. There was blood in the sink but it could have been my own. I'd torn up my fist, standing there in my pajamas looking absurd and teary-eyed.

"Are you all right?"

I whirled around, ill at the thought of an observer, and saw

Charlotte. I could not tell if she was a better or worse witness than somebody else.

"Precious?" Her eyes, steely as ever, flicked down to my hand, still bunched up in its seeping fist. "Are you okay?"

"Are you?" The words were more hostile than I expected them to be. Her face, after they'd been spoken, less so.

Charlotte had never been a paragon of self-discipline, especially when it came to her temper, but now when I looked at her shadowed eyes, I didn't even see a single spark of anger.

"I heard about Ellie."

I didn't say anything. Gossip always traveled fast at Lady Hawk, but it would have taken some while to reach Charlotte as she was, secluded in an annex and without any friends. I wanted to ask her the time but could not.

"Are you going to go to Matron about your hand or do you want me to do it?" Charlotte had quirked an eyebrow, and her sight still cut like steel, a fierceness of insight that I thought had been drained out of her with the fire. She didn't bring up Ellie again.

I managed to bandage myself up all of last year, I wanted to say. But I didn't.

Charlotte had always been able to read the unspoken words.

She took me to her annex. *If he is in there*, I thought, *if he is in there I will hit him again*. But he was not. In fact, Charlotte's room lacked herself, let alone another; it was frighteningly clean and sparse, scrubbed of all personal possession aside from a vase of drying lilies on the windowpane. In contrast, the way she bathed my hands felt achingly intimate, almost nostalgic, although the motions themselves were stronger, more practical, than I remembered.

She had cleaned wounds since I last saw her.

"There's no monster," she said, interrupting my thoughts. I couldn't read her tone. "Here, or back home. It really is just a baby boy."

I stared at her, at the vase behind her, and suddenly did not believe her. The lilies encircled her head; her face was serene,

timeless, marble; I could see him gnawing at her again. *Gaia.*
Bound to the monster at her breast.

"Precious?"

"It got Ellie," I choked out, pulling my hands away from her.
She held onto them; tight, fast. 'It stole Ellie—"

"No, Precious—"

"I've seen it too."

She stared at me, then back at my hands, and her lips
thinned. I thought, finally, that she was going to shout, but she
didn't.

Just said, "I'm glad I wasn't here last year."

Good. I didn't miss you. I didn't say it. I couldn't. Unable to
meet her eyes, I focused on her vase, those pale sickly lilies.

"He's not here," she promised to my upturned palms, breathing them out like a prayer. "I promise, Precious. He's not here,
and he's really just a boy. Ellie...Ellie...they think she hurt herself in the shower."

My response was not to Charlotte. It was to the sagging petals of the tallest flower, which seemed to be withering to my
very sight. "I saw Ellie. I *saw* her. She was mauled."

I did not look back at her face. I hoped that it did not show
hurt.

The teachers told us that it was monthly troubles. That, in truth,
Ellie had been struggling with them for quite some while, but
had felt embarrassed to say. There was no need to panic, but
after the most recent escalation she had gone home to see a city
doctor. Further, and most importantly, this was not the sort of
information that Ellie would like us to repeat. Our dorm should
keep it to ourselves.

And so we did, even though everybody else was saying that
it was the beast. Winter was bearing down upon us, and with it
the expected festivities, despite strong reservations from parents. As soon as it was announced that a Ball would be going
ahead, the murmur of dwindling gossip had once again become
a roar; the beast had claimed its first victim in Charlotte around

this time last year, and everyone was chattering that he might do so again.

June was marching through the school like a soldier, scolding and intimidating the gossips, but I found myself mostly ignoring them. I didn't know what to do, especially now that I had finally spoken to Charlotte; what was I to believe? I hadn't seen the boy since that morning in the bathroom.

"You're going to get yourself into trouble," I said to June one evening, watching her storm to bed in her nightshirt. She prepared for sleep as if she was going to battle these days. The anger never quite left her.

"I'm always in trouble."

"Yes, but not for flattening third years."

"They should keep their mouths shut if they don't want to be flattened." She scowled, and I wondered how she had come to be so defensive of Ellie. "It's all utter shit."

Deirdre, predictably, rose at the crudeness, neck straining with the effort of lifting her head from her pale pillow. "You shouldn't curse," she said. "And besides, it's not though, is it?"

June glowered at her. "What?"

"You both saw it too. The beast."

I frowned. I hadn't told Deirdre about my experiences with the beast, and June had been vehement that she'd never seen anything. "I don't know what you're talking about."

"Please! The sheets were all torn. Her uterus grew claws, did it?"

June gaped, perhaps genuinely unable to comprehend the beast, maybe simply nonplussed at hearing Deirdre say the word uterus. I thought about repeating what Charlotte said, that the teachers thought Ellie had harmed herself, but couldn't imagine admitting to the others that I'd talked to her.

"It's evil for them to make us stay here," she announced. "Right beneath that woman and her son."

"There's no son, Deirdre," said June, frustrated. "At least, not here. And he doesn't have claws, he doesn't have teeth."

"Believe what you like," she bit back. "I know what I saw.

And so does Precious."

She didn't blow out her candle that night. I could see her lying there, open-eyed, Bible clutched to her chest. June, as ever, was snoring in what seemed like minutes, unaware of the strange shadows that the night made on the walls. Deirdre must have known I was awake but she didn't try to whisper to me. The dorm had never felt emptier.

I tried to will myself to sleep, and I think I did, although it wasn't very restful. I slid from dream to dream, taunted with images of bleeding boys with sharp teeth and Charlotte and her lilies and then poor, gutted Ellie crying over an empty cradle. Before I woke up, I was on some kind of plain, surrounded by pale twisted trees bursting with rotting fruit. Every time I blinked, the new crop had fallen, flooding to the ground in grotesque purple splashes for the worms to rise up and the vultures to swoop down. The grass was writhing with feasting vermin, and I seemed to be no better than them, up to my knees in the sticky kicking soil of the vile garden. I cried out, and there was nothing. Looked up, and there was nothing, for what seemed like years; but I could eventually make out a distant bright pinprick, a pale gleaming thing that seemed to me like it might have been sunlight. It did not warm me but I reached for it regardless, willing to endure any alternative. And, indeed, it took me away from the field, and into the routine stillness of a Lady Hawk Academy dorm room.

Deirdre stood above my bed.

She had lit my candle—which pulsed still, that pale strange Sun—and bore over me in its dim sickly light, flaming match in hand. Her flushed skin was damp like she had been boiled, and water stained the carpet beneath her flexing feet and her nightgown at the shoulders. She was breathing heavily and shaking with cold, or rage; I could not tell.

"What on Earth are you doing?" I managed. The words sounded sensible. I did not think that Deirdre was in the mood for sense. She made a strange, guttural noise at my words, and before I knew it, she was upon me.

My leg had kicked, before my brain had understood what was happening, into the crook of her arm, which made her shriek, but successfully fling the candle to the other side of the room. Deirdre was above me, grabbing at my neck and my hair; her nails, which I knew she so carefully trimmed and polished, felt sharp and jagged. June, blearily, woke from her bed.

"What are you two *doing?*"

Deirdre had both of her soft, small hands pressing down on my neck. I thought, wildly, that this would be an absurd way to die.

"Get her off me!" I managed.

June leapt forward and separated us with ease. Everyone knew June was by far Lady Hawk's best athlete, but there was something incredible in the deft way she threw Deirdre back on her own bed, utterly unafraid.

"What is the matter with you?" she demanded.

Deirdre snarled in response. It didn't sound like her because it wasn't—no; it wasn't Deirdre at all, but the boy, the beast. He unfolded himself from her and emerged growling, all bared teeth and sinew. I could see from June's expression that, at last, she could see him too.

He hissed and jumped at her, and she jumped back, to her own bed, to her bedside drawer where, in clear violation of multiple Academy policies, she always kept a pocket knife. She would hide it every Monday before they cleaned. It was with that courage that she met the monster's panicked, frantic eyes and slammed into him.

He howled. His hands were filthy, stuffed with grime under thick fingernails like talons, and as he flew backward he dug the left one into her shoulder. June swore, grunted, hissed something I could not hear. She twisted and then they were writhing and she was on top of him, pinning him to the ground. Their eyes met. She slammed his head unto the ground, but he would not disentangle himself.

June took her knife and savagely sliced off the paw that was still stuck in her, and the Beast began to transform in front of my very eyes.

It fell as Deirdre's hand. Pale, a long pianist's fingers, almost surgically clean.

There was silence until Deirdre herself began to sob. Damp, again; the sweat poured from her. There was too much blood. June went very pale.

"But I thought...I saw..."

I wanted to say yes, yes, I saw him too. But how could I? Besides, she told the teachers that she thought she had seen a lion, and, of all the things I had seen, I had never seen that. So I said nothing as they were both taken away. Deirdre, of course, to a hospital, and June in a cloud of fiercely muffled disgrace.

I tried to speak to her before her parents arrived, but she still looked white and sick, and they had whisked her away come morning. There would be no public scandal this time and, I was sure, no invitation to return.

The empty beds, in the quiet of the night, looked to me like graves. So I crept that night upstairs to Charlotte, into the annex where the Beast was born.

I think I wanted to fight something, but it wasn't to be. She looked very frail when she opened the door.

Up to that point, to my mind, her son had taken that from her too. She would surely have to be at her most elevated to withstand the indignity that he represented. Cold white marble to the core. But when she met my eyes, I thought perhaps that she had not withstood it at all.

"I heard about June," she spoke in a whisper, although nobody remained to hear us. "And Deirdre. Did...did something happen?"

"June hurt her."

"*June?*"

"She thought she saw the beast."

Charlotte's whole face pulled taut. I saw lines; I saw veins. And I heard, as she shrieked, like some kind of monster or banshee, "Precious, there is no beast!"

We stood there in silence. Me, numb at the door, and her, hunched over her dressing table. Her legs were trembling as if they were going to give way; her breath was rushed. Before I knew it, I found myself supporting her, taking her back to the bed. She threw her head forward between her legs. I thought she might be sick, but she wasn't.

Minutes had passed by the time she craned her neck up to look up at me, hands supporting her face. "I would never have come back here if I thought I could stand home. Do you think that I *chose* this?"

"June thought she saw him." I didn't know what else to say.

Charlotte glared, but it had no bite. She brushed an exhausted hand against a wet mouth. "Everybody has, it seems."

I swallowed, nodded. Shame pricked me again. But then there was joy; joy, that there was not *everybody* anymore, that I was alone and myself, that I could go up the stairs and Charlotte could descend them and all could be equal between us. I looked at her and hoped that she could read it in my eyes.

Charlotte. Beautiful Charlotte. Wonderful Charlotte. Charlotte who had always been able to understand me. She sat up to look at me. The moon had pulled light all through the room and the lilies in her vase bloomed in it.

"What did you think when you heard that I was pregnant?"

"Stupid," I confessed. My shoulders hunched, as if anticipating that the blow would fall once again. "I just wanted to know why you didn't tell me."

Charlotte laughed, but there was no humor in the sound. She looked out of the window again. "I really couldn't say."

"I suppose you couldn't," I agreed, the acknowledgment sliding between my teeth before I had time to catch it.

Charlotte smiled.

We laid and looked up at the ceiling and it might have been carpeted with stars. I told her about sixth year. She told me about a baby, a baby called Thomas, and from her descriptions, he did not seem a miracle but I wondered that I had once thought of him as the Nemean lion. All night I drank and drank and drank from her, and everything was wonderful and deca-dent; there may have been monsters hiding, but they kept themselves confined to the shadows.

I had missed her.

By morning we were tired, but she wasn't ready to sleep. Ap-parently, she had nightmares.

"About what?"

"About the Ball, mostly." The moonlight made a cross on her face. "I don't want to go again. But I'd rather die than not go. You know what they'd be like."

I smiled, despite myself. "Pride's a sin, you know," I said, alt-hough it had always been my favorite one. Charlotte wore it so well.

"What's yours?" she asked, before I left. I had to before morning, even though there was no one left in the dorm. Surely if I were to wake in Charlotte's bed instead of my own, the very walls and doors and foundations of the Academy would all crumble on top of me.

I could not answer her.

The days drew themselves out in brief, dreamlike bursts, mere blips of life before the Ball. No one spoke to me; they thought my days were numbered, that soon I would be gone like Ellie and Deirdre and June.

And, like a woman in a witch trial, survival would simply be proof of guilt.

I could see the corpses of everyone else's gowns floating like spirits before me, as I did my hair. Ellie's had been frothy yel-low, skirts upon skirts. It could have been done elegantly but it wouldn't have been; I easily imagined her, all frizzy hair and ruffled taffeta. Deirdre's was metallic silk, long sleeves, a high neck. It would have looked regal with her dark hair. It was pressed beautifully, waiting for her to return home like a golden ghost even though it would likely be some time before she could attend a gala.

June's navy gown was still curled up like a snake underneath her bed; she had abandoned herself by the roadside. I found myself understanding the urge.

In her image, I enclosed a knife in my purse.

It wasn't a proper knife like June's; that had been taken away, of course. It was a silly snap-off blade from the workshop, unlikely to do much damage.

I was no David, to kill a beast with a stone. But it could cut all the same.

That night, all my thoughts bled into new ones about bleeding, until even my reflection in the mirror was smeared with red. I knew that it wasn't real. *It'll be them instead*, someone in me vowed. *I'll hurt them instead.*

In my mind I drew a tall pale tower, and locked that girl inside.

I was wearing white. I knew it would be striking, but as I sat there laying pearls into my tightly bound hair, I wanted nothing more than to cut the dress into pieces. A white dress was oddly final, bridal; it felt like I was walking to my death when I finally stepped through those big wooden doors in slightly-tight silver shoes. I was very nearly late. It seemed that the whole school craned their necks to look at me. They were organized in rows, looking in their colored gowns like a box of macarons.

The stares were followed by a gasp. I frowned at the gasper; it didn't seem complimentary. But then the whispers started. First gentle, then rushing, like an angered river. And I knew what had happened.

Charlotte was behind me.

She wore white too, a mockery. She had pasted a pair of red and wryly smiling lips atop her face, and I thought that only I could see the brittleness behind them. Her hair bobbed behind her all-in-one movement, a soft yellow cloud. It was pulled back from her face at the front with pins, two severe diamond lines. I started stepping, and so did she, and we took our place at the end of the line together.

"Ladies," Mrs. Priam said, stiffly.

Other than that, silence.

And then sound again.

Time flooded out; at some point there were violins. I wasn't paying attention. No, I was staring at Charlotte, who, even in the garishly lit hall seemed to be threading moonlight down the room.

We didn't dance together. Of course not, that would have been silly. I took a partner and so did she. The boys at Ashwood seemed to know who she was—because one of them, I thought furiously, perhaps *him*, has pointed her out. Hers smiled smugly the entire time. He spoke as they danced, and I could see the fire and steel cutting at her pale perfect face.

He wants to peel away your skin, I thought, mindlessly stepping alongside my partner. His name was Tom. He liked cricket and mathematics. He seemed perfectly polite.

He wants to leave you bare, Charlotte. Don't let him.

Although I was supposed to be paying attention to Tom, I found myself looking at Charlotte's partner instead. He was vile, I could tell; she was not smiling anymore, her lips were pressed together, but if she were to abandon him during the dance everyone would see. I stared at his squirming pink hands sticking out the ends of his dark suit and they wriggled and writhed and melted into trotters.

Charlotte was dancing with the beast.

I did not want to see the beast here. So I looked back at Tom, but his face was jumping beneath the brows, his strange small nose twitching and jumping, flesh hanging from his protruding teeth. I wanted his hands off my waist; they felt to me damp, furry things, the paws of a horrid hare. His mouth was moving but all I heard was grunts.

Past him, the girl behind us was swelling out of her dress—a pink, princess, fairy-like affair, into a great furry grizzly. Her partner had iron nails and teeth and he did not seem to notice.

Nobody seemed to notice. I danced waiting for screams that did not come.

The room moved to the violins, but I was distracted from the sound. All I could see were snakes in suits and twirling boars and prancing goats cloaked in glittering shawls. White cats swayed round and round in a circle. There was a squat, shimmering toad sat in the corner of the room, wearing a glistening gold tiara.

The music stopped. My partner made noises. I nodded, breathless, and then rushed out to the first door I could see.

I didn't want to be there when the beasts started to draw blood.

The door lead to a door. That door opened to glass windows; those framed a balcony, although it was only the first floor. Out there I could only just hear the music.

Was this the place the beast had been conceived? I wondered. Surely, the teachers would have blocked it off, if so. But perhaps not, because in a matter of seconds, I could see Charlotte behind the glass.

She pushed her way out onto the balcony, eyes creased with concern. "Precious?"

"It's too much in there."

"Well, you can't wait here." I glared, but she just jerked her chin at the grounds. They stared back, silent and still in their silver veil. I saw the Moon coming closer and closer to me, one big white spinning pale Medusa Eye.

"Precious." Charlotte's voice was oddly calm. "Priam must have been watching me like a hawk. Our partners saw us leave too. We either go back in, or we *go*."

I turned in a fury to look at her, not sure if I was ready to break her neck or fall to my knees, and the longer I stared and loved and hated, the more her diamond pins began to grow. They twisted up, in strange aborted tangles, until they were great horns like tree branches burning bright and brilliant white. I couldn't imagine their weight, but still her neck would not bow. I stared at her perfect face beneath it and wished it would crumple; in response, her teeth started to sharpen, great fangs ready to bite me.

"*Precious.*" Her voice was urgent because there were footsteps; footsteps that seemed to echo and tremble like the workings of some great clock, ones that surely signified the end that I had imagined. The sensible clack of undeniably heeled shoes made me think that it was Miss Priam, doubtlessly horrified despite the lack of male presence on the balcony.

Before I knew it, we had taken hold of one another and leapt downwards. I found Charlotte, a beating heart encased in silk, in the air.

It was not a long fall, but the landing showed well enough on our white dresses. The sight made something inside me curl in on itself.

I looked up at Charlotte, successfully struggling to her feet in her pretty heeled shoes. They were a soft white satin to match her dress; they must have been costly, and were now irreparably ruined. She came closer, and closer, and closer, still crowned with her horns. Our foreheads met. Her face blurred beneath the stars and her eyes shone like mirrors.

I saw myself in them, and then I stabbed it.

Charlotte's small mouth parted, but her eyes were not surprised. The silly, inefficient craft knife stood embedded in her breast; she bled only at the sharpest point, a scarlet sphere of blood. She caught the wrist of the hand that had struck her, but did not pull back from me; our hands stood as separate entities between our bodies, each of us struggling against the other's strength. When she spoke, her voice was hot.

"I'm glad we put so much of ourselves into each other, even if you're not," she hissed, eyes wet. "But whatever it is, you don't have to attack me."

I said nothing.

"I'd have died if I didn't share something with someone," she admitted, voice soft and small. It didn't fool me though, not when I saw her eyes. "It wasn't like that with him. I thought it might be."

The confession surprised me. I looked down again at her quivering wrist, flesh, not marble, and it began to reach out, morphing and twisting into and around me.

I felt myself curling into her too, like that poem about the trees that grew intertwined with one another. My eyes were changing. Her horns were growing. My head was pounding.

This would be visible even in the hall; *that*, we knew for sure. So we hobbled on four legs to her blank, bare room, to bathe her wounds and haunt the school, where they now tell rumors of the four-horned fairy that still roams the grounds. They say that our spirits are bound to the dorm; that they have ascended to Heaven or tunneled down to hell. That they rot, unclaimed, in the lake with our earthly bodies. Some girls dare to dream that we have left, that we live in a little cottage of roses, that a beastly boy with a spider's hands jumps up to pick the plums from our garden. No one thinks to check their mouths or their mirrors. But that, of course, is the one place where the Beast of Lady Hawk Academy will always be sure to reside.

A . A . B L A I R

And She Cried Out, Unseen

Kayri was born with half her soul in the beyond.

She been touch, her gran would say when someone told the story, eyeing the patch of skin that had been left faded and colorless from the cord around her neck. *Like somet'in try come wit' yuh ta di side-or keep part uh yuh back there.* Many dismissed the old woman's words, but there'd been moments that had certainly made Kayri feel like something was always kinda...there.

Like when she'd been three and had tried to reach her favorite woven baby doll that had been shoved to the top of the shelf out of her reach. She couldn't get it. She was too small. But some faint glow had blossomed and floated and, then, her dolly was in her hand. Or when she'd been five and her father had come home much too early from work, a shadow silhouetted against his back; it had lingered even as he shut out the sun with a slam of the orange door riddled with shard scratches from a flung beer bottle. Or like when she turned ten and had been sitting at the feet of her gran's rocking chair and saw a faint flicker of white and silver matter at her shoulder. It had blossomed in, just hanging there while her gran laughed over memories of crab-crawling through dense bushes and the heat of outdoor kitchen fires. Unlike before, this one never went anywhere. It just hung there. Lingering. Floating. As if waiting.

But when she pointed this last moment out to her mumma, the petite woman just looked at her strangely. A full minute ticked by, then two, before her mother finally sucked her teeth and waved her off to go play.

Dat eye uh yuhs ain't see not'in, chil'.

That eye. Her left eye, her mumma meant. That eye was nothing more than a haze of glassy film, worthless for seeing, another leftover mark of her harrowing entry into the world. *Not enough oxygen*, the doctor had explained, even if it didn't sound quite right. It left her blind in one eye, in addition to looking like her discolored neck didn't quite belong on her gangly body. But something had been there, and no one else believed her. No one else saw any of those things: the glows, the shadows, the monochrome scope of blacks and grays and whites and dulls that hovered any and everywhere. Floating matters that came in uninvited. Kayri did, though. Kayri saw everything even when her mumma claimed she saw nothing.

And the next morning, when her gran lay still and stiff in her bed and had to be hoisted into a black bag that crinkled and screeched as they zipped it up, Kayri still saw it.

Only when they wheeled her gran's body out and away, did it finally dissipate. Kayri never understood it. What were these things that she was seeing?

The answer came on the day the shadows did.

She woke up that morning feeling dizzy. Groggy. Throat drier than burnt banana leaves. Her eyes throbbed, even the useless left one. Her head felt heavier than normal. She simply thought she needed sleep. She'd been up late trying to read *Beka Lamb* with a flickering flashlight, using imagination and the story of another girl somewhere else far away to drown out the muffles of angry shouts, crashing glass, and eventual grunts of forced pleasure echoing from her parents' bedroom just beyond the threshold of her bedroom sanctuary. She hadn't fallen asleep until the sounds were gone.

Blinking now, against the glare of sunlight through the corner of her dusty curtains, she pulled herself out of bed. Everything looked strange. Even when she yanked her curtain all the way over to block out the rising sun, balls of light remained. Spots flickered like tiny floaters on her pupils; each time she looked left, then right, they'd move, too. She pressed a palm against her lid. When she opened her eyes again, there were more. Seemingly thousands of them.

"Mumma," she called out, dragging hard-heeled feet into the

kitchen where her mother stood fiddling with the garbage bin. The woman jerked up suddenly and yanked her half-splayed robe shut, though Kayri swore she saw a flash of purple skin before the material covered it.

"Wha's yuh stress, chil'? Why yuh ain't in da tub, yet?" An arm of pepper-spice and faint freckles waved at her.

"Muh eye," Kayri said, fingers splayed over her forehead where she still covered it.

Her mother released the bag she'd been manhandling. There was a rattle of bottles that made Kayri look over with her one good eye, but her mother's furrowed brows just as quickly blocked her scrutiny of the bulging bag. She saw the question in the furrow and frown of her mother's brow and mouth.

"It hurtin'. Keep seein' all kinda lights. Flickerin' everywhere."

"Yuh probably pressin' too hard on it wit' yuh hand. Move it, lemme see." She yanked Kayri's arm down and hummed, mumbling under her breath.

The lights were still there, a little fainter than earlier, but a new anomaly appeared. There was a shadow. A dark one. Just at her mother's shoulder. But it didn't behave the way the lights and floating matters she often saw did. Those ones moved like shapeless clouds, almost transparent and dismissible. This one hung like a tattered, hovering cloak from a small distance, gray tendrils ribboning as if from behind a translucent screen. It was opaque, nearly visible. It gawked. Bobbed. Leered. With eyes of mist and a jaw of black smoke. Open. Smiling. Grinning.

Kayri screamed and shoved away from her mother's grip. Shocked, she blinked rapidly a few times—and it was gone. Breathing hard, she barely registered her mother's fussing. Her mother's voice came slowly behind the ringing that had, unbeknownst to her, filled her ears from the residual screech of her own scream.

"—matter wit' yuh? Trynna scream me ear off?" Her mother sucked her teeth with a *tcha* and stood. "Yuh eye look fine. Gone go bathe 'n get ready fa school." There was a faint hesitation as she shuffled forward, as if it hurt to move, and Kayri swore she saw another hint of purple skin at the part of her mother's thigh that peeked from beneath her robe.

"Mumma. Yuh leg—"

"Tub." She slammed her hand on the counter and there was a flicker of a shadowy grin over her shoulder before it blinked out. Like static. "Now."

That day in school, it only got worse. Every time she looked, there were lights and shadows. Glows and orbs bouncing, flickering, moving. Solidifying in ways she had never seen before. And each time something appeared, her eyes pained her. Like they couldn't tolerate the sights but still wanted to see them. Even stranger, each time she spotted them, it was from the left.

Always from the left.

By the time she got home, her head felt like it was being split open and her left eye throbbed. She refused supper, much to her mother's annoyance; she waved her to her room with another suck-teeth and a grumble. Kayri was trembling by the time she made it into bed, skin still warm from the steaming bath and smelling like coconuts and Dettol.

That night, she dreamed. Of red trees and green soil. Of waving limbs and spiders the size of houses. Of burning incense and a never-ending whirlwind of powder and ash and gray specks that filtered by as if microscopic clouds. It was a wilderness of magic and lore, of the beyond.

And she could see it. All of it. Fully. With *both* eyes. Kayri gasped and touched her face. She looked at her hand. Traced the movement of fingers and knuckles, and the etchings of palm lines. She glanced down. Her body was bathed in white, the color clinging to her like a robe. She touched it and felt...light. Did light have a texture? It did here. Wherever she was.

"'M dreamin'," she whispered.

And her own mind responded. *Yuh ain' dreamin', gyal.*

She could feel colors, hear sights, taste sounds. See everything. If not a dream, then what?

She moved barefoot atop perfectly shaped leaves that had

fallen to the ground in a natural pavement of a path, their greens shining through a kaleidoscopic earth. Her feet felt like yellow, warm yet cool. Her skin prickled in an orange-ish way, a hum of skin and bones and sensations.

Noises peppered in the distance. She tasted a mingling of accented voices on her tongue. Speaking languages she did not know but somehow understood. Yoruba. Taino. Igbo. Papiamento. Faint silhouettes of gold moved alongside, but still within the thick choir of red swaying trees.

"Hello?" she called out; her voice bounced like chalky skipping rocks through the waterless forest, each ripple a different language. *Nle o. Tau. Ndeewo. Bon dia.* There was no response. She walked on. Trusting her feet to follow, Kayri turned her gaze to the sights. A flock of birds took flight, soaring into the sky with a chorus of blues. It was breathtaking. She wanted to keep watching. To see it all. To see so fully for the first time was simply...everything.

And, then, a scream shattered the song. It rang through in a voice so shrill that it waved toward Kayri in a rushing sandstorm of raw umber. It washed over her, engulfed her and yanked her. She glided through the sand into time and space and came out the other side.

Darkness. A pool of clearness below, but black all around. She stepped into it but it was not wet. Just warm. The sounds continued but it was softer, now. Whimpers.

"Ah beg ya. Please. Dun'."

She knew that voice. "Mumma?"

The pool jittered and before her emerged a scene: her mother on her knees, nightgown ripped and hanging from her shoulder like rags, arm up in supplication and a man before her. Bare-chested, a belt in hand, and eyes redder than blood. Her father.

"No."

Beside them, something else manifested. A shadow of spindly limbs and mist. She could taste its crackling exhales. Hear its odor of rot and sewer. Putrid. Its tattered shrouds swam into her nostrils. Nearly drowned her. She coughed, choking, only to see her father's hand tensed around her mother's neck.

He squeezed, Kayri choked, and the shadow laughed. It was there. Then it saw her. *You.*

Me? Kayri took a surprised step back.

You're not supposed to be here. The screech of rot crept toward her. As it moved, Kayri became frozen. Bones were rattling, a choke of charcoal on her tongue. *The void is not meant for you. Not since we took your tether. You're not supposed to be able to get here.*

It stopped. This close, Kayri could smell nothing but sulfur. Rotten eggs and something else charred. She could barely speak. "Ain'...wha'...."

But the thing had fallen silent. It stared at her. Directly in her eyes. No. Just one eye. Her left eye. The clattering in its voice could only be described with one word: panic.

It has come undone. You can see us. You can see it all.

As she stared, caught, her mind split deeper. There were flashes of color and sound. White masks. Blue sheets. A wheel screech. Dark laughter. A frantic wail. Tightness. A cord around her neck. A burning in her chest. In her face. Fingers down. Up. Moving. Scraping. A slash across her lids. A clamp. Then a release. She crashed to her knees, choking on the memory of her birth with the knowledge of what had happened. She could see. She'd always been able to see, but her eye had been purposefully shielded. Blocked from whatever lay beyond by whatever had wanted to keep her from seeing them. Could this be what her gran meant? A clinging. Something from the beyond that had ruined her when she'd been born with only half her soul. Shadows and light, blinding her in the waking world, but granting her clairvoyance in the...wherever this was.

Her stomach suddenly dropped. Kayri felt the formless space that was this strange place open beneath her. She fell. With no warning, the universe realized its folly in her learning. She shifted back and fell through her death and landed into life. Right back atop the comfort of her bed.

Awake.

Kayri bolted upright and slapped a hand to her eye. It was wet with tears but, much like in her dream, she could see. Her hand, the blue lilies on her wrinkled sheet, the crumpled uniform she'd tossed down as soon as she'd gotten home. She could see all. Clearly. With both eyes.

"Ain' a dream..." And if that had been real then everything else...

Her feet slammed onto the floor. She ran, leaping through the hall and bursting through the door of her parents' bedroom. There they were, the same as in her dream only surrounded by a bureau and bed rather than a weightless pool of shallow water.

Her father spun toward her, enraged, belt aloft. Her mother looked at her, face trekked with dirty, bloody tears, and an arm pleading for her to go back.

Kayri had a flash of another memory: peering through the bars of a crib as her mother's arms and legs waved about in an ensemble with the whap-wish-clang of a thick buckled-belt. The sounds. The sights.

Kayri ran forward.

"Stop!" she cried, putting herself between her parents, but her gaze shifted elsewhere. "Yuh leave her be, yuh hear. Leave 'em alone!"

The latter was shouted into a corner where she could see it, again. The dark figure. Leering. Her father had always bore a darkness in him. She'd seen it as shadows. As bits of murk that never quite left him even when he was sober. Her eye had known. Had been spotting inklings of the truth from as far back as she could remember. And now she knew, too. That the shadow had always been there. Not her father, but a being of the beyond invading him.

"Yuh ain' belong here."

The figure lunged. When it came forward, she reached out and grabbed it, not knowing but hoping. Her hand only shoved through. She gasped. It felt like ice water instantly numbing her limbs. It grew heavy, then suffocating, and Kayri felt foolish in her actions. But as she gasped for air, she pinned her gaze on the creature of mist and darkness. It stared back, its growls tasting like poison and sounding like the deepest onyx. She willed it away. Forced it. Demanded it. And, soon, the pressure eased until she exhaled, coming to the surface for air.

The shadow. The darkness. It was gone.

The girl fell to her knees trembling, as her mother caught her. Out of the corner of her eye, she saw her father collapse, a river of deep purple and gray seeping from his fingertips into the ground. Light bathed him as he inhaled a stutter then went silent but breathing. Still breathing.

"Kayri?" Her mother's hiccupped whimper drew her gaze.

She saw the moment her mother recognized that her eye was seeing. A matching shade of brown to the other. Opened. Connected.

"I can see," the girl exhaled and then inhaled deeply, breathing in the view of her mother's whole face for the first time. "I can finally see."

Mud

The first time that Monica Freeman met her fiancée's mother was the day they buried Gwen Beaumont in the ground. The day was heavy and humid. The Alabama heat felt suffocating and even more claustrophobic than the New York City streets that Monica was accustomed to. Her kinky curls stuck to her skin and she was the only one that wore color in a sea of black. Only one of color besides the house staff.

Monica was raised in New York but her roots were in the South. Her grandfather had warned her of the way that old Southern towns stuck in old Southern ways stayed haunted. So, she wore blue as a safeguard. Didn't matter that her dress set her apart, that she was out of place. She was never meant to feel in place on the Beaumont plantation, which was why Gwen had never brought her home in the first place.

The large three story antebellum home loomed over Monica as if it stood still in time, the white pillars and wraparound porch of the setting that people still called idyllic, looked ominous. If she squinted, the white pillars, the wrought iron fence around the property, could have easily been prison bars.

The maid that opened the door was silent. Stoic. Skin dark like the bark of the willow oak out front. Lips pinched into a thin line and for some reason Monica felt as if the woman's lips had been sewn shut. As if her brown eyes wanted to scream. Monica almost opened her mouth to scream for her but she noticed a blemish on the green manicured lawn. Her gaze zoned in one a grassless patch of earth, the red clay revealed underneath.

The maid cleared her throat and Monica jumped.

"Gwen used to sit out there and make mud pies," she told

Monica, "Dug at the earth and would eat the clay like it was the only thing that sustained her."

Her voice was raspy. Low in that easy way that reminded Monica of Jazz, of lullabies. Of simplicity. She could tell the tone was practiced. Monica was herself an artist. Always seeking patronage. Funding. The New York elite was a different animal but not so different from those with money in the South. She'd found that domestics tended to be the same everywhere. Careful. Poised. Always aware. Always subdued. Non- threatening. Appeasing until out of the space of the wealthy.

"What's your name?" Monica asked.

The woman looked startled as if she hadn't been asked that question in a long time. "Camellia," she responded after a moment. "After the Alabama state flower."

Gwen had told her about Camellia. About warm hands, warm meals, and a smile like sunshine. There was no smile now. Whether it was from mourning or a tiredness that came from years of servitude Monica wasn't sure. Wouldn't ask.

"It's pretty," she commented instead, allowing herself to be led into the house, glancing one more time back at the patch of open earth. The imperfection amongst the seemingly picturesque.

Monica navigated the funeral the way she would've an art opening. Her expression portrayed a false sense of calm, hiding the turmoil and anxiety underneath. The grief was a new thing to navigate but well within her limits. She mingled. She gave off the impression of being mournful but well put together. Always well put together.

She didn't react when she was referred to more than once as Gwen's roommate.

"Isn't the roommate such an articulate thing," murmured just loud enough for Monica to hear as she crossed the room. "I was respecting the roommate to be someone a bit more unrefined given the way Charlene spoke about her."

"She's refined enough I supposed, for an..." a deliberate

pause, just long enough to be grating, and then, "artist."

"What was her name again?"

"Camellia, I believe."

"No dear," a tittering laugh, "Camellia is the maid."

A shrug, a glance in Monica's direction. "Roommate. Maid. Doesn't matter much. Neither are family. We won't see either after this. Why keep track?"

Monica pasted on a smile as she passed. The frozen sort of Colgate smile that used to make her laugh when she saw it in commercials because it felt so uncanny valley. So unnatural. Lacking humanity. But she wasn't human here, to these people. She would save her emotions for those who saw her as such.

Monica didn't react when she saw the tears on Gwen's mother's face. A face that looked too much like Gwen. The hazel eyes. The dark brown hair. The tiny nose that Monica used to kiss. Only Charlene Beaumont had a sharpness to her features like the edge of a knife, but angular in that disjointed way of portraits by Picasso that were distorted and could've been seen as monstrous or beautiful depending on who was beholding them.

Monica managed herself until she saw Gwen in the casket. The pale lifeless figure incongruent with who Gwen was. Even the funeral was against her wishes.

She'd wanted to be cremated, she'd said once.

They never talked about death. Not really. But the first portrait Monica had ever painted of Gwen she'd fused her with a phoenix. Gwen laughed and said, "I always wanted to go up in flames. I always figured if I was cremated it wouldn't be death, but a sort of rebirth."

Their wedding had been three weeks away when the car ran Gwen off the road. Three weeks and they would've been married. Monica would've been her next of kin. She would've been able to carry out her wishes. Three weeks.

Instead, her mother had taken Gwen home to Alabama. Hadn't met Monica. Hadn't bothered to tell her anything. Monica hadn't even been certain until she'd receive a funeral invitation a week later. One that came on the condition that she not cause a scene of any sort. Not sully their daughter's name.

She hadn't wanted to come. She wanted to curl up in the bed that Gwen no longer shared with her until her scent faded. She wanted to cry and scream and tear down the little matchbox apartment they had shared. She wanted to set fire to every canvas and let the flames consume her. Let herself be reborn wherever Gwen was now.

But that wouldn't bring peace or closure. So she got on a plane. She put on the mask she wore for investors and buyers and hadn't taken it off since.

As she looked at Gwen's still form in the casket, she realized this wouldn't bring closure either. That this would only bring anger. Resentment. Gwen couldn't even die on her own terms. They couldn't acknowledge Monica or the life she'd built with her even after losing their daughter.

Monica walked out after seeing Gwen in the casket. She didn't speak. She walked out of the home and onto the lawn. She sat down on the bare patch of earth and cried. She cried until the clay became mud beneath her fingers and she could've sworn she felt warmth. Heat. Flesh. She brought her fingers to lips. Tasted the clay. Tasted Gwen.

***

In exchange for a few large bricks of clay from the yard, Monica agreed to play host to Charlene Beaumont for two days. One weekend seemed long enough to gather her daughter's belongings. Belongings that Charlene didn't want but Monica knew that she didn't want Monica to have.

Charlene could've easily stayed in one of New York's premier hotels. She had more than enough money. Could've hired someone else to retrieve Gwen's belongings. But that wasn't really what the visit was about. It was an intrusion. An invasion. Colonization in order to pass judgment on her daughter even in death. Gwen was no longer there to hear the criticism but that didn't mean that Monica would escape. She was an easier target.

Vulnerable. Hadn't had the release that death brought Gwen but would be punished for Gwen not living the life Charlene hadn't wanted her to.

It didn't matter in the long run. The more sentimental objects were at Monica's studio. Everything she wanted to keep moved there before Charlene Beaumont moved herself into their small apartment, the walls becoming even more oppressive when she walked through the door.

Charlene looked unimpressed. Called it a hovel. Scowled at every bit of imperfection.

"The appeal here escapes me," Charlene said, upon walking through the door, "though I suppose I never saw the appeal of anything Guinevere did. Any of her choices. You included."

Monica ignored it. Wasn't surprised by it. Was more offended by the use of Guinevere because she knew the way that Gwen hated to be called by her full name.

The other stuff she had dealt with her whole life. It ran off her like water off a duck's back. Could've been white noise.

"Will be until it catches up to you," her grandfather always told her, "We all gotta break some time. But don't you ever let their voice be stronger than your own."

The Beaumonts came from old money. Even older bigotry. Lived in what was once and likely still was a sundown town. Their daughter living in a rundown apartment with a Black girl who grew up in Harlem and made abstract art for a living was never going to be the life they wanted for her. Monica had always known that. Had never cared. Had never planned on meeting her in-laws.

It should bother me, she thought. Having the woman in her space. Having her eyes that were too much like Gwen's scanning and judging. But Monica's focus instead turned to the bricks of clay that had been delivered before Charlene's arrival. The clay that spoke to her in a voice that was louder than some over the hill bitter Southern belle that wanted to lash out in her grief.

Monica could find focus in creation. A way to channel her own grief. She touched the clay and once again felt heat. A warmth that she had been starved of.

The clay became an easy distraction. A welcome one. Felt more human and malleable than the sharp angles of Charlene's face. She didn't bother to have it moved to her studio. She worked with it on the floor in her living room. Ignored Charlene's words of protest and looks of disgust as she began to sculpt and mold and shape. The clay felt alive and thrumming under her fingers.

***

Monica didn't sleep the first night. The first morning, Charlene awoke to find her still sculpting, the clay covering her skin, her clothes, her hair. The creation took shape. The shape of Gwen. The shape of her curves. Of her nose. Her mouth. Her lips. Her eyes. She couldn't stop touching the clay. Couldn't keep her hands from running over it again and again.

It drew all of her focus. This resurrection of her beloved. It was better than looking at Charlene and her too expensive clothes. Her pristine demeanor. Her eyes that were all wrong.

Better than thinking about how too much of her life had been dictated by people like Charlene. People with money. With resources. With status. People that got to decide what was art. What was love. That got to decide the worth of the beauty that Monica created with her hands. Her blood. Her sweat. Her tears. Her lips on Gwen's skin.

People like Charlene that stripped humanity from people like Monica. That would never understand people like Gwen had been. Open and vulnerable and artistic, and unwilling to fold in on herself or create an acceptable image of herself for the rest of her world. For her mother. Monica wished that she wasn't too hollow now to be that brave. Wished she had the privilege to be.

She had lost herself along the way. Pleasing critics. Pleasing people with deep pockets. Smiling false smiles. Listening to others dictate what she and her art should be. The only thing that had been left untouched by outside influence was Gwen. Now Gwen was gone.

But the sculpture felt real. Organic. True. Untouched.

"Is this your way of mourning?" Charlene asked.

Monica didn't answer. She moved to the sculpture's head, her hands molding the hair.

"She would've drowned in you," Charlene continued, when Monica didn't speak. "You ruined her. Even if she had lived. You would've ruined her."

Monica blocked out the words and instead picked up a sculpting tool.

Charlene packed another box.

***

The next night, sleep came but it was restless. Fitful. Monica fell asleep in an empty bed still covered in clay. She woke up covered in sweat. She came out to the living room and frowned at the sculpture. Somehow it moved. Reformed. From standing to sitting. She blinked. Walked over to the couch and shook Charlene awake.

"What did you do?" Monica demanded.

Logically she knew the woman was no artist. No sculptor. She couldn't have reformed it, so perfectly reshaped its position while keeping its torso intact.

"What are you talking about, *girl*?" Charlene grumbled in her sleep. Said girl as if it were something foul. As if it were bitter on her tongue.

"You moved it," Monica said.

Charlene looked at her in confusion.

"The sculpture," Monica pressed, "You moved it."

"You awoke a guest in your home for something so trivial? I knew you were ungroomed but this is a bit much even for you." Charlene sat up, looked at the statue bleary eyed. "Are you mad? It hasn't moved. It's the same as it was."

Monica wouldn't put it past the woman to gaslight her. To hire an artist to come in while she was sleeping. But when Monica looked back at the statue, it was standing again, the same position it had been before she fell asleep. She blinked. Rubbed her eyes. The statue winked at her. mocking . Perhaps it had been in her head. The constant unrest since Gwen's death finally had overwhelmed her.

"As if I would dirty my hands with it. Really, Camellia." Charlene huffed.

Monica felt herself break.

"My name is Monica," she said, and then yelled, "Not *girl*. Not Camellia. Not roommate. My name is Monica. Monica. And l loved your daughter in a way that everyone wants to be loved and no one could dream of. I loved her in a way that you never did."

Charlene laughed. "You loved her to death. To ruin. She died to me the moment she took up with you. It doesn't matter what your name is. You could be anyone. You were an act of rebellion, not love," she shouted back. "I gave her a life everyone dreams of. She left it for an over emotional destitute artist she knew I would loathe because she wanted my attention. Even your precious love wasn't about you, *girl*. Your name doesn't matter."

Monica opened her mouth to retort but felt tired. Bone deep exhaustion. She saw movement out of the corner of her eye and glanced at the statue. The face was distorted. Enraged.

She heard Gwen's voice in her head.

Don't listen to her. I loved you the way that fires burn. Endless. Consuming. Stronger and larger as it breathes air. Leaving ashes and embers in its wake but never dying. Living anew in lunges and singed wallpaper. I loved you. I loved you. I love you, still.

Monica's eyes stung with tears. She crossed the room. Rested her forehead against the forehead of the statue. Let the sculpture's hand cup her cheek, the other run down her arm the way that Gwen's used to.

"You can cling to that hunk of mud if you like, but it won't bring her back," Charlene's voice said from somewhere far away, "It's about as real as your little relationship was."

Monica pressed trembling lips to the statue's. Felt the sculpture respond in kind. Felt herself slowly losing what was real but she knew that the moment was more real than the sentiments of a mother lashing out at her dead child's lover that was too broken to fight back. More real than a Colgate smile. Than art produced for money. Real in a way that comforted and suffocated her all at once. Flesh. Heat. Gwen. Fire.

Monica closed her eyes. Willed her grief to let go of her mind. She took a deep breath. Counted to ten. She went back to her empty bed. Dreamed of Gwen. Dreamed of holding Gwen's head under water. Drowning her the way that Charlene had accused.

Gwen let her. Welcomed Monica's hands around her throat. Smiled as water burned her lungs like fire. Whispered long after her body went still.

I loved you. I loved you. I love you, still.

***

In the morning Monica woke covered in sweat again, this time with the statue curled around her. Spooning her, the clay hands stroking her hair. She embraced it in return but the touches faded to nothing. The heat turned into an empty chill.

She sat up to find the statue laying across her bed, lifeless and frozen. *Charlene must've put it here*, she thought. *Another trick. Another game.*

She got out of bed. Went to confront Charlene once more, only to find the woman on the couch covered in water and clay. In mud.

The woman's eyes were open wide. Blank. Lifeless. Clay dripped from her mouth, her nose, the corners of her eyes. Monica approached slowly. Reached out. Felt herself tense at the rigid cold of Charlene's hand.

She opened her mouth to call her name but, "Your name doesn't matter," came out instead. Because it didn't. Not anymore. She would just be a rich white woman found dead in a poor Black girl from Harlem's apartment. Monica would be a statistic. If they even took her in. If she even stood trial. If she survived beyond a call to the police and an explanation she didn't have beyond a statue that lay cold in her bed.

Monica let out a laugh. Hysterical and broken.

She felt arms wrap around her from behind. Looked down and saw red Alabama clay. She could feel it again, flesh and bone where there was no flesh and bone. She turned and faced the statue. Looked into eyes that had no color. No light. Kissed lips that were hard and malleable.

She smiled to herself as the statue let her go. One clay hand wrapped around a discarded bottle of paint thinner. The other holding a lighter next to a candle on the kitchen counter.

Monica closed her eyes and prepared for rebirth.

The Witnessing

The headlights of Gina's old Hudson Wasp opened the night like a wound. Born and raised in Micanopy, she'd driven down US-441 a thousand and a half times, but never like this—in the dark. When Gina was still small, before the grand lie began, the three of them—Gina, her momma Lottie and her stepdad Clay— would ride down 441 to Mount Olive for Sunday service with the windows down; let the Hudson fill up with the sound of the old WRUF broadcasts and swamp smell, the earthy aroma of rotting vegetation. Now, though, as Gina sliced the dark open on this old familiar road, the windows were rolled up and the radio was off. The stations were all news of disruptive sit-ins and bus boycotts and colored student protests. Nothing Gina wanted to hear as she drove back to the boondocks of Alachua as another lie grew in the bottom of Gina's gut like mildew, appearing first as a rust-colored smudge in her unmentionables.

The smudge hadn't begun as a lie, not exactly. Her fiancé Dale drove them the hour from Gainesville into Jacksonville to see a doctor and they'd cried when they heard the news. On the ride back, he'd alternated between kissing her fingers and calling her Momma—*What does Momma want for lunch? What station does Momma want to listen to? Does Momma want to split a cola?* Gina had been drunk with joy beside him, giggling at the feel of his stubble against her fingers and playing along—*What do you think about Cotton's Barbecue, Poppa? Oh, stop the dial here, Poppa, I love that Bobby Darin. Can I get my own cola, Poppa? I'm drinking for two after all.*

Their still-pending marriage made it a secret between them, but when Gina noticed the regularly returning coil at the root of her hair, angrier and wilder than the last time she'd touched

up her relaxer, the secret began to turn and curdle into a lie she
thought was long-buried. A lie that threatened to take everything from Gina: her job at Juniper & Assoc., every opportunity
that lay ahead of her and her unborn baby, even Dale's license
to practice wasn't safe, not if word got out that he was engaged
to, much less fathered, a mulatto. And the wedding? As much as
Dale believed in Gina's ambitions—Alachua county's first
woman solicitor—Dale's ambitions were more realistic and in
closer sights, and the one-day county prosecutor couldn't be
married to a spook.

Then her roommate Lily Lancaster came home with a wrig-
gling cocker spaniel in her arms. First, Gina thought Lily had
gotten a replacement. A *very* good copy. As the days passed, the
dog picked up Winnie's old ritual of scratching at Gina's door to
go out when Lily slept passed her alarm. Preferred Winnie's favorite sniffing spots when they went for a walk. The new dog's
coat, that salt and pepper brindle pattern, was too identical to
Winnie's, and when Gina finally asked Lily hadn't been shy. *"I
saw a root-woman. She's the real deal. If you need a miracle, Orula
is the one to call."*

This was why Gina now traveled south. Why she'd asked after the root-woman with the strange name. Why she drove this
road to a town she'd tried to leave behind. Gina and the lie
growing inside her needed a miracle desperately.

She nearly sailed by the turn-off that led to the lake. Her mus-
cle-memory was trying to take her back to Mount Olive AME,
back to that lichen-caked headstone she hadn't seen since the
funeral. The Hudson banked right onto a narrow county road;
the canopy of trees overhead was donned in Spanish moss and
darkness. Gina had made the call. Had whispered through the
phone to somebody who told her to come to Tuscawilla Lake.
Told her that Orula would meet Gina at the water, and that she
preferred cash to personal check. Fifty dollars and serving as
witness was what her roommate paid for calling on Orula. *A witnessing.* That's what Lily called it.

Gina had pushed her, begged to know what her roommate had witnessed, to know what exactly she was getting herself into, but Lily wouldn't give an inch. *I'm sworn to secrecy, I don't wanna undo the magic.* She didn't bother asking if that was something the voice on the phone or Orula had told her or something Lily had created in her own imagination. Besides, why risk it? Gina didn't want to go back to the sight of Winnie caught under that truck, spread across 9th street like jam on toast.

The road ended at an unpaved empty lot, and she stepped out onto the uneven sandy soil. The night sang, and the muted crunch of Gina's old saddle shoes on fallen twigs and leaves were an out-of-time metronome. She breathed in the familiar sappy smell of the trees, the water. Years ago, the three of them would spend Sunday afternoons on the far side of Tuscawilla Lake, where the trees grew thick enough for them to go unnoticed from the street or across the water. Between bites of cucumber sandwich, Clay and Lottie would sit in the car to listen to the football game and Gina in the shady grass, looking across the lake at the crawfish-colored children on the beach splashing and churning the water with games she didn't know the names of, wondering why they couldn't sit on that side of the lake. Why Gina couldn't get in the water like *those* kids.

Gina looked across the shore, trying to find the silhouette of this root-woman meant to meet her. Gina imagined sharp shoulders, body draped in oriental fabrics, a turban-topped head. Instead, knee deep in the lake, rising from the water like a mangrove, was a wide-set woman, her face still round with youth, dressed in waders. Her hair—Gina had been wrong about the turban—bloomed out and up from her scalp in a wide gravity-flouting halo.

"You the lawyer lady?" she called from the lake.

"Paralegal," Gina said. "You're the Root Worker?"

The woman in the water propped her fists on her hips and snorted. "Is that what they're calling me in the land of milk and honey?"

Gina tried to kill the grin on the corner of her mouth.

Gainesville was the land of malt liquor and mosquitos at best.

"Enough yap," Orula said. "Roll them pants up and kick them shoes off."

"You want me to get in?" Gina said and swallowed. "I thought I was just the witness."

"And just what you think witnessing means? You ain't gone witness shit from the shore, Lawyer Lady." The woman bent, her hands disappearing into the shallow water, searching for something. Then, she looked up, her obsidian halo bouncing at the edges, and said, "Or do you got a problem getting in the same water as a *Negro*?"

Gina went hot and kicked off her shoes. "No! I'm voting for Kennedy."

The icy water stung at her ankles as Gina waded through the dark to where Orula still shuffled like a crab.

"What are you looking for?" Gina asked.

"I buried supplies out here a while back. Should be somewhere about here," Orula said, gesturing vaguely, first in one direction then the opposite.

"What sort of supplies?"

"Start searching along the shore. It'll feel like a vase, with a handle on either side."

"How do you know it's still here?" Gina said, and moved to mirror Orula's bent, hands-in-the-water posture.

"It's here. Keep looking."

A pile of rotten branches and abandoned Coca-Cola bottles sat at the edge of the water, growing with each tossed piece of refuse Gina pulled from the silt.

"Do you think someone found it?" she said, standing and stretching her back. "Maybe it drifted deeper?"

"No. It's here."

"Will your supplies have survived the water?"

"You gotta lot of questions," Orula called from several feet away. "Makes for a good lawyer."

"I'm just a paralegal," Gina said again. Her fingers looped around something in the water. Excited, she yanked up and scowled when she saw it was an old, mud-caked pair of Levi's, her fingers looped where a belt might go.

"You always wanted to be a *pair-uh-legal*?" Orula asked. She lifted a twisted branch from the water and cast it onto the shore with Gina's collection.

"No," Gina said with a dry laugh. "I wanted to be a bonified lawyer. Put bad guys away." Gina's fingers met something curved and heavy in the water. She pulled. A sand-filled milk jug rose from the lake, and she tossed it onto the shore.

"So, how come you ain't?"

"My fiancé does enough lawyering for us both. Besides, no one wants to be represented by a woman. Too hysterical."

"And is that true? Are you hysterical?"

"Doesn't matter if I am or not," Gina said, sweeping a bare foot across the lakebed for something vase shaped. "All that matters is if the jury thinks I am."

"How do you convince them?" Orula asked.

"I suppose I'm still figuring that out."

Beneath the water, Gina hooked onto something weighty. Gina brought her other hand down to the mass under the water's surface, followed the curve of the thing up to a second fist-sized handle. Gina squatted for more leverage and pulled; when the mass wouldn't budge, Orula waddled over with a toothy grin—one that said *Told ya*. When the container finally broke free of the muck and shot from the water, one woman on each handle, Gina thought it looked like a mighty clay catfish leaping from the water into hungry, waiting hands.

***

Twin beams, headlights, shot through the tree-lined lot and cast the shore in a grimy yellow. The petitioner was actually *petition-ers*—a colored man Orula called Nate and his wife Bernie. Nate barreled down the shore like a locomotive; shoulders bouncing with each step like pistons; his face, steely and wide like a cow-catcher. Bernie trailed him, clutching something the size of a holiday turkey in her arms.

Gina shifted nervously and watched the two out-of-sync petitioners' approach. If Nate was the train, Gina thought that Bernie was the coalsmoke, dark, cloaked in something heavy, and dawdling on the air her husband left behind. Beside her, Orula smacked on sticky caramel, without a care.

The supplies they'd plucked from the river were more mundane than Gina had expected, or maybe hoped; from inside the sealed clay jar, Orula had recovered, triple-bagged, a firestarter, a spool of fishing line, a fist-full of sinkers, a miniature E&J, and five tumbleweed-looking plants the size of Gina's fists. Most underwhelming from the jar: a Baby Ruth bar that Orula peeled open with the efficiency of a trapper shucking a rabbit free from its tiny pelt.

"What's up with the white girl?" Nate asked when he made it to the water's edge.

Gina's blood went molasses-thick. The words—*white girl*—floated on the muggy air and wrapped around Gina like a wet coat. The words were true, Gina supposed. That *was* the character she was playing. Some mornings she'd stand in her vanity and look for echoes of some invented man, a father who'd left her only hazel eyes and fair skin. Maybe a sailor from some faraway place. A traveling salesman, spellbound by Lottie's plump lips and wide hide hips, the same parts she'd given to Gina. Maybe he was a man who Gina walked by in town, someone who passed her childhood home on his way to work, never knowing Gina was his.

If she sat in the vanity long enough, Gina could see him in the round of her eyes, the angles of her heart-shaped face, different from Lottie's almond eyes and round face. But inevitably, Gina's relaxers would start to go, and her roots would begin to crimp. Then, she would find herself wrapped in scarves and hiding behind sunglasses on the city bus—the Hudson was too recognizable to be seen in the lot of Tanya's Afro Beauty Supply. Then Gina would stare into the mirror, her scalp ablaze with PermaStrate, and all she could see were the parts Lottie had given her, the parts Gina feared would pass to her and Dale's child. These were the parts that could topple this lie, end Gina's grand performance.

Nate folded his arms, thick as pecan trees, across his chest and gave Gina a hard stare. Gina was used to stares but this was something else. He didn't stare at the width of her nose, the bulge and wide spread of her hips and mouth. This wasn't like the leers she'd gotten used to at the office; ones that felt like being backed into a corner by a bigger, stronger animal. Gina had watched Lottie be cornered like that, cowering under Clay's booming voice and quick hands. Girl-Gina hadn't known then what she knew now: that the world women walked was a labyrinth with infinite corners and, when she was done with this world, someone would stuff her with woodchips and slide her into a box; enclose her in corners forever.

No, this was a stare Gina remembered wearing herself before she started relaxing her hair, before she left Micanopy for the anonymity she'd found in Gainesville, back when the *Whites Only* signs hung across her hometown might as well have been armed guards, their barrels pointed right at Gina and Lottie and Clay and all the rest of the colored folk in Micanopy. His was a stare to know when the strikes were coming, like an animal watching its predator stalk them. Nate's watchful eyes said *I know what you're capable of, I know your kind of claws.*

"You know how it goes," Orula said around a mouth full of peanuts and nougat. "She's your witness."

"It's nice to meet you both," Gina said as Bernie finally made it down to the shore to hover behind her husband.

"This ain't no wishing for a good hand of cards or the right bolita numbers," he said, ignoring Gina. "Get her out of here."

"You *know* how it goes," Orula said.

"You didn't say nothing about white folks being here."

Again, that strange heavy feeling crawled up Gina's back. Wrapped around her middle and squeezed. She pulled her lips in, biting down on both. He was right, but Gina's face still felt hot, her hands still nervously fidgeted.

On one Sunday, the summer that Gina turned twelve, Clay caught her dipping her toes in the lake. He pulled Gina up the grassy bank and back to the car by her curls. *Have you lost your damn mind? Just cause you could pass for one them don't mean you one of them.* Gina had cried in the backseat and Lottie had scowled at her husband, *you ain't have to pull her like that.* Clay's hand caught the side of Lottie's face and Gina remembered the wail beginning in the back of her throat and the sight of her stepdad's fingers wrapped around her Momma's face. Clay's fingers, the color of cast iron, locked around Lottie's brown jaw, and he screamed something Gina couldn't remember now. But Gina could remember reaching into the front seat, her hands trying to pry her Momma free. Remembered her fingers, pale as maggots trying to dig into tightly packed earth.

This was where the lie began, as a seed, an idea that germinated in the backseat of the Hudson on the ride back home, as Gina watched her Momma's shaking brown fingers—much darker than her own—fiddle with the radio dial. When Gina was alone in her room, she began practicing *being* one of them. Talking like them. When she went out alone, she practiced smiling and nodding at them and, to Gina's surprise, without the shadows of Clay and Lottie, they smiled and nodded back. And when Lottie died and Clay took off, Gina could finally leave this Micanopy backwater for Gainesville. Then the lie finally took root.

"If you got a problem with your witness," Orula said, "bury your boy and be done bothering me."

Gina's chest felt tight, she chanced a look past Nate to Bernie and their bundle. Orula walked from the water past Nate and his demure wife, Orula's boots caking with soft sand, and made to undo her waders. Nate grabbed her roughly by the arm, the force knocking the candy bar from Orula's grasp and into the sand, and said, "Where you think you're going?"

"Nate, let's just get out of here," Bernie said in a small, pleading voice behind him, clutching her turkey-sized bundle close to her chest.

"And who the fuck is talking to you," he said, half turning to look at his wife.

Orula looked down at the fallen candy, her eyes lazily pulled back up to Nate, and she nodded toward the lot. "You better have another Baby Ruth in that lemon y'all drove here."

"This some kind of joke to you?"

"So, you *don't* got another," Orula said with a heavy sigh and shook his hand from her arm. "You already paid, so I'm going to do you this one. But if you can't replace my Baby Ruth, you're staying on the shore. Consider it mercy."

"*Mercy* my ass," Nate said, pulling Bernie to his side, one big hand resting on the bundle in her arms. "We're paying customers and I want to see the services I'm paying for."

"Look around. Where you think you at, boy?" Orula said, gesticulating wildly. The sudden movement made Nate flinch and, in that half step backward, Gina saw fear. Gina recognized it, had felt that same fear toward Clay.

This was the kind of fear felt in the moment after a dish clattered to the floor, in the silence on the ride home before the three of them got behind closed doors and out of sight of neighbors. This was the fear Lottie chose over and over, the pyre she threw herself on when Gina asked why they didn't leave, why they didn't pack up their things and creep away in the dark. *I do all this for you*, Lottie had whispered angrily as Clay snored on the sofa. *So that you got some place to sleep, food to eat.*

Orula's snort and the water licking her legs pulled Gina back to the present. "You think this is Woolworths? The Winn-Dixie?" Orula waved her hand at Nate. "Ain't no *customer service* out here, fool. Ain't no *manager* to talk to. We dealing in the land of the Spirits. God's country. *My* country. You hear me?"

Nate's jaw clenched; his eyes buried in the sand. Gina's skin rippled with goosebumps as Orula stepped toward him.

"Do you hear me?" she asked. Gina reached for her shoes, but Orula clicked her tongue and held up her finger, like a mother telling her child I don't think so. "The lawyer lady stays," she said, her eyes flicking to Gina and back to Nate. "And *you* either wait on the shore, or you gather up your wife and head home to start planning a funeral."

Nate's mouth unfurled into a hard line. "I'll be in the car."

He turned to his wife and Gina thought she saw Bernie wince, and in that quick furrowed brow she thought she saw a little bit of Lottie. In a voice that rose from deep in his belly and slithered from between his teeth, Nate said, "I swear to God, Bern. Don't fuck this up like you do everything else."

"I won't," Bernie said, biting her lip.

"Won't what?"

She closed her eyes. Gina felt her face go hot; her jaw clenched tight. Bernie shifted on her feet. Gina watched the gathering of her brows, the roll of her tongue over her gums. Finally, Bernie swallowed, and said, "I won't fuck this up."

When Nate raised his eyebrow, his wife took a shaky breath and continued, "Like I do everything else."

Something in Gina curdled. She had seen this performance before with different actors. Had seen this, acted out by Lottie and Clay. Gina knew what happened in the third act of this play and knew the chaos of being a child watching it unfold. Gina watched Nate chug through the sand to his car and wondered if this was Bernie's opportunity to run, start over someplace new. Wondered if this was more than just her child's opportunity to grow up. Maybe this was the chance to know a life outside the heavy gaze of their father's patient, looming violence, the kind Gina had known under Clay.

Almost like the old violence of those *Whites Only* signs, one Gina had to mine her memory to remember. That was the kind of violence she'd run from, the kind she'd unshackled herself from when the relaxers began, when she enrolled and started classes at the all-white University of Florida, when she got the job at Juniper & Associates, and when she met Dale in the copy room. Inside Gina, the lie pulsed. That was violence Lottie and Clay, Bernie and Nate, couldn't outrun. The violence that she feared would return to her should her baby come out with the wrong hair, the wrong skin. But when the sound of a car door slamming shut sounded through the trees, Gina wondered if this was Bernie chance to outrun Nate's violence, to leave with her son and start someplace else.

The night was loud, full of cicada screams and toad croaks. Gina shivered, tossing ripples across the water while Orula finished anchoring the last tumbleweed—*Rose of Jericho* she'd said, correcting Gina—and arranged them in a circle where the water rose to their waists. When the last weed was placed, Orula brought Bernie into the center, bundle in tow.

Bernie unwrapped her parcel and the boy's fingers emerged first, curled like the legs of a dead spider. Gina followed the gradually emerging line of his small arm, around his shoulder to his small face that peeked at Gina in profile. He could have been sleeping if not for his dull skin and the whisper of blue Gina thought she saw around the boy's nose and mouth. Outside the rose circle, Gina's face tightened, her hands clenched around the spool of fishing wire and small brandy bottle.

Bernie's trembling, breathy voice, broke through the night lake's night song. "Don't make me do this," she said, "it's not right. Please, don't make me."

Gina recoiled. Bernie's words upended Gina's thoughts, derailed their momentum, and ripped away something that Gina hadn't realized was so precious until tonight in the Tuscawilla water, until she stood at the precipice of the miracle. She couldn't stop the words that tumbled out of her mouth, "What do you mean?"

"I don't wanna do this," Bernie said, her voice quaking, tears threatening to come. "It's my husband. He wants this. But it's wrong. Wrong. You hear me? I'm not trying to upset nobody, Miss Orula," she said, her frantic words rushing out. "I'm a God-fearing woman. And I know this ain't right, bringing my boy back to this world after the Lord called him up."

Gina swallowed. Fear had pulled Lottie back from right choices when Gina was a girl. Fear was the thing settling into Bernie's hands now, into her throat, pulling her back from what she knew was right, the thing keeping her from the chance to give her baby something better, like what Gina was trying to give her own child.

"You don't have to be afraid of your husband," Gina said, flicking her eyes to the lot and approaching the circle. Bernie's eyes, unreadable, peered from under her side-swept bangs and high bouffant that lifted her hair off her neck and from Gina's spot in the water, she could make out the speckled purple of new bruises curving around the back of her neck. Cautiously, Gina reached toward her. Bernie flinched, tried to angle away. Orula held up a hand, a silent command to not butt in, but Gina placed her hand on Bernie's shoulder. "You don't have to bring him back to *that* world. You can resurrect him and leave this place and never look back. Show him a new kind of living."

Bernie's mouth twisted, her eyes narrowed, and she stepped out of Gina's reach. "What are you talking about? I'm not leaving my husband."

"But you can," Gina said trying again to rest her hand on the woman's arm, but Bernie took another half step back. "You can show him a life that isn't *this*. A home where you don't get bruises on your neck, on his face."

"What do you know about my life?" Bernie said, her temples pulsing, nostrils flaring, grip tightening on the cold skin of her boy. "What do you know what kind of home he had? You don't know me or my family. You don't even know my son's name."

"I just want to help," Gina said, trying to keep her voice even.

"You think you're better than me?" Bernie asked, straightening her back, standing up taller than Gina thought possible. "She might be the one with the black magic," she said, nodding to Orula, "but you? You the devil. I see you, you know. You think I'm stupid. I see it in your face. How you pity me. How you think you could do my life better than I do. *Don't* talk over me. You only saying all this so you can get your own ask. You and all your white friends from town, running to the root woman to pass a test. Win the lotto. Raise a damn dog from the dead. What you need, white girl? Hmm? Is your car broke down? Your man running around on you? Your fancy office job not *exactly* what you want? Well? Don't get all quiet now. You got so much to say? Say it now."

Gina flushed and bit down till she thought her jaw might snap apart at the hinge. She wondered if Lottie would have fought sense, if she would have dug her heels in, even at the cost of Gina's life. If Lottie's imagination, like Gina imagined was the case with Bernie, was too smothered under years of this poisoned kind of living.

"I don't need his name to know he's better off alive than dead," Gina said through her teeth. A shudder rippled across her chest, Gina thought she sounded almost—just a little—like Nate. But she wasn't. She didn't beat babies or women. Didn't bully her way about the world. "Better off away from your husband than he is with him. And if you can't see that, you never deserved that baby."

"Hey, Lawyer Lady," Orula said, and Gina turned.

The back of Orula's hand caught Gina off guard and she stumbled back, dropped the fishing line and the E&J, and sent small quakes across the water. The sting of the root worker's slap made Gina's face buzz with heat as her throat swelled with remembered panic, a spilled tea, a backhand, a grand lie. Orula raised a pointed finger to Gina's face, like she was reading a book, and said, "You got one job here: hold my shit." Orula lifted her hand, palm up, like she was waiting for Gina to put something in her grasp. "Where's my shit, Gina?"

Beneath the water, Gina thought she felt the shape of the fishing line spool bump against her toe. Gina swallowed, tried to will the angry tears welling at the corners of her eye away. Why couldn't Orula see? Bernie was kissing the gun in her mouth. Willing to throw away this chance, willing to risk herself to make the wrong choice. Bernie was willing to pay the cost of staying beside that beastly man with her own son's life.

Orula turned to Bernie, and said, "I don't do refunds. And I'm not the one who's got to deal with Nate. You sure you want to do this?"

Bernie nodded, the boy's hands bouncing with the ferocity

of her movement.

Gina opened her mouth, but Orula's quick hand, that damned finger, held up stopped her.

"Ah-ah-ah. Hear that?" Orula asked. "You can head on home."

"I'm not leaving," Gina said. "I came to witness. I got a petition to ask."

"What? Your *baby* problem?" Orula said with a chuckle and Gina's cheeks went pink, her hands reflexively cupped the barely-there curve of her abdomen. "You wanna make sure that child don't spill your black beans, huh? Well," Orula continued. "Let me put it to rest. I'm gonna do that."

"What? Why not?"

"'Cuz I don't want to. Consider it a lesson."

"I'm not going anywhere," Gina said, trying to sound assured. "I'm not afraid of you, root worker."

You keep calling me that," Orula said, and walked past the floating Roses of Jericho to where Gina stood. "I don't know who told you that's what I am. Or if that's the rumor floating about that swamp-town. But, you way off. Ain't no magic or root work can do what I do."

She came close enough that Gina could smell the patchouli wafting from her hair, the lingering smell of something, jasmine maybe. Gina had that feeling again, that feeling of being in a corner, of being stalked by something more dangerous than her, but she fixed her jaw, squared her shoulders, and said, "What *can* you do? I haven't seen you do nothing but send a man time out. Is that why you won't? Because you can't?"

Orula laughed, a hearty, wheezy sound, and when she caught her breath, said, "You wanna see something I can do?"

Orula's eyes rolled back, her pupils vanishing so her eyes looked like twin moons in their sockets. Gina gasped and stepped back. As her foot hit the sandy lake bottom, something beneath the water grabbed hold, yanked her foot down so she stumbled. That hold pulled again, wrenched Gina down so that her right leg was buried up to the knee and the water rose to her collarbones. Gina tried to cry out, to push off with her other foot, but when she opened her mouth, another hard tug down and her head disappeared below the water, buried in the lakebed to her hips.

Gina tried to free her leg, tried to pry her way back to the surface. Her arms could reach the surface and she reached for Orula's, or maybe Bernie's, outstretched hand. But her hands found nothing, and only clawed at the air. Another tug down and Gina screamed, water filling her mouth, sand gripping around her waist.

Only when Orula's hand reached under the water, hooked under Gina's armpit, and pulled her up, did the sand finally release her. When she broke through the water, Gina gasped wildly, her breath turning to rough, wet coughs.

"Go home, Gina," Orula said, her voice flat and hard like a slap to the face.

Gina bit back her tears as she walked, dripping, up shore to the lot. She chanced a glance back down to the water but saw only silhouettes. One, she couldn't tell this far away if it was Orula or Bernie, held that boy.

She passed Nate and Bernie's car first. A beige Lincoln Continental. Easy enough to remember. Gina wondered how many silent car-rides that Lincoln had seen. Wondered if that gun in Bernie's mouth would go off when Nate found out she hadn't gone through with it. Stupid girl. Nate was slumped, snoring and open-mouthed behind in the drivers' seat and Gina took the opportunity to linger. To memorize that license plate. To put to memory Nate's physical description, the sight of that bruise around the baby's face.

Gina bit her lip. Climbed into her car. Shut the door. If she brought them this, the case was sure to be an easy win. And if they couldn't get him on this? *Well*, Gina thought as she cranked up the Hudson, *men like that? People like this? They always have something they were hiding; always had something you could pin them down for.* A man like that? He had it coming anyway. And

Bernie? Well. One day, Gina was sure, Bernie would thank her.

Gina rolled the car slow over the dirt road, still feeling the phantom grip of that thing, that force, around her leg. Pulling her down, into the earth. She held her breath. Gripped the wheel tight. Turned onto US-441.

Welcome

The unseasonably high winds blew the corner of the mat so the letters in the beginning were covered. Rheeta stood back from her front door to survey her newly inspired décor. She hadn't decorated the yard since the kids were in middle school, and now that the last of them was gone away from home, having something to focus on other than the loneliness of her empty nest spurred her excitement about mundane things like mats and garden accessories.

She bent down to straighten the "Welcome" mat so that it read more than "come." Rheeta had always teased the kids that she never put out a mat before, so their friends couldn't read and interpret it to mean they were supposed to come to their house every day. "Until I can find a "Please bring food—starving teens" mat, I'll keep using the generic ones without any messages."

Her babies, birthed and found, had known she was joking because all the friends had always ended up in Rheeta's game room to hang out anyway. Eating her out of house and home. Sometimes breaking things that had to be replaced. Definitely harassing poor old Harry, their long suffering dog.

In the end, it was all in good fun. She missed the chaos of a house full of rambunctious teens running around with a small elephant masquerading as a dog.

Her Louis had often been right in the middle of the disarray, introducing the next generation to the virtues of old school Hip-Hop and jigsaw puzzles. He lit up when he was able to provide anything for the kids and their friends. And for Rheeta. That husband of hers had an impeccable work ethic that had driven her nuts sometimes, but mostly kept her worried for him.

That worry came to pass when he suffered a heart attack in the warehouse he supervised and died instantly. Rheeta always thanked goodness he hadn't suffered or lingered. He would have hated wasting away, with her having to care for him in a sick bed. The way he went was the way he would have wanted. And her last memory of him before the closed casket ceremony was of virility, him unfolding his large frame from their bed that morning, kissing her on the forehead.

Her smile faltered a bit. A part of her hoped that maybe someone *would* see the sign on her doorstep and come visit with her for a little while.

The kids had scattered in the four years since Louis passed and Rheeta wouldn't have had it any other way. She'd often joked with her husband that they were supposed to raise their kids to leave them, to live independent lives. Louis would jump up and down in a faux victory dance and exclaim, "Well, hot dog! We're on our way to a retirement filled with lazy days and good food nobody else will eat before we can get to it."

She'd swat at him playfully. "As if you're ever going to retire."

He'd kiss her. "Of course I will. Then we can spend forever together, doing nothing except whatever we want."

Their forever never came, and now Rheeta faced her autumn and winter years all alone. She folded her arms across her torso against the chill in the air that blew the leaves in the yard up into a swirl. The mat folded over again. Come.

The wind blew her front door wide open and it banged on the wall, startling her. She stepped over the mat, half-heartedly trying to move it back into place before giving up in the onslaught of the kick in the air. She closed the door and locked it, standing in the foyer of her family home.

Memories washed over her. Of her and Louis touring the inventory home when she was pregnant with their daughter, their third child, wondering if they would ever grow into the enormous space of five bedrooms and three and a half baths. Of bringing the baby home. Finding out she was already pregnant with the last child at the baby's first birthday party that they held in the yard. It was baby number last who covered the foyer wall with little brown paint handprints. The massive formal dining room table sat solitary in the room that used to be alive with fancy family meals Rheeta insisted on cooking regularly so they could eat together. The slight sprinkling of dust reminded her to clean soon.

The scent of Louis' cologne assaulted her nose and she swooned against the stained glass center of the door. She had first bought it for him when they visited Cabo years ago, and she smelled it as they walked through the airport on the way to the resort.

"You spoil me, sweet wife of mine." His white teeth beamed from between those sensuous, thick lips that Rheeta loved.

"It's selfish, really. Now I have an excuse to get close to you all the time so I can smell you."

"You never need an excuse."

The scent enveloped her. She could feel his presence around her and her heart fluttered. What she wouldn't give to be held by him once again.

The familiarity faded and she was once again in her lonely reality in a giant, empty house. Needing solace, she decided it was the perfect evening for a cup of tea before bed.

She turned the porch light on. Humming to lift her spirits, she went into the large kitchen she'd always loved and put the teakettle on the stove, laughing as she put a mug on the counter next to it.

Her oldest daughter had bought her one of those fancy coffee makers that heated water and poured it through little plastic pods. "Ma, it's faster and the tea tastes just as good."

It might be faster, but the tea did not taste as good. She used the machine whenever one of the kids decided to visit, which wasn't very often. Otherwise, it sat alone on the counter as she continued to use her old, stainless steel teapot on the stove.

Rheeta wiped down the space around the sink and washed the lone glass nestled inside. She then busied herself with putting it and the scant few dishes in the rack up into the cabinets.

Something large brushed against her legs and she grasped the counter to regain her balance. Harry used to love running between her and the counters in the kitchen, as if he were a small dog that could easily fit into small spaces.

He wasn't small at all, weighing in at around one hundred pounds. She felt the familiar sensation again, and tears welled up in her eyes. She missed Harry almost as much as she missed Louis. Her husband had gifted him to her one Christmas and her special boy had mourned the loss of their Louis together. Harry was already elderly but she knew he had held on to help her as much as he could.

Finding him dead at the foot of her bed had almost destroyed her. He had gone peacefully, wrapped up in one of Louis' favorite blankets. It was a befitting end to a valiant companion who had put up with their kids because he loved her and Louis. She was sure he had loved the kids, too, but he was her boy. She lifted her eyes toward the mantle on the fireplace where both his and Louis' urns sat, in spots of honor, where she could keep them around.

A slight sound to her side in the kitchen caught her attention. She turned around and gasped. The mug she'd placed beside the stove was filled with steaming water.

Rheeta hadn't filled the cup. The teapot hadn't even gone off. The water she could see through the glass top as she walked closer popped sporadically with the faintest beginnings of a boil that hadn't yet flourished.

She didn't want tea anymore.

She turned the fire off. Unable to bring herself to touch the mug to dump and wash it, she left it sitting where it was.

She turned and walked slowly into the living room to watch television. She sat down in the recliner she had inherited upon Louis' death and sighed. She debated raising her feet, thinking of her grandmother who always insisted that her feet stay on the floor. *Feet wasn't meant to be propped up like that. Makes a body lazy.* Granny's voice whispered in her ear and Rheeta sat straight up.

The wide screen of the television came on, stunning Rheeta. Her eyes searched frantically for the remote control so she could turn it off. Before she could find it, the television screen went blank again.

Rheeta could hear a faint hum, picking up the tune she was humming to herself in the kitchen. The tone was ominous. That wasn't her Louis. Or Granny. Definitely not Harry. Not waiting around to hear it get louder or become identifiable, she walked as quickly as she dared to her bedroom and slammed the door shut. One of the hardest things about growing older was not being able to make your body do the things you wanted it to do, and as badly as she wanted to break into a run, she knew it to be unsafe while she was at home alone. Always alone.

She waited long moments with her back against the bedroom door, rationalizing what had happened.

The television was old. Maybe it had a short. She probably just forgot she had already poured the water into her mug. The water in the kettle was hotter than she thought. She was thinking of her dead beloveds and they had come to comfort her. They hadn't meant to scare her. They loved her. And wanted her to know they were still with her.

A loud crash and the sound of breaking ceramic came from the direction of the kitchen and Rheeta eased away from the door, deeper into her bedroom. Another door slammed somewhere else in the house. Something rustled in the hallway outside her bedroom door. Multiple sets of footsteps ran up, closer. Closer. They stopped right outside the door.

Silence.

Rheeta trembled and waited for the noise to start up again. She thought of calling one of the kids to come over but embarrassment stopped her. They would tell her she was imagining things. And start up about her selling the house, again. In that moment, she knew they were probably right. The house was too much for her alone. She didn't need all the space. She'd contact a realtor first thing in the morning.

She didn't call anyone right then. She stood in her bedroom with her hands pressed over her mouth, willing herself to breathing while the destruction of her house continued behind the door.

After the longest time, she realized whatever was happening might be over. Rheeta went into her bathroom and brushed her teeth with shaky hands. She always showered in the evenings or took a long bath. She didn't do either and instead pulled on her nightgown and burrowed underneath her covers. Sleep came more easily than it usually did and Rheeta didn't have time to wonder how she could sleep in the middle of the madness over-taking her. She welcomed the slumber.

Three loud knocks pounded on her bedroom door. Rheeta couldn't shake the cover of sleep and mumbled.

"Come in."

The kids always waited until she was deep into sleep to come asking for stuff in the middle of the night.

The door to her bedroom slammed opened. Rheeta sat up, fully awake.

The kids weren't at home anymore. She was alone.

Flurries of whispers met her ears as she sat with her back pressed against her headboard, mouth agape. She strained to see in the darkness.

Not alone.

Shadows played against the wall where her alarm clock shone dimly. Rheeta could make out human forms filling her bedroom, surrounding her. The temperature dropped.

Thank you.

Weights landed on her bed in multiple spots. She screamed and couldn't untangle herself from the blanket.

We come.

Rheeta felt hands pressing her down, into the bed, icy ten-drils surrounding her as her lungs constricted with her breath leaving.

We are welcome.

Flower Girl

There was a one-of-a-kind girl, exceptional. She was obsessed with flowers, for reasons none of her relatives could understand. She came from a long line of bakers, you see. Flour (not flowers) was the life of their line. But man cannot live on bread alone. Unbeknownst to them, God had placed a new thing in the soul of the girl, yet they did not know it. So it was a mystery why she studied stems and petals ardently, as religion. And if she would have continued to navigate the narrow path determined long before her birth, untethered by the prison of tradition or sentenced to its death row of domesticity, she would have discovered—as she was meant to discover—the two flowers which, if cross-pollinated, would unify into a super-plant, spawning a mystical new fruit with infinite uses, mundane, practical and divine.

If only someone told her how important it was to keep busy in her little garden; that a tough skinned acorn of persistence could yield an oak tree for the world. But you know how it goes; she fell in love.

Her man nicknamed her Bug, since she was always on her back for him, with her legs stuck up in the air. Then she graduated from her back to her knees, squatting, birthing, washing, scrubbing, while the babies bloomed one after the other, like a pot of devil's ivy, until the dinner table was full and the tasks sisyphean. At first, when there was a pause in the din, she would sneak away and tend to her blossoms. But each time her focus narrowed to the point of concentration, a child would come from somewhere and rip-whine-ruin, or her man would clear his throat, rub his belly and sniff the air, and so on.

No one spied the rope burns from her personal tug of war.

Eventually weeds overtook the garden. The Mother drowned her hands in flour, resigned to make dough.

Like all God's chosen, the Mother had a growing hand. She was the sunshine of her family's life, beaming with devotion, warming them with the suppressed light of her obedient soul. Whatever she touched, improved. Whether in flavor, quality or comfort. She feathered her nest, even if she had to pluck her own hair to do it. But then years later, subtle as a cataract film, Mother's light clouded over. One day someone—it could have been a neighbor, lover, child—said (alarmed), *Mother, you don't look well.* They took her to lie down. Her cheeks were sunken, her collarbones sharp. Her dress hung, shapeless and embarrassingly flat. And for weeks now, her fingers had given up their clockwork touch that polished and shone the world. There were crumbs in the corners and food in the drain. Stains on the bedspread. Dust in the air.

They begged Mother to *Get well soon,* and then grumbled among themselves about who would do all that she had done. But Mother got worse. She grew delirious, then comatose. In her sleep, she dreamed a doctor that no one called appeared at the door. His specialty was tragic irony. You see, the only medicine that could have saved Mother would have come from the fruit of the cross-pollinated superplant that she accidentally never invented. Remember? How her arms shook with exhaustion whenever she tried to carve out the time? How her tools grew dull? How she lost the point?

In her haze, it dawned that what she'd failed to do would remain undone, for gifts are as singular as thumbprints. She dreamed the doctor brought a bouquet for the occasion.

"One must leave gifts at the altar," he said, though he was visibly perplexed that his gift was the only one. Her own lover, children, neighbors, never even thought of it, even after all Mother had done.

"You know how much she needs them, yes?" the doctor asked.

"Needs...flowers?" her family repeated, incredulous. *Maybe long, long ago.* Pictures of grandchildren eating perfect pies were shoved in the doctor's face. *This is what she needs now. This is all that matters.* They eyed him suspiciously for causing trouble. *How did he hear about Mother's sickness, anyway?* they wondered aloud.

The doctor waved away their questions. He focused only on the sick bed thrown together in the corner of the room. Then Mother saw herself lying there rocking back and forth underneath a pile of covers, her body's outline no bigger than a child's. The doctor reached over and raised the blinds just above her pallet, and Mother turned her pinched face toward one last merciful ray of sun.

Then she lay still.

***

She knew she dreamed, yet seeing herself on the bed made her feel uneasy. She couldn't understand why she was dreaming from outside of her body. Not that she particularly wanted to be inside her body, either. She had not felt at home inside herself for a long, long time. She watched as the doctor sat on the edge of her bed and laid a gentle hand on her back. He pulled up her covers and tucked them around her.

"Mother," the doctor said softly.

She stared at the pair, doctor and patient, curious whether the figure on the bed would respond. But then the doctor hung his head, shifted his gaze and looked right at her, at the real Mother watching from the corner of the room. They locked eyes and she remembered. Oh! This was no dream! He was no doctor. He was her very own Self, come to claim her. Mother looked down and saw she'd shed her skin and limbs, was back to being a shimmer of gold ink on the page of infinity. The man rose from the sick bed and stepped into the black, joining her in the bosom of the All. Behind them, the breathing world rolled shut like a scroll, taking her tired old body with it.

"Praise the Stars for bringing me home," she said.

Indeed, agreed her Soul. *Living is hard and dying ain't easy.*

But she'd already forgotten she'd ever lived or died. It seemed she'd always been here, hovering over the fathomless. If remembering a dream when you wake up is difficult, remembering awake when you dream up is nearly impossible.

Does anything remain? her Soul was obligated to ask.

She was quiet for a moment. Or a lifetime. Finally, a ripple of recognition rose from her interminable depths and she was rocked with wave after wave of mourning. "Oh my Soul," she cried out, "how many do I have?"

How many what? he asked, knowing but pretending not to know. He'd rather she didn't remember them. Their demands made hell on earth.

"My babies," she whimpered.

An untold number, her Soul confessed. *We've returned infinite times. We almost always make more. I've lost track.*

"We've been the grandmother & the newborn," she said.

Perpetually, her Soul agreed.

"Well. They need us," she announced, choosing again the ways of the World.

At the thought of returning, her Soul despaired. He was strong, but not invincible. *No*, he cried. *We've given them enough! Love in that place is slavery! They use your heart...*

"Against you," she finished, another dark click of memory puzzling into place.

Is that enough? Her soul was desperate. He had reached the limits of his limitlessness.

She was quiet for a millennia. It was a lot to think about. Finally, she said, "Yes."

Yes, what?

"Yes. It is enough."

Enough for what? he persisted. He needed to hear her say it.

"Enough to... let the dead bury the dead."

An opening appeared as a golden slit in the cosmos; an emerald path spilled from its depths. She had uttered the key words that unlocked the one true door. They were light enough to enter since the world was no longer a weight. She finally understood there was no sweeter mercy than relief, no greater goal than to set your burden down. For the first time in forever, it was well with her Soul.

***

Someone finally thought to check on Mother. The one who checked was traumatized to find Mother had breathed her last. Not even her ghost remained. There was great sadness and much wailing from the shock of her departure. And then her bones were *gathered to her people,* as is written in the Good Book. There is a proverb that says a house does not rest on the ground, it rests on a woman. So the family mourned the loss of their foundation and searched for someone willing to lie down so they could rebuild.

Naturally, they thought of Oldest Daughter. She was young, but old enough to gather the crumbs from the sink, dust the corners, inherit the heft and weight of dough. She was found in her usual place, with her head in a book, a pen in her hand. You see, there was a new kind of idea the Good Lord wanted to put on the earth, about the power of language over the tongue of life's circumstance. The girl was wise beyond her years. She had what they called an old soul and for good reason: there was an epidemic of the newly dead refusing to return and guide the living. No matter how much ancestor money, or candles, incense, flasks and cigars were heaped upon the altars, no matter how many petitions buried or incantations moaned, none of the prayers were heard. The situation grew dire, for now it was up to the living to guide themselves. And don't run off thinking God abandoned His creation either, because that ain't it. The truth is people have always had trouble hearing the Lord because He speaks in thunder and lightning, and folks tremble themselves to death before He's done clearing His throat. That's why the ancestors went between, to carry the prayers up and bring the answers down. But over time, their knees creaked into stardust and their weary Souls cried out. *Mercy*, they begged. *Surrender*. So the Most High began seeding wise youth among his people, with the answers born inside. They knew how to hit a straight lick with a crooked stick. How to make a way out of no way. How to be still & know. Even so, the road is broad and the gate is wide. Many are called. But few are chosen.

Suddenly, Oldest Daughter became aware of her father and another young man behind her, the shadows of their hungry bellies blocking the sun. She had snuck long glances at the young man before, but seeing him close up doubled her heartbeat. He was near enough to touch. Involuntarily, an image arose in her mind of his long, hard body stretched against hers. She saw herself holding tightly to his neck as he rocked her and filled her with life's joy. Her left ankle twitched, wanting to throw itself in the air. She sensed that her father meant for her to marry this man. She did not object.

"It's time to put that away now," her father said, gesturing toward her papers. He took her pen out of her hand, shoved it irretrievably in his pocket, fished a potato peeler from its depths. "Here," he instructed, his stomach growling. "There's more important things to do."

Oldest Daughter gathered her things and followed them, free and willing—until she spied the sunset, a masterpiece of rose and gold, preening for a tribute in stanzas and verse. She longed to cool off at the creek, lie down with the crickets and catch the lightning bug poem flashing across her mind. But Daddy sensed her resistance and quickened his stride. Oldest Daughter lamented, but did not halt her step. For Mother raised her properly, that is, to put herself aside. *Be a good girl.*

The poem ran off to find somebody who would take it seriously.

The Favor

"You know," Shawna said between grunts and strained breathing, "he's exactly as heavy as he looked."

No response. Just the rhythmic, alternating crunch of dead leaves under Carrie's boots as they walked through the woods. Shawna watched the frame of Carrie's body a few steps ahead of her own in the darkness. Carrie's grip on the flashlight showed how much her hands were shaking. Shawna guessed the tremble wasn't just because of the crisp autumn breeze that pushed against their jackets.

Shawna joked, "Nothing? You got nothing to say?"

"Shut up, this isn't funny," Carrie snapped without turning around.

Shawna dropped the rope in protest. Behind her, an area rug tightly wound but oddly shaped, hit the ground. The leaves underneath it screamed and echoed in the forest's night air. "That's it. I'm done," she said abruptly, as she squeezed the tip of the glove on her middle finger to remove it from her hand.

Carrie whipped around and the beam of light followed, cutting across Shawna's torso and causing the shovels strapped to Carrie's back to clank together. "Wait, no," she pleaded, holding out her other hand. "I'm sorry. Please."

"I don't have to be out here," Shawna hissed through gritted teeth. "Remember? You called me."

"I know." Carrie took a step forward with her hand still outstretched as though Shawna was a wild animal in need of a calming presence. "Please. I'm sorry. I'm just...I'm so scared."

"Well, so am I, but you're not helping."

Carrie's big brown eyes began to twinkle through a welled-up wall of tears.

Shawna took a deep resigned breath and reassured, "It's gonna be okay, all right? We got this."

Carrie shifted her weight from one foot to another and looked more like a nervous child than a thirty-three year old woman. "Are you sure?"

"We don't really have any other choice now, do we?" Shawna slapped Carrie's upper back. "Come on. Keep walking."

"Do you need help with...?" Carrie's nodded toward their cargo.

They surveyed the mesh underbelly that, by now, had gathered dirt and blades of dead grass. It was two rolls deep, bulging in the middle and bound with cables that hooked together, hugging it close. The rope, which looped under the cable, snaked along the mesh and draped over the opening. Cocking her head to the side gave Shawna the right angle to see the top of a head, full of short brunette hair matted with dried blood.

"Nah," she replied. "You need to stay in front with the light and make sure we're going the right way. How close are we?"

Carrie traced the ground with her light. Off to their left buried in debris, a small stone angel sat cradled in gnarled roots peeking out of the dirt. She approached and examined it under the spotlight. Turning back to Shawna, "This means we're close. A hundred more yards maybe?"

"I don't know how far that is," Shawna confessed flatly. She leaned down, grabbed the rope, hoisted it back over her shoulder, and continued to drag the carpet through the leaves.

"Let's just keep going this way." Carrie pointed the light between two trees, leaving the angel in the dead foliage.

The wind hollowed and Shawna noticed the forest getting thicker every few paces. At her pull, the carpet pushed its way through fallen sticks and rubbed against tree trunks through Carrie's path. Despite the ambient noise, the silence between them made her even more uncomfortable than she already was.

"Your uncle owns all this?"

"Yeah, from where we parked to the railroad tracks."

"Does he know we're out here?"

Carrie's steps seemed to slow. "He passed away last year. He left it to my cousin Dee, but she's not home. And she never ventures out this far anyway."

They walked side by side now with only the light in front of them. Shawna looked over at her friend a couple of times to gauge how she was feeling. Her profile was pensive. Ashen trails cut through the caramel colored foundation on her cheeks, full lips pursed together beneath a shining layer of pink gloss, still shone with lip gloss, forcing exhales out of her nose. Her hair collected under a black Yankee ball cap, a long braid bounced against her puffy vest with every step. Always the pretty one even when you're scared shitless, Shawna thought and looked away before she was caught staring.

Carrie didn't notice. Her gaze was transfixed on the ground just a few feet ahead of her. "I used to play out here all the time when I was a kid. It was perfect for hide-and-seek." An awkward laugh bubbled up from her throat. "My friends didn't want to play with me after a while because I was so good at it."

She tilted the light up to show more trees clustered together into a maze ahead of them. She went on, "Then when I got older, this became my quiet place. It's really pretty in the spring when everything is in full bloom."

Shawna's eyes surveyed what little she could see in the dark and had a hard time imagining the woods being beautiful. At that moment, it seemed more like the setting for a Grimm's Fairytale or the *Blair Witch Project*. She shuddered and pushed the thoughts out of her mind. "Never took you for a country girl," she said, changing the subject.

"You never came home with me on breaks." One corner of her mouth curled into a half smile. "I asked every Spring and Fall."

"And what would I say?" Shawna couldn't help but crack a smile too.

"'Why would I leave the best city in the world?'" They recited in unison, laughing lightly at Carrie dropping an octave to match Shawna's feminine, yet baritone voice.

"But why would I? It was New York, baby!" Shawna waved a hand as if they were in the city marveling at the hustle and bustle. Her hand came back down on the rope with a slap that hurt underneath the glove, but she didn't care. The memory of their senior year at NYU kept her warm and almost happy in the moment. "Breaks were the only time I could get out of the books and have some fun."

"You didn't have to study so hard."

"I did if I wanted to keep my scholarship. I wasn't just about being good at Judo. They cared about my grades too."

"God," Carrie said between chuckles. "Your Judo uniform used to smell so bad after competition."

"For the last time, it's called a judogi," Shawna corrected warmly, "and I still resent you making me put it out in the hall."

"Remember when I threw it out the door, and it hit Taraji, and she got in my face about it?"

Shawna nodded. "She was about to kick your ass. You're lucky I was there." She adjusted her cotton beanie over her short cut and a few black coils peaked out from the edges.

Carrie admired Shawna's dark skin and her natural-but-always-got-mistaken-for-falsies lashes that curled up to her eyebrows. Shawna, the cool one, the strong one, the one who wasn't afraid to get a septum piercing and a tattoo on the same day. Carrie went with her but chickened out on both opportunities, which became the perfect metaphor for their friendship.

"I'm glad you're here now," she said, still crunching leaves under her feet with each step.

"You better be." Shawna let the rope fall again in exhaustion and bent over. "Fuck."

"Ugh, I'm sorry. Here. Let's take a break."

Carrie slid the makeshift harness holding the shovels off her back and laid them down the ground. She turned off the flashlight. Darkness enveloping, they sat on the rug that had little give underneath them. Carrie's legs were pinned together, leaning to the side as though she wore a dress and needed to stay "lady-like."

Shawna spread wide, resting her forearms on the tops of her thighs, and caught her breath. Her hands ached so she let them dangle down over her knees. She looked up and the canopy of trees broke, showing just enough sky for her to see a collection of stars.

"Since we're reminiscin' and all," Shawna said between exhales, "can we speed up to the more recent past?

"What do you mean?"

"Really?" Shawna scoffed. "I haven't heard from you in months."

"I know... but we do that sometimes." Carrie shrugged. "We go a few months without talking."

"Not like this," Shawna said, the toe of her own boot drawing a circle in the dirt.

"I don't remember that last conversation going so well."

"'Cause you had something to say about Rita."

Carrie leaned forward, switching her legs to her other side, away from Shawna. "Rita," she repeated.

"If it makes you feel any better, we broke up."

Carrie was grateful Shawna couldn't see her eyes widen at the news. "Oh."

"Don't act surprised."

"I'm not. I'm just—"

"Just nothing. You never liked her. And you saw straight through her bullshit. It just...took me a little longer."

The wind blew through the space between them. Carrie burrowed her hands between her thighs for warmth

"I'm sorry," Carrie finally said.

"Don't be. You called it. She was a liar and a narcissist. I've been glad she's gone." Shawna grabbed her fingers and pushed down to crack her knuckles. "It just didn't feel good hearing you shit all over our relationship and you'd just gotten married... like you were doing any better."

Carrie lifted her hands back up and twisted the engagement ring stacked on top of her wedding band around her slim finger. "I didn't mean to. Rita was just so obviously not the right person for you."

"And you said that. Actually you said that a lot. About her and me." Shawna paused. "'Willing victim'...yeah, that's what you called me. "

"I know." Carried scooted herself forward a bit on her uneven seat.

It wasn't a comfortable seat for an even more uncomfortable conversation.

Shawna waited a beat before breaking the tension. "You know she took the lightbulbs."

A laugh burst through Carrie as though it was dying to get out. "What?"

"That bitch took all my lightbulbs," Shawna snorted. "I once called her my light when we first got serious, so when she left, she said she was taking her light with her."

They both cackled, but hushed when it echoed against the nature sounds of the forest.

"God, she was crazy," Carrie said.

"Yeah, truth, I'm glad she's gone. I had to go buy out an aisle of the Lowe's in Brooklyn, but still. Glad she's gone."

"We should have celebrated."

"We would have if you'd answered a text afterwards."

Carrie pretended to recall with a dramatic cock of her head. "Uh, no, it was you not answering my phone calls. I called you twice."

Shawna shook her head. "I couldn't talk to you. I was embarrassed and I was still mad. Then, I don't know. Everything got weird. But you're right, we should have celebrated. There's still time."

Carrie fell silent. Was there time? The wind died down and her sniffles resounded in the darkness.

Shawna reached out and massaged her shoulder.

"Carrie, it was an accident."

"It was an accident," Carrie repeated, taking another big, wet inhale." I should have called the—"

"No," Shawna snapped, giving Carrie's shoulder a pinch that

shook her into focus. "What did I say? The ambulance and the cops would have shown up. What do you think they'd do seeing you with a white boy face down on the living room floor? You know how that looks."

Carried nodded. "I know. We gotta do this."

"Yes." Shawna let go of her. "Now, tell me we're getting closer. Is a hundred yards up yet?"

Carrie pressed the button on the flashlight, allowing the beam to stretch back out in front of them. She flipped it in her hand so it was pointing straight down, and she cleared some dead leaves away with her foot. "Oh wait, I think this is good." She stood and did a 360-degree turn. Nodded vigorously, she declared, "Yeah, we're here."

"Good," Shawna said, getting up with a slap to her legs.

"Let's clear out this area right here." Carrie swiped her foot along the ground.

They moved the fallen leaves enough to find an oval shape that was just long and wide enough. Carrie let the flashlight rest on the ground to provide light for their space. When they were ready, they picked up the shovels and started digging. Shawna awkwardly held hers too high on the handle, taking shallow scoops out of the ground.

Carrie scoffed, "Who taught you how to dig? Damn, you city girls..."

"Oh, you a landscaping expert now?"

Carrie answered by stabbing the head of the shovel into the earth, pushing it deeper with her rubber soles. "Lemme show you." She pulled back on the handle and heaved a mound of dirt off to the side with a grunt.

Impressed, Shawna didn't hide her smirk. "Okay then," was her only reply and she used what strength she had left to follow suit.

They shoveled without talking, only their short groans of effort passing back and forth with every scoop.

"This looks so much easier on TV."

"They usually skip past this part," Carried explained. "Digging any kind of hole takes a while... especially one this deep."

Shawna paused, resting her hands on the tip of the erect handle. "Well, since we got time..."

Carrie flung another shovel-full out of the ankle-deep crevice that was forming. "Yeah?"

"What happened when you left me and Rita that summer?"

Carrie shrugged. "We were smack in the middle of that damned renovation on our new house, which in hindsight, was a mistake as newlyweds."

"Why?" Shawna started digging again.

"You've never worked on a place before. It's stressful. Every time we turned around, something else needed to be done. You tear down this wall and find six more problems. It got expensive. So we started our entire marriage already arguing over money."

"I liked your house. I mean, what little of it I saw on Instagram."

"Yeah, it looks good now. That took a year off our life to get it livable. By then, some of the damage was done. We'd had so many blow-outs. Already said some regrettable things to each other."

"I didn't know you weren't getting along."

Two fingers still wrapped around the shovel handle, Carrie turned up her hands as though weighing options. "It wasn't as bad as how my parents used to get when they were about to separate. And I think that's what I had in mind. Like, if Mom and Daddy could hold it together, we'll be fine. We haven't had the cops called on us, so..."

"Where would we be without our parents' shitty marriages setting the bar so low," Shawna chuckled darkly.

"Yeah," Carrie agreed and dug another divot in the dirt. "But things did get better. They were good for a while. Then we started trying to get pregnant, and it was like a reno all over again. This time it was my body all busted and needed repair."

Shawna stopped and shoved the shovel into the ground.

"Don't say that. You know that's not true."

"I know," Carrie said. "But that's how it felt. My uterus didn't work." She paused, staring down at the ground. "After two miscarriages—and the last one was so bad—I said I didn't want to keep going. He said he was fine with it but I knew he wasn't. He was never okay not being a dad."

"I'm not an expert on men, but I hear that's unusual."

Carrie's gaze turned to his encased body and sighed. "Some guys, after they finally settle down, really want to be dads. Devin was that guy."

Shawna wiggled the shovel out of the ground and dug again. "So he resented you?"

"Felt like it. I mean, he never said he resented me, but you can just feel that shit, you know? Like everything else we did after that was never as good as it could be because we weren't a family."

They kept digging. Occasionally their shovels would hit each other on the way up and one of them would take a step back.

Shawna noticed Carrie kept looking back at the hole's intended occupant, and she pushed away the thought that Devin might still be alive and slip out of sight. That only happens in the movies, Shawna dismissed, although she was painfully aware of how the current situation looked.

By the time the ground was level with their hips, Carrie took a breather, setting the shovel against the newly formed wall that surrounded them. She leaned back, trying to keep her braid out of the dirt.

Shawna took her cue to do the same, except she tossed the shovel out of the hole and lifted herself up so she could sit on the edge. Brushing specks of old grass off her jeans, Shawna spoke up, "So, this morning—"

"Shaw, please," Carrie groaned, pulling the lid of her ball cap down to shield her eyes. "I can't."

"You got me out here in the middle of nowhere with your dead husband in a piece of carpet," Shawna gestured toward him. "And you still haven't told me what happened."

Carrie looked around nervously but Shawna's stare never lifted.

"Tell me," Shawna said pointedly.

Carrie's heart pounded through her chest. She leaned off the wall, grabbed the shovel, and pushed the head in and out of the earth to distract herself. After a hard swallow, she began. "Everything was fine. I mean, we'd been fighting a little, but we followed up with our usual I'm sorry texts. He went to the gym and he must have hit it too hard, because when he came home, he was all sweaty—like more than usual. We talked for a bit in the living room, but then we were back at it arguing again. He got all hot in the face and it was like he couldn't catch his breath between yelling at me." She paused. "It kept getting heated and he shoved me so I shoved him back."

Shawna resisted saying, *That's my girl.*

"But he lost his balance and fell. Hit the coffee table on the way down. It was this freak thing," she began to sob. "He was bleeding all over the place and then he grabbed his chest—like he was having a heart attack or something. I ran to grab some towels to stop the bleeding, and we didn't have any because I was doing laundry. So I had to go down to the laundry room in the basement, but when I came back...he wasn't moving."

"You didn't do this," Shawna reiterated, gripping the ledge of her perch to keep her anger at bay. "It was an accident."

"But I ran," Carrie wailed. "I was in shock and I just left the house. I went to Starbucks. I walked around the mall. I-I-I didn't know what to do so I just left him there on the floor to bleed out." She took a deep breath and finally looked up at Shawna. "That's—"

"That's when you called me," Shawna finished.

Carrie nodded.

"He wasn't a bad man," Carrie added, her voice gravel-thick trying to return to normal. "We were just in a bad spot."

"I know." Shawna hopped down in a leap that brought her within reach of Carrie for a tight hug.

Carrie buried her face in Shawna's neck and limply held on

as more tears flowed.

Shawna cooed, "Shhh. It's gonna be okay."

Carrie lifted her head and they were face to face.

Shawna cupped Carrie's wet cheek with her hand. "We will fix this," she assured. She was so close that her gaze moved between Carrie's big brown eyes but she only let it bounce down to her lips once. Shawna's own mouth grimaced in painful frustration. *If anyone else had called me this morning–anyone else but you...* her thoughts trailed off.

A gust of wind ripped through their bodies and the flashlight spun around, draping them in darkness.

"Oh shit!" Carrie broke out of their embrace to jump out of the hole and grab their only source of visibility. "We gotta hurry this up."

"Yeah," Shawna agreed, brushing a few leaves off her shovel. "I don't wanna be out here any longer than we have to. This place gives me the creeps."

The air got colder the more they dug, but they still began sweating under their layers of clothes. Shawna's back ached with every heave of the shovel, but she wouldn't let herself stop especially once it looked like they were getting close.

"Hold on," Carrie said breathlessly. "I think we got it. This is deep enough. We don't want to make this so deep we can't get out."

Shawna leaned up to see the edge was now chest level. She hoisted herself out and lent Carrie a hand, pulling her out.

"Now this guy," Carrie muttered, looking at the rug that thankfully hadn't moved all night.

They walked over to it and Shawna untied the cables and the rope, then bent down to shift it over to the hole with her hands. When it reached the edge, Shawna stood up and Carrie came to her side.

"And we still gotta cover him back up," Shawna said bitterly.

"That's the easier part," Carrie replied.

They stood over the tube of carpet in silence. The wind whistled past their faces and Carrie pulled a few stray strands of hair from her face, never breaking her glare. She whispered something that Shawna couldn't make out and snapped her foot out in a kick that sent the it rolling forward and unraveling quickly.

"Carrie! Wait!" Shawna's arms jetted out, but it wasn't fast enough. Devin's stiff lifeless body fell into the pit without his covering. His feet clumsily tipped the flashlight into the hole with him.

"Oh shit," Carrie mumbled.

"It can't be good that he's down there like that. Aren't bugs or animals or something gonna sniff him out?" Carrie gave her a confused look and Shawna bellowed, "What? Are you some kind of true crime expert?"

"This is fucked." Carried walked away, putting her hands on top of her head, elbows splayed in opposite directions. "We're fucked. What do we do?" Half of it lay on the ground while the rest draped over the grave's edge down toward the body.

Shawna's hand covered her mouth as she calculated their next move. "Maybe," she finally said. "We take it with us and drop it in a lake or something."

"The nearest lake that's that kinda deep is like two hours away."

"Well, what's your idea then?"

Carrie came back to Shawna's side. "Let's put it in the hole too."

Out of options, Shawna groaned, "Okay."

"The flashlight though. We still need it," Carrie said. They met each other's gaze, hoping the other would retrieve it.

Shawna could tell Carrie's eyes were begging her to do it. "Fine," she sighed.

Devin's body stretched the length of the hole, so when she jumped in, she toppled unsteadily onto his legs. She reached down and grabbed the flashlight that fell head first into the dirt. When she lifted it up, the beam moved along his body. She re-called that she hadn't seen Devin in person since the wedding. Only Instagram pictures existed of him in her mind. Even that day, Devin was firmly rolled up in the carpet before Shawna arrived to the house. It felt like an awkward reunion.

Her foot kept slipping on his smooth gray trousers. His hands covered his pelvic area with his wrists against a brown belt Shawna instantly recognized as Armani. His white collared shirt, though speckled with blood, still managed to look crisp and pressed. Shawna's pulse began to race as her eyes darted down to Devin's feet. The laces of his leather shoes were still tied.

"Carrie?" she asked softly, her eyes glued to the well-dressed corpse.

No response. Her gaze shot up but Carrie had moved to the opposite end of the pit. Her fist was tight around the shovel handle as she propped it up. Her ball cap created a canopy over her eyes that were sharp as slits and her face seemed harder than before.

"What?" Carrie's voice was low, but not in a playful way like before. Her tone was almost harsh.

Shawna could hardly get the words out. "I thought...I thought you said Devin came home from the gym."

Carrie's eyes widened and her face softened. "He did." Her voice bouncing unusually high and light. "He, uh, he came home from the gym, then he, um, he changed. He showered and he changed clothes."

Shawna eyed the body again. "Into a suit?"

"He was going to work," Carrie said matter-of-factly, a slight tilt to her head.

"Okay." Shawna felt weak. She put the flashlight back on the ground. She palmed the ground with both hands just past the edge to pull herself out, but her arms went numb with fear.

Carrie moved slowly, dragging the shovel along to meet Shawna at the other end, eventually standing over her.

Shawna looked up to see Carrie gently kick the flashlight away from them. It rolled around so the beam pointed back into the woods. In what little light they had, Shawna saw Carrie's frame crouch down closer to her, still holding on to the shovel.

Carrie dipped her chin, her voice back in that low, deadly serious tone. "It was an accident, Shaw."

The words were like a chokehold on Shawna's throat and she squeaked her friend's name hoarsely.

Carrie repeated, "He fell. It was an accident...." She gave her a vacant smile. "Just like you said." She put out her hand. "Now, can I help you out of there?"

Shawna grabbed Carrie by the forearm and used her other hand on the ground to get out. When Shawna was steady on her feet, Carrie picked up the flashlight, walked over to the rug and pushed the rest of it in. Without a word, Carrie started filling the hole back in.

Shawna stared at her friend. The sweet one. The one who needed protecting.

Carrie caught her gaze. "Are you gonna help me or not?"

Shawna gulped what little saliva she had left in her dry mouth. She eyed the shovel that was pitched in the ground.

Gripping the handle, she shimmied it out of the earth.

Bios

Fatima Abdullahi is a writer of literary and speculative fiction, a poet, and a photographer. Her works have been published or are forthcoming in various publications, including Dark Matter Magazine, Lunaris Review, The Decolonial Passage, Libretto Magazine, Arkore Writes, The Best of Africa, EboQuills, and elsewhere. She lives in Nigeria with her family and tweets @SolitaryWriter_

Camilla Andrew is a born and bred Black British Londoner. She cut her teeth on fairytales and has been delving into the speculative ever since. She currently lives with her mother, younger brother, and tabby cat in Worcester Park.

Azure Arther, a Flint, MI native and Dallas transplant, is obsessed with literature and has found that her passions are evenly distributed between writing, teaching, and reading books with her son. Azure's stories and poems have appeared in more than a dozen publications, including a winning story in Writers of the Future 38. She is also a 2023 Marble House artist. You can keep up with her at azurearther.com

Megan Baffoe is a freelance writer currently studying English Language and Literature at Oxford University. She likes fairy tales, fraught family dynamics, and unreliable narration. She does not like Twitter, but can be found @meginageorge. Her published work is available at meganspublished.tumblr.com.

A. A. Blair is a writer and teacher out of The Bahamas. She has taught Language Arts and Literature for over ten years where she aims to instill a love of reading and culture in the minds of her students. Her free time is spent penning her own stories, poems, and essays that focus on the realities of a region that is paradise to many, but that has its own inherent traumas that often go unspoken. Her stories are about identity, magic, culture, and truth.

Kayla Cayasso is an Afro-Latina writer and poet from North Florida. Her stories, poetry, and essays have been published or are forthcoming in Jabberwock Review, The Amistad, Saw Palm, River & South Review, and elsewhere. Kayla graduated with her Creative Writing MFA from the University of Central Florida, where she studied fiction and was a recipient of the FAMU Feeder Fellowship. Currently, Kayla is an English PhD candidate at the University of Missouri, where she is the recipient of the GW Carver Fellowship.

Jasmine Griffin currently serves as the Learning and Outreach Manager at the Taft Museum of Art in Cincinnati. She's previously held the roles with Lighthouse Writers Workshop, the Mercantile Library of Cincinnati, and Carve Magazine. Jasmine was recently published in Vast Chasm Magazine, Eunoia Review, Random Sample Review, Cincinnati Refined, Genre: Urban Arts, and Cleaning up Glitter. She received her MA in Creative Writing from Wilkes University and has participated in several fellowship and mentorship programs including, Voodoonauts, AWP's Writer to Writer Mentorship program, and Pitch Wars. Jasmine is currently at work on her first novel, *Blackbird at the Crossroads*, which is set in New Orleans and steeped in Southern lore. Follow on Twitter @jcgriffinwrites.

Elnora Gunter is an author of contemporary, contemporary romance, contemporary fantasy, horror, and speculative fiction mainly in the young adult space but also writes select genres in adult and short stories. No matter the age group or label, her stories will always include love, family dynamics, the weight of decision-making, and a thread of hope. She received a BA in English from LSU (Geaux Tigers!). When she's not spinning tales, Elnora spends her days breaking down prose and literature to teenagers, binge-watching entirely too much TV, and cooking with her husband. She lives in southern Louisiana but spent her early childhood in New England and Appalachia. She is represented by Katelyn Detweiler at Jill Grinberg Literary Management.

Ashley J. Hobbs is a writer, voice over artist, all-around creator, and award-winning podcast producer. She enjoys crafting stories that honor the moments when Black women and girls are allowed to explore and assert their agency, gifts, femininity, and spirituality without interference. To learn more about Ashley's projects, visit ashleyjh.com. You can also follow her on Twitter @ashleyjhobbs.

Jennifer E. Jones is a writer and editor living in Florida.

Toni Jones is a Black University of Tampa graduate who writes domestic superhero fiction out of a compulsion to combine her love of Tennessee Williams and comics. Her work has been published in Madcap Review. It has also won honorable in the L Ron Hubbard Writers of the Future Contest and semifinalist in the Stories That Need to be Told Contest by Tuliptree Publishing. IG: ball_of_oddity.

Rhonda Jackson Garcia, aka **RJ Joseph**, is an award winning, Stoker and Shirley Jackson awards nominated writer who earned her MFA in Writing Popular Fiction from Seton Hill University and currently works as a professor of English in Houston, TX. Several of her works have appeared in applauded venues. Her horror story collection, Hell Hath No Sorrow like a Woman Haunted, was released in August 2022 by The Seventh Terrace.

Hou Rhyder is the unapologetic alter-ego of an introverted assistant professor who writes tales of neighborhood doings, outer space, and interesting mythical creatures. She wants to change the world, one word at a time. Find her work at amazon.com/author/arneal

Lorraine Rice is a writer and educator learning how to care for a very old house. Her work appears or is forthcoming in Witness, swamp pink, Scoundrel Time, Philadelphia Stories, and elsewhere. She received a fellowship from Kimbilio, and has had work nominated for a Pushcart Prize. Originally from South Carolina, she currently lives in Philadelphia with her family.

Nortina Simmons has been writing since the age of three, inspired by her songwriting, guitar-playing father who was known to tell a spooky ghost story or two. Her stories typically fall in the categories of romance, speculative fiction, and Christian fiction. Nortina has stories and poems published in Agave Magazine; FishFood Magazine; Cease, Cows; Meat for Tea: The Valley Review; fēlan; Twisted Vine Literary Arts Journal; and Minerva Rising. nortinaswriting.com.

Karla Tiffany is a Black poet and fiction writer from Oakland, CA. She holds a BA in Writing and Literature from California College of the Arts. She is a recipient of the San Francisco Foundation/Nomadic Press Literary Award for Poetry (2021). Her work has appeared or is forthcoming in the San Francisco Public Library's Poem of the Day series, Second Stutter, Gulf Coast Journal, and Augur Magazine.

Oubria (Ooh-Bree-Ah) Tronshaw is a writer and spiritual entrepreneur. She is the creator of the Melanated Classic Tarot Deck (illustrated by Julia Goolsby) and the facilitator of the Melanated Classic Tarot Academy, a self-guided online course that spies the system of tarot through the lens of memory, personal narratives & the wisdom of divine order. She is also the mind behind Marrow Women, an ongoing collection of anonymous interviews by and for Black women. Originally from Chicago, she and her fiancé are happily settled in the Bay Area raising her five children.

Desiree Winns is a graduate student of international relations at the George Washington University. She enjoys writing stories about interpersonal relationships and ethical dilemmas with introspective and dynamic Black characters. A lifelong writer, Desiree has been published by midnight & indigo and khoreo magazine. She aspires to attain a PhD in Political Science and write fiction and nonfiction books. In her free time, Desiree enjoys chess, reading about history, overanalyzing everything, and playing with her cockapoo, Wuzwee.

About The Editor

Ianna A. Small is the founder of midnight & indigo Publishing and creator of midnight & indigo, a literary platform dedicated to short stories and narrative essays by Black women writers. m&i is her love letter to Black women like herself, who long to reach the pinnacle of their purpose.

A media marketing executive, Ms. Small has 20+ years of experience developing partnerships, distribution and content marketing initiatives for entertainment brands including BET, Disney Channel, ESPN, ABC, FX, VH1, MTV, HOT97, and more. As the executive editor of midnight & indigo, she oversees editorial and creative direction for the digital and print platforms, and oversees the writing program.

An avid fan of Black and South Asian literature, British television, and all things Jesus + The Golden Girls + Michelle Obama + cultural food documentaries, she dreams of one day running midnight & indigo from a lounge chair overlooking the archipelagos of her happy place, Santorini.

Ms. Small is a proud graduate of Syracuse University, daughter to Nadia, and mother of an amazing son, Jalen Anthony, who is simply: her reason.